PRAISE FOR DA

TIN CITY

"Twists and double-crosses, exciting car chases and gun battles, leavened by plenty of laughs."

—*Boston Globe*

"Channeling Raymond Chandler with tongue-in-cheek humor, Housewright delivers plenty of action, a pinch of romance, and more than a few surprises."

—*Publishers Weekly*

"An amiable throwback to Marlowe/Archer. Housewright has a keeper in McKenzie."

—*Kirkus Reviews*

"This series may be seriously habit-forming."

—*Booklist*

"A nicely crafted combination of procedural and character-driven crime story."

—*St. Paul Pioneer Press*

A HARD TICKET HOME

"A true son of Spenser."

—*Publishers Weekly*

"Captivating…a series worth watching."

—*Booklist*

"An exciting, action-packed thriller."

—The Best Reviews

"David Housewright has written a stunning novel."

—William Kent Krueger, author of *Blood Hollow*

"I didn't so much read *A Hard Ticket Home* as inhale it. The action is superb, and the tour of the Twin Cities is a delight."

—Nevada Barr, author of *Hunting Season*

"David Housewright's McKenzie is a smart-alecky, wisecracking, two-fisted, soft-hearted, and very human addition to the PI field. Get to know him—you'll be glad you did."

—S. J. Rozan, author of *Absent Friends*

THE VOICE ON THE PHONE

"McKenzie, you're just gonna screw up everything, aren't you?"

"I might."

"Ahh, man. I was gonna cut you some slack cuz you have balls, but you're just too big a pain in the ass to live. Go look outside your window."

"My window."

"Go 'head."

I crossed the room, dragging the telephone with me. When I reached the window, I used the muzzle of the Beretta to push the drape out of the way. It had become dark, but not so dark that I couldn't recognize Michael and Lawrence. They were standing in the rain in the parking lot just below my room, the Ford Ranger between them. Michael waved at me.

"Hey, McKenzie," the voice said.

"I'm here."

"You see 'em?"

"I see them."

"One last time—you gonna back off or what?"

"It's not that I don't trust you to get Frank. It's just that my dear old dad taught me, if you want something done right, you have to do it yourself."

"Uh-huh. Well, tell me this. Just out of curiosity. How are you going to get out of the room?"

The phone went dead before I could answer.

Other *Leisure* books by David Housewright:

A HARD TICKET HOME

DAVID HOUSEWRIGHT

TIN CITY

LEISURE BOOKS  NEW YORK CITY

For Renée,
as always.

A LEISURE BOOK®

October 2006

Published by

Dorchester Publishing Co., Inc.
200 Madison Avenue
New York, NY 10016

Originally published by St. Martin's Press

ISBN 0-8439-5762-X

Printed in the United States of America.

Visit us on the web at www.dorchesterpub.com.

ACKNOWLEDGMENTS

I would like to thank Tammi Fredrickson, Alison Picard, Ben Sevier, Michael Sullivan, and Renée Valois for, well, everything.

TIN CITY

Chapter One

The old man held three dead honeybees in the palm of his caramel-colored hand.

"Here," he said.

"What?"

"Take 'em."

I took a step backward. "What do you mean?"

"Take 'em."

I kept retreating until I was hard against the kitchen counter.

"What's the matter with you?" he wanted to know.

"They're bees."

"They're dead."

"So?"

"They can't hurt you."

"Who says?"

"You big baby." He dumped the bees on top of the kitchen table and sat down. "Honest to God,

McKenzie—a grown man afraid of harmless honeybees." He shook his head like he felt sorry for me.

It disturbed me that Mr. Mosley would question my manhood. But twenty-five years ago I had been stung no less than sixteen times by "harmless" honeybees in his own backyard, and the incident had stayed with me. Once I even abandoned my Jeep Cherokee along I-94 because two wasps had flown through the open window. When I explained it to the state trooper who was going to cite me for illegally stopping on a freeway, he put his ticket book away. He understood, even if my own father had not. But then my dad was a big believer in the Nietzschean philosophy—"That which does not kill me makes me stronger"—though I doubt he knew who Nietzsche was. Mr. Mosley was the same way. He and Dad had fought together with the First Marines at Chosin Reservoir. They weren't afraid of anything. Not even God.

"You gonna sit down or what?" Mr. Mosley asked.

I sat in a chair on the other side of the table and as far away from the bee carcasses as possible. The tall black man ran his fingers through the fringe of silver hair just above his ear while he stared at me. The hair seemed thinner—and so did he—than the last time I had visited him, and it gave me a small jolt. My dad had died two years earlier, and he and Mr. Mosley were the same age.

"I need a favor." He said it like he wasn't sure he was asking the right person.

"Sure." I answered automatically. If Mr. Mosley had asked me to jump off the Lake Street Bridge I would have said yes. Yet it occurred to me in that moment that

I had never heard Mr. Mosley ask for assistance from anyone. He was like my dad, one of those guys who was quick to help others but would never ask for help himself. It gave me another shock of anxiety. He really was getting old. Either that or it was his way of persuading me to visit more often.

"It involves my bees," he said.

"Just as long as it doesn't involve handling them."

"I can't believe you used to be a cop. Man, you went up against some nasty people."

"And not one of them tried to sting me."

"You tellin' me you're more 'fraid of harmless honeybees than you are of crim'nals with guns?"

There's that word again—"harmless."

"I'm also afraid of heights," I told him.

Mr. Mosley rested his forehead against the tabletop. "Unbelievable." When his head came up again, he said, "I've been losing bees. And it's gettin' worse."

"What do you mean, losing bees?"

"I mean they're dying. What do you think I mean?"

For a moment, I flashed on the old nursery rhyme—*Little Bo Peep has lost her sheep and doesn't know where to find them*—but I didn't say it out loud.

"Last year I lost maybe twenty percent of my population."

Leave them alone and they'll come home, wagging their tails behind them.

"And this year it's closer to a third. Do you want some joe?"

"Sure."

Mr. Mosley went to an ancient percolator plugged

into the wall near the sink. My first cup of coffee had been poured from that percolator decades earlier, and I was amazed that it was still working. He filled a mug that was adorned with sunflowers. He served it black—"the way God made it"—without bothering to ask if I wanted cream or sugar. When he had poured that first cup, Mr. Mosley informed me that spooning "additives" into good coffee was like putting ice in bourbon (which I sometimes do but always feel guilty about).

"I started noticing strange doin's couple years ago but didn't think nothing of it."

"Strange doings?"

"The queens," he said. "The young ones would be takin' on the older ones, which is what they supposed to do, 'cept they wuz doing it in the fall, which they ain't supposed to do. Wrong season. Then I start noticin', man, my bees are dyin' all over the place. In the winter, I lose as much as 10 percent of the hive. That normal. But now, man, it up to 30, 40 percent. That bad."

"What's killing them?" I asked. "Pollution?

"Somethin'. You watch 'em and sometimes the bees go insane like, jerkin' all around and bouncin' into each other and then they lie down and die. It's ugly."

I looked over Mr. Mosley's shoulder and through the back door screen. I could see three hives arranged on a wooden pallet. Each hive contained a queen and approximately sixty to seventy thousand worker bees that produced 120 pounds of honey a year—sometimes more, sometimes less. Mr. Mosley sold the honey for $6.50 a pound. There were forty-seven hives scattered over his property. That amounted to well over three million "harmless" honeybees and for the first time since sixteen of them had chastised me for thumping one of the hives with a football, I actually felt sorry for the little buggers.

"Something from around here is killing them, you think?"

"It's gotta be 'round here cuz this is the only colony that's hurtin'," Mr. Mosley said. "My other colonies—I keep hives in five locations now, I don't know if you know that."

Last I heard it was four.

"All but this one are located on the western side of Minnesota, near South Dakota, cuz there ain't much people or insecticide spraying over there. And those colonies, they fine."

"Are you sure?"

"I talked to my man out there just this morning. Lorenzo says there're no problems. Nothin's changed since I was out there last week. Lorenzo, though, he isn't the sharpest knife in the drawer. I might have t'—I haven't fired anyone before. You ever fire anyone?"

"I've never been in a management position."

"It's not somethin' to look forward to." Mr. Mosley gave his head a frustrated shake. "You watch your bees, man, and they'll let you know if somethin' gone wrong with the environment. Like them birds they use t' bring down in them mine shafts—if 'n there a problem, boom, they the first to die. Now, look at my bees—yeah, we got a problem."

Mr. Mosley shook his head some more.

"When I moved to Young America back in '61—that was way before the city merged with Norwood and became Norwood Young America—there weren't nothing out here and I didn't have to worry about DDT and such. DDT was used a lot back then. I was thirty-five miles from downtown Minneapolis. Now with the people and traffic and pollution, I might as well be *in* downtown Minneapolis."

"Urban sprawl," I told him.

"Whatever they call it, it ain't healthy."

"What do you want me to do?"

"I want you to earn all those free jars of honey I've been giving you and your girl all these years."

"She's not my girl."

"I 'member the first time you brought her 'round, way back when you was in college. She wasn't afraid of a couple a' well-mannered honeybees, didn't mind 'em at all. Last summer she visited with her little girls, they were still babies almost—they weren't afraid of the bees, neither. Unlike some people I could name."

"Yeah, yeah."

"That Shelby, she's a looker."

"You do know I've been seeing someone else."

"The jazz girl?"

"She owns a jazz club."

"I notice you ain't never brought her around," he said. Mr. Mosley didn't ask "Why not?" but the question hung between us just the same. I didn't have an answer for him.

Mr. Mosley said, "You shoulda married her. Shelby, I mean."

"She married my best friend."

"You shoulda married her."

I didn't have anything to say to that, either.

"Agatha thought so, too."

"I know."

"So why didn't you?"

"She married my best friend," I repeated.

"That Dunston fella . . ."

"Bobby Dunston."

"Was a cop, like you."

"Still a cop. A homicide detective in St. Paul."

"He's okay. Agatha liked him—but not as much as she liked you."

Agatha was Mrs. Mosley. It was she who treated my bee stings all those years ago, telling me it was all right to cry, telling me to ignore the disapproving glares of my father and Mr. Mosley, who figured I got what I deserved for playing where I didn't belong. "They're just jarheads," she told me. That was six months after my mother had died of a cancerous brain tumor. Twenty years later, the Big C also claimed Agatha.

"She was a good woman," I said.

"Yes," Mr. Mosley agreed.

"My mother was a good woman, too. You were the only one who would tell me that she was dying. Not even my father had courage enough for that."

Mr. Mosley refused to linger over the memory. My father had been the same way. I learned from them.

"What about my bees?"

"I know a guy . . ."

Mr. Mosley smiled. "I knew you would."

"At the University of Minnesota. A professor of entomology. What we'll do, we'll ask him if he can determine what actually killed the bees. Then we'll have to decide what to do about it. Might have to sue someone."

"I don't want to sue anyone."

"That's okay, Mr. Mosley. I know plenty of lawyers who'll be happy to do it for you."

He grimaced at that but didn't say no. Instead, he swept the three deceased honeybees into a plastic sandwich bag and sealed it. He held the bag by the corner.

"Be careful, now." He didn't actually say "wuss"—I don't think the insult had ever passed Mr. Mosley's lips—but I heard it just the same.

I slipped the bag into my jacket pocket.

"Before you go." Mr. Mosley produced a sixteen-ounce jar with a colorful Mosley Honey Farms label and slid it across the table to me.

I caught the jar. "Thank you, sir."

"Take two." He slid another jar in front of me. "Give one to your girl."

"She's not my girl."

"Sevin XLR Plus," the young woman said.

"Is that some kind of new coffee drink?"

She didn't so much as bat an eyelash in response.

'That's a joke," I told her.

She glanced at Professor Buzicky and shrugged. He shrugged back. The silent message that passed between them was unmistakable—there's no accounting for what some people call humor.

We were sitting at a small table inside Lori's Coffee House on Cleveland Avenue North, across from the St. Paul campus of the University of Minnesota. Among other things, the St. Paul campus housed much of the university's agricultural college. I had gone there with my Baggie of dead honeybees an hour after visiting Mr. Mosley, dropping them on Buzicky's desk. I had told him what I needed, and he said he'd take care of it. I had introduced him to his wife fifteen years earlier, and the success of his marriage was such that Buzz still felt obligated to me. Three days later, he arranged a coffee meeting with the graduate student who had tested the dead bees. "When I said I'd take care of it, I didn't actually mean *I* would take care of it," Buzz said at the time.

"Sevin XLR Plus is an insecticide," the student told me. She spoke slowly, as if she were instructing a dull child.

"Is it particularly virulent?" "Virulent" isn't a word I use often, but after the coffee joke I wanted to prove that I had gone to college, too.

"No more so than any other insecticide when used properly."

"Ahh."

She glanced at Buzicky and shrugged again.

Her name was Ivy Flynn. She was five-foot-nothing with Irish-red hair that she wore in a severe ponytail and emerald-green eyes that she muted behind thick, large-rim glasses. Her clothes were baggy—she was dressed for winter instead of a warm day in May. When he introduced her, Buzz said she was one of the brightest students he had ever instructed. Her lips curled slightly at the compliment, the closest she had come yet to a smile. She reminded me of a character in one of those makeover movies, the kind where the plain Jane takes off her glasses, lets down her hair, and is suddenly transformed into Sandra Bullock.

"Sevin XLR Plus controls important crop pests," Ivy said. "It is approved for use on alfalfa, corn, dry beans, small grains, soybeans, sugar beets, and sunflowers. Unfortunately, it contains an ingredient called carbaryl."

"Carbaryl," I repeated to let her know I was paying attention.

"I should emphasize that carbaryl is not illegal by any means. It is, however, toxic to bees. Apparently, Mr. Mosley's honeybees came in contact with the insecticide and brought it back to the hive, where it built up over a period of time, resulting in his current predicament."

"So what we need to do is find the source of the Sevin and ask the perpetrator to stop spraying it."

Again her lips curled upward just so.

"I like that word—'perpetrator,'" Ivy said. "Unfortunately, it's not that simple. Even if we do locate the source, convincing the 'perpetrator'"—she quoted the air—"to cease and desist is problematic at best. It is extremely difficult to demonstrate cause and effect."

"We'll worry about that later," I said. "Right now, we need to find the source of the Sevin. How would I go about that?"

"We know that Sevin is employed to control insect pests on certain crops. We know that honeybees have a range of four miles. It should be comparatively simple if somewhat time-consuming to fan out in, oh, let us say a three-mile radius initially from the infected colony and take samples—soil samples, water samples, plant samples—from likely locations and test them using equipment here at the U."

"Would you be interested in undertaking such a task?"

Ivy turned to Buzicky.

"It'll be good practice for you," he said. "I'll even give you academic credit."

"And I'll pay you," I added.

"You will?"

"What's the going rate for something like this? Twenty-five hundred?"

"Dollars?"

"Yes."

"Yes. Of course, I'll do it. For science." She smiled, really smiled. If it had been any brighter I would have needed sunglasses.

I gave Ivy Mr. Mosley's address in Norwood Young America and directions on where to find it, along with his phone number. I gave her my address in St. Paul and phone numbers—home and cell. I wrote out a personal check in her name for $2,500. She took off her glasses like she didn't want them coming between her and the number. Forget Sandra Bullock. I swear she looked just like Nicole Kidman.

Shelby Dunston didn't look like anyone in particular. Instead, she always reminded me of a southern Minnesota wheat field, all golden and windswept. She met me on the old-fashioned wraparound porch of her pre–World War II colonial wearing a white sleeveless shirt and khaki capris. She probably hadn't dressed to look sexy but managed it just the same.

The Dunstons lived across the street from Merriam Park in St. Paul in the house that Bobby had grown up in; he and Shelby bought it from Bobby's parents after they retired and moved to their lake home in Wisconsin. There was a low-slung community center in the park with a decent gym, plus baseball fields, and in the winter there was a hockey rink where Bobby and I played when we were kids. There was also an enormous hill dotted with large oak trees. When we were teenagers—before driver's licenses—we spent many a pleasant summer evening wandering from the top of that hill to the Burger Chef on Marshall Avenue, where thirty-nine cents' worth of Coca-Cola bought us loitering rights in a corner booth, and then back again in an endless search for friends, acquaintances, and any kind of excitement. Some nights we'd make the trip several times. Occasionally we would venture to the other side of the hill, out of sight of Bobby's front porch, and make out with the Catholic girls from Our Lady of Peace and Derham Hall high schools. It was there that I kissed Mary Beth Rogers—the most beautiful girl of my youth—for the first and only time. Glancing up at it now, I wondered for a moment if Bobby had ever taken Shelby over the hill, but I didn't ask.

Shelby's daughters were delighted to get a jar of honey from "that cool beekeeper guy," even though it had been four days since my visit with Mr. Mosley and one day since meeting Ivy Flynn before I had found time to deliver it. They were even happier with the small bags of mini-donuts I doled out.

"Where did you get these?" Victoria wanted to know.

"I made them."

"You made them?" Katie asked, her mouth full. "These are just like the donuts you get at the state fair."

"I should hope so."

"How did you make them?" asked Victoria.

"I bought a mini-donut machine."

"Really?"

"Really?" echoed Shelby.

"I bought it off the Internet," I told her. "Belshaw Donut Robot Mark I. It can make up to a hundred dozen mini-donuts in an hour."

"One hundred *dozen* mini-donuts?"

"No home should be without one."

"If you say so."

"Let's go to your house right now," Katie said.

"Let's do your homework right now," Shelby said.

"Ahh, Mom," both girls replied in unison.

"Ahh, Mom," she repeated, folding her arms across her chest, giving her daughter the don't-mess-with-me look that she claimed was being challenged more and more as the girls grew older. To me, she said, "A mini-donut machine. To go with the sno-cone machine you bought last fall, I guess."

"Four flavors, no waiting."

"Uh-huh. What's next? Cotton candy?"

"I was thinking one of those machines that make corn dogs. I was never much for cotton candy."

"Oh, I love cotton candy," said Victoria. "The pink kind, not the blue kind."

"Really. Well, I'll have to give that some thought."

"You would buy a cotton candy maker just for me?"

"Sure I would."

I think she would have hugged me except both hands were filled with donuts.

"Homework," Shelby said. "Go."

Victoria left for her bedroom, muttering, "What a grouch," just loudly enough to be heard.

"What did you say?" Shelby asked.

"Nothing."

Katie, who was younger and consequently more cautious, followed her older sister out of the room without a sound.

"Honestly, McKenzie," Shelby said when they were gone.

"What?"

"You're trying to buy their love."

"Hey, if it's for sale, I'll take it." I held out a small paper bag for her. "Donut?"

Shelby took the bag and the jar of Mr. Mosley's honey and went into the kitchen. I followed.

"How is Mr. Mosley?"

"Okay, I guess. It's just that he seems so . . . old."

She set the jar on the counter and turned toward me. "What is he, now? Late sixties, early seventies?"

"Seventy-two. He's as old as my dad would have been."

"My dad just turned sixty-five. He thinks that's young."

"I just turned thirty-seven, and I don't."

Shelby popped a mini-donut into her mouth. She closed her eyes while she chewed.

"Rushmore, these are amazing."

Shelby's the only one who gets to call me by my first name. I was christened after the national monument in whose shadow I was conceived while my parents were on a motor vacation through the Badlands. I liked to joke, "It could have been worse, it could have been Deadwood." But that line was getting as old as I was.

"I'm still trying to get the sugar and cinnamon mixture right," I told Shelby.

"No, no, this is good. This is perfect just the way it is."

She had another donut, and I told her about my visit with Mr. Mosley and his bees. I deliberately edited out his "your girl" remarks.

"When will you know?"

"I have no idea. Ivy—Ivy Flynn, she's the grad student doing the fieldwork—she just started gathering samples this morning."

"You enjoy it, don't you?"

"Enjoy what?"

"Helping Mr. Mosley. Helping any of your friends, for that matter."

"I like to be useful. I think everyone has that desire. I think we want that more than cash."

"Or love?"

"Maybe that, too. Besides, it gives me something to do when I get up in the morning besides count my money."

"There are a lot of things you could do besides what you do."

"Go fishing? Play golf?"

"Why not?"

"I do go fishing, I do play golf. It's just . . . People retire. They scrape enough money together so they don't have to work and they say, 'I'll go fishing, I'll play golf.' It's what they squeezed in during those brief periods when they weren't working, and they enjoyed it. But take away the work and suddenly the fishing and golf become their whole lives. And it's not enough. They go nuts. Some manage it, of course. My dad enjoyed retirement. But he had a hobby. Doing stuff for other people was his hobby. Shingling roofs and building decks and plumbing. He was even a volunteer firefighter for a while. 'Live well, be useful,' he used to say. Words to live by."

"Words you live by."

"They're good words."

"Except you're not particularly handy with a hammer or a wrench. So instead you perform other—what do you call them, chores?"

"Favors."

"And the more difficult and dangerous the favor . . ."

"The more fun," I concluded.

"And if someone tries to kill you like they did last fall?" There was anxiety in Shelby's voice, but I pretended not to hear.

"People tried to kill me when I was a cop, too."

"You and Bobby." Shelby turned and looked out her back window. There was a swing set that the girls were starting to outgrow and two bikes lying on the grass. Moments passed before she spoke again.

"I thought you were going back to the cops. I thought you were going to take a position with the St. Anthony Village Police Department. Chief of detectives, wasn't it?"

"They offered me the job, but . . . The thing is, being a cop, you have to follow an awful lot of rules."

"You didn't mind when you were with St. Paul."

"That was before I spent two and a half years obeying

my own rules, coming and going as I please. It's hard to go back to the everyday grind after that."

"I suppose."

A few moments later, the front door opened and closed. A male voice announced, "I'm home," without much enthusiasm.

"In the kitchen," Shelby replied.

Bobby Dunston entered. He was the same size as I was, as well as the same age. I can't remember a time when we weren't friends.

"Hi," he said. He wasn't surprised to see me. I had spent a lot of time in his kitchen when I was a kid, too.

"How's it going?" I asked.

"Murder and mayhem abound."

"So business is good."

"Too good."

He went to Shelby, wrapped his arms around her, and held on tight. She returned the embrace. It seemed to last longer than a welcome-home hug should, or maybe it was just me being embarrassed by their obvious affection for each other. After a few moments, Shelby gently nudged him away.

"You're not going to believe this," she said. "McKenzie bought a mini-donut machine."

"I'm going to take a shower," Bobby said. "I'll be right back."

There was a look of concern in Shelby's eyes as she watched him exit the kitchen.

"He does that a lot lately," she told me.

"Take a shower? I should hope so."

"As soon as he gets home from work, before he talks to me or the kids. It's like he feels he needs to wash off the day first."

I understood completely. I had been a cop for eleven and a half years before I quit in order to collect a three-million-dollar bounty on an embezzler I had tracked down in my spare time—St. Paul cops aren't allowed to accept rewards and finder's fees. Back in those days, I had taken a lot of showers, too.

For dinner Shelby served pasta with a light sauce consisting of olive oil, onion, tomatoes, shrimp, dry white wine, and Italian parsley. However, the girls refused to eat it, insisting instead on smothering their noodles with butter and grated Parmesan. That was fine with Bobby, but Shelby glared at me like I was responsible for corrupting her daughters' eating habits. Honestly, I don't see them that often.

After dinner, Bobby also inquired about Mr. Mosley's health and welfare. I told him the same thing I had told Shelby. That prompted another discussion concerning the aging process, during which Bobby announced that he did not look old, feel old, or behave in any way that could be construed as old, as he was sure his lovely wife would testify, but that I was free to seize any excuse—including advanced age—that might explain my obvious dilapidated and sorry physical, emotional, and mental condition. I would have raced him around the block but I was afraid I'd lose.

During the bottom of the third inning of the Twins-Angels game, my cell phone sang "Don't Fence Me In."

"I bet that's the girlfriend," Shelby said.

"Ahh, Nina," Bobby cooed.

Nina Truhler was the "jazz girl" Mr. Mosley had referred to. Only it wasn't her. It was Ivy Flynn.

"Oh, God, Mr. McKenzie . . ."

"Ivy?"

"Mr. McKenzie, unbelievable . . ."

"What?"

"The guy . . ."

"What guy?"

"He shot at me."

"What?"

"He shot at me."

"Who shot at you?"

Bobby Dunston's eyes grew wide. He rose from the sofa where he had been sitting with his wife and stood in front of me.

"Ivy? Are you all right?"

A deep breath. "Yes."

"Who shot at you?"

"Some guy. In the ditch. He shot at me in the ditch."

"Where are you?"

"I'm in a bar."

"Are you safe?"

"What do you mean, am I safe? I'm in a bar. I don't go to bars."

"Did you call the police?"

"Should I do that? If I was trespassing—that's probably why the guy shot at me."

"Tell me what happened."

Another deep breath. A second. A third. I didn't rush

her. After a moment, Ivy began speaking again in the same patient voice she used when I met her at Lori's Coffee House.

"I was collecting samples. I came across a large pasture. I might have neglected to tell you, but Sevin XLR Plus is often sprayed on unbroken ground such as pastures and roadside ditches. That's because grasshoppers tend to lay eggs in undisturbed ground and, after they mature, disperse into neighboring crop systems. Although there are as many as one hundred species of grasshoppers on the Northern Great Plains, only five rate as the most important crop pests—the two-striped grasshopper, the migratory grasshopper, the clear-winged grasshopper, and the red-legged and differential grasshoppers."

This was more than I needed to know, but the longer Ivy spoke, the calmer she became, and I didn't want to disrupt the process.

"I halted my vehicle and climbed down into the roadside ditch. There were no grasshoppers there, Mr. McKenzie, which I find telling. I began gathering samples. I heard someone calling something, but the words were snatched away by the wind. I looked up and saw a man approaching. A big man. Fat. He was carrying a gun—a shotgun—I recognized a shotgun. And he started shooting—he just started—I saw muzzle flashes and puffs of smoke—at least I think I saw . . . Mr. McKenzie, I wasn't trespassing, it was a public road, a county road."

"You're sure you're all right?"

"I scrambled out of the ditch, climbed into my car, and drove off. I drove very, very fast. I drove for a long time. I'm not actually in Norwood Young America anymore. I'm in—" She stopped speaking. I heard the sound of music and her voice calling, "Where am I?" The question was followed immediately by laughter and the murmur of voices. "I'm in Glencoe," she told me after a few moments.

Glencoe is nowhere near NYA.

"Tell me where you are and I'll come get you."

"That's not necessary. I'm okay."

"Ivy."

"No, really, Mr. McKenzie. I'm fine. It was scary, but I'm fine now. I'm going to get something to eat and then drive home."

"Are you sure?"

"Yes, sir. But what should we do about . . . about the guy?"

"I'll deal with it."

Bobby shifted his weight and sighed.

I asked Ivy if she had noted the address. She had. She had written it down along with the approximate distance from Mr. Mosley's hives when she catalogued her samples.

"You collected samples from the ditch even with the guy shooting at you?" I asked.

"Only one. I labeled it before entering the bar. I kinda like this place."

I kinda liked her.

"It is my intention to begin testing samples tomorrow," Ivy said.

"Begin with this one."

"Yes, sir."

"I'm sorry about all this, Ivy."

"Oh, don't be. Actually"—her voice dropped an octave or two as if she were afraid to hear herself say it—"it was kinda fun."

She fear'd no danger, for she knew no sin. John Dryden had written that over three hundred years ago. Now I knew what he meant.

Bobby Dunston was still standing above me when I deactivated my cell phone, his hands on his hips.

"Someone shot at someone?"

"Not in your jurisdiction," I told him.

"Does this involve Mr. Mosley's bees?"

I smiled at him, although I don't know why.

"The game's afoot," I said.

"Ahh, man. Not again."

Chapter Two

The next morning I found Mr. Mosley working the hives near a shed about the size of a two-car garage—the "bee barn," he called it. He was wearing a white hat with a round, flat brim not unlike what you'd expect park rangers to wear, with a light-colored wire-mesh veil that hung down over his shoulders. He was carrying a smoker, a galvanized metal container resembling a large thermos with a narrow funnel at the top. You light a fire inside using old newspapers and kindling such as pine needles, cotton rags, corn cobs, tree bark—whatever—and puff smoke into the hive. The smoke masks the pheromones secreted by the sentry bees at the entrance of the hive so an alarm isn't sounded when you approach. The smoke also compels the bees to gorge themselves on honey, presumably because they believe the hive is on fire and they'll need to swarm and find a new home. As a result, you're able to go about your work unmolested. At least that's what I've heard. I've never actually tested the theory myself.

I watched Mr. Mosley move among his hives, wondering not for the first time how he did it so fearlessly. I called to him through the screen of his back door. He waved at me to join him near the hives. Yeah, like that was going to happen.

Eventually he moved back to the house. I watched him slowly remove his gloves, then his hat and veil, watched him fluff what remained of his white hair with both hands. Again I was jarred by how old he appeared. It seemed like only ten minutes ago he was telling me to choke up on the bat if I wanted to get around on a fastball. And now . . . I promised myself I would spend more time with him.

He said, "I liked that little girl you sent over. Ivy Flynn? She knows her *Apis m. mellifera.* Ain't afraid of 'em, either."

"Yeah, she's tough as nails."

I deliberately crossed my arms over my gray sports coat and Minnesota Wild sweatshirt, knowing what was coming.

"Pretty eyes. And hair. I don't recall ever seeing hair that shade of red. Are you involved with her?"

"Stop it."

"Uh-huh. Well, you should be."

"She's a kid."

Mr. Mosley raised an eyebrow.

"She's my employee."

He raised the other. "I'm startin' t' wonder about you, McKenzie."

I doubted my love life could stand much more scrutiny, so I changed the subject, telling him of Ivy's encounter the previous evening with the shotgun-wielding fat man. Mr. Mosley became so concerned over her safety that I had to assure him twice that Ivy had escaped unscathed.

I told him that earlier that morning I called up Carver County's Web site on my computer. "Did you know that Carver County was named after a Massachusetts explorer who may or may not have ever set foot in the place? Guy named Captain Jonathan Carver. He had gone west in the hope of gaining fame and fortune, failed, and then wrote a book—*Travels Through the Interior Parts of North America in the Years 1766, 1767, and 1768.* The book did pretty well until it was discovered that much of the manuscript contained plagiarized accounts of the adventures of other explorers. Carver died penniless."

From the expression on Mr. Mosley's face, I might as well have been lecturing him about the properties and characteristics of dirt.

"Anyway . . ." I told him that I fed the address Ivy had given me into a search engine on the Web site that allowed citizens to access their neighbors' property tax information and was instantly informed that the primary taxpayer/owner of the property was a finance company called Lundgren-Kerber Investments. A phone call to Lundgren-Kerber and a little fast talking revealed that the tenant was named Crosetti, Frank—which made me think of Frankie Crosetti, the great shortstop who helped the Yankees win eight world championships between 1932 and 1948.

"I know most of my neighbors," Mr. Mosley said. "I don't know him."

"Crosetti moved in just over six weeks ago," I said. "Which means he probably isn't responsible for the Sevin XLR Plus that had been sprayed on his land—if, in fact, Sevin XLR Plus had been sprayed on his land. Still, I'm a little annoyed about what happened with Ivy. So I figured I'd wander over there and have a friendly chat with the man. Explain the situation. Ask him not to shoot at Ivy anymore."

"I'll go with you."

"I rather you didn't. I mean, if he shot at Ivy—"

"He's my neighbor, I should say hello. I'll bring him a few jars of honey, welcome him to the area."

"If you say so."

Crop and dairy farming had been the chief occupation of Carver County for over a hundred years. But in a blink of an eye most of the farms had vanished and the county was suburbanized by housing tracts, strip malls, and sixty-four thousand additional residents, most of whom commuted to Minneapolis. You could still see a few farms sprawling west of Braunworth Lake where Mr. Mosley lived, although it was just a matter of time before they, too, disappeared. One of them already had a huge sign attached to its fence posts announcing that it soon would be transformed into a housing development called Carver Hills. There wasn't a hill in sight.

"I hate farming," Mr. Mosley said as he studied the sign through the passenger window of the Cherokee. "I used to work a farm like this one. When I was a youngster.

They sent me there in '45, after they closed the Minnesota State Public School for Dependent and Neglected Children—now, ain't that a mouthful? It was kinda like an orphanage down near Owatonna, 'cept most of us, we wasn't orphans. We was abandoned, signed over to the state by our parents like we was property, like we was nothin'. That's the way we was treated, too. Kept in cottages, thirty of us to a room. Made t' work in the fields. Workin' on our hands and knees pullin' weeds. Catch a whuppin' if'n we didn't work fast enough. They'd beat you with a radiator brush, man. Pour kerosene on your head. Somethin' like two hundred kids died in the place 'fore they get around to closin' it.

"After they did, they sent me to a farm near Waseca. Foster care, they said it was. More back-breakin' work for no pay is what they meant. I figure I learned everything there is to know about slavery from workin' that damn farm. After I got some size, I ran off and joined the Marines. They sent me to Parris Island for training, said it was gonna be tough. Tough? Boy, after what I been through, the Corps was like heaven on earth. That's where I met your daddy, in the Corps."

"I know."

"That's right. You've heard all my stories."

"A couple of times."

Laughter rumbled out of Mr. Mosley's throat. "Well, you'll probably hear 'em again."

One can only hope.

The house was old and small, a simple two-bedroom split-level with attached garage. Yet it seemed much grander than that, perched on top of a hill at the end of a long gravel driveway, surrounded by a huge green lawn and, beyond that, by acres of shrubs and prairie grass. What would you call it, I wondered as we approached. Not a hobby farm—there was no indication that any work took place there, except perhaps the work of mowing the lawn. A kid could retire on what he'd make mowing that lawn. Not an estate, either. Just a small house in the country, I guessed.

I pulled off the county road and accelerated up the hill, stopping the Cherokee at the top of the driveway. We left the SUV and started toward the house. We didn't take three steps before a man rounded the corner of the garage.

"Freeze, assholes!"

I saw the shotgun first, a dangerous-looking over-and-under 12-gauge with the barrel sawed off. Then the man's enormous gut stretching the material of his gray polo shirt—he looked like the "before" picture of every diet ad ever printed. He was wearing black dress pants and a pair of black wing tips that seemed at first glance to be rooted to the ground. They weren't. He stepped toward us, moving carefully, the shotgun leading the way.

"Freeze," he said again.

His hair was the color of potting soil, and he was losing it starting in the front and moving back. His eyes were so dark brown that it was impossible to see his pupils. The expression on his face made me think he was entertaining a private joke and that it was on me.

I flashed on the guns that I keep locked in the safe embedded in my basement floor, yet only for a moment. I could have been carrying as many weapons as a character in a Schwarzenegger movie and it wouldn't have done any good. Crosetti had us cold.

"Don't move," he screamed in case we didn't know what "freeze" meant.

"Whoa," I said, showing him my hands. "There's no need for that."

"Whaddaya want?"

I was closer to him, but he wasn't aiming the shotgun at me. He was pointing it across the hood of the Cherokee, glaring at Mr. Mosley with unblinking eyes as if willing him to melt.

"I'm talking to you, nigger."

Ahh, fighting words.

I stepped toward him.

He swung the barrel in my direction. "You want some of this?"

I showed him my hands again, both sides this time, making sure he could see that they were empty.

"Mr. Mosley is your neighbor. We just dropped by to welcome you to Norwood Young America."

"Fuck that. Who sent you?"

"No one sent us."

"What do you want here? Talk."

"We wanted to give you a couple jars of honey."

Mr. Mosley was behind me and to the right, the Cherokee between us. I don't know what he did, but Crosetti didn't like it. Again he swung the shotgun in Mr. Mosley's direction.

"Somethin' funny, nigger?"

I said, "Mr. Crosetti, please—"

"You know my name. How you know my name?"

Explaining to him that I looked it up on the Internet somehow didn't seem like the wisest course of action at that moment, so instead I started backing slowly toward the Cherokee. I hoped Mr. Mosley would do the same.

"Mr. Crosetti," I said carefully, "I promise we mean you no harm. We're going to leave now. And we're not coming back."

"Don't move."

I stopped moving. I stopped breathing. I stopped blinking my eyes. If I could have stopped my heart beating, I probably would have done that, too.

"First the girl yesterday, now you. What's going on? Tell me."

It was a cloudless day in mid-May, warm but not hot, yet Crosetti was sweating. Beads of perspiration formed on his forehead and ran in rivulets down his temples and cheeks. His shirt under his arms and across his chest was wet. Suddenly it occurred to me that even though he had the shotgun, Crosetti was more frightened than I was.

"The girl you mentioned is a student at the University of Minnesota."

I started to lower my hands, but he flicked the business end of the shotgun at me and I raised them again.

"She was taking soil samples to test for traces of an insecticide called Sevin XLR Plus. The insecticide has been killing off the area honeybee population—"

"You're here because of some goddamn bees?"

I heard the car before I saw it, heard the engine racing as it accelerated up the hill. I didn't turn my head to look until Crosetti did. A yellow Mustang convertible, its top up, coming fast, tires pitching gravel and dirt behind it. It swung off the driveway, arced across the enormous lawn, and cut between Crosetti and the Cherokee. The driver was out of the Mustang before it came to a complete stop.

"For God's sake, Frank," the driver shouted. Crosetti lowered the barrel, but he wasn't happy about it.

"What's going on here?" Now he was shouting at Mr. Mosley and me. "Answer me."

I gestured at Crosetti.

"Get in the house," the driver yelled. Crosetti didn't move. "I mean it. Get in the house, now."

Crosetti gestured toward me. "Fix this."

"I'm going to fix it."

"You'd better."

"Don't worry about it."

"I'm not worried. You're the one better be fuckin' worried."

"Get in the house."

Crosetti looked about to say something, thought better of it, and retreated back around the garage. I didn't know whether he had left or was just lying in wait.

"What do you want?" the driver asked. He was wearing a dark blue suit, a white shirt, and a dark blue tie flecked with red and tied in a Windsor. I nearly asked what he was doing driving such a beautiful car in such an ugly color. Instead, I said, "Who are you?"

"Never mind who I am. Who are you?"

I introduced Mr. Mosley and myself. I explained about the insecticide and the bees.

"Honeybees?" The driver made the word sound like a felony.

I explained some more, told him about Ivy Flynn.

"I'm sorry about the girl. But she was trespassing. So are you. Leave now. Do not return." He spoke like a man who was used to having his own way.

I glanced at Mr. Mosley.

He didn't say a word—hadn't said a word during the entire incident. He opened the door and slid inside the Jeep Cherokee. I did the same. I backed all the way down the driveway, watching the driver as much as the road behind me. He didn't move until we were on the county blacktop heading east.

We drove for what seemed like a long time without speaking. Finally Mr. Mosley said, "Once before a white man pointed a gun at me, called me nigger, and laughed. That was back in 1950. Know what I did?"

"What?"

"Nothing. And I've been angry 'bout it ever since."

"You know, Mr. Mosley, it's not 1950 anymore."

"Tell me about those lawyer friends you mentioned."

Sweet Swinging Billy Tillman, the fastest man alive, aka Tilly, aka Tilly the Swift, aka Wild Bill, had become an attorney—a fact that astonished all who knew him, including Tilly's mother, because no one ever misspent his youth more recklessly. I remember dodging a bowling ball that he once rolled down the stairs at me when I visited his second-story duplex—I felt like Indiana

Jones in *Raiders of the Lost Ark.* On one memorable occasion, Tilly and his cabal of miscreants laid siege to a hamburger joint on Marshall Avenue with bottle rockets because the establishment refused to buy union lettuce. For three consecutive years he water-skied down the Mississippi River in nothing but swimming shorts, in February, evading ice floes for the benefit of a local TV station; I remember because I drove the boat. Often he would travel to Wisconsin, where the drinking age was nineteen, purchase assorted alcoholic beverages, smuggle them across the border, then sell them out of the trunk of a car at grossly inflated prices to college kids in Minnesota, where the drinking age was twenty-one; I remember because I drove the car. Then there was his annual Pub Crawl. Tilly would rent a school bus, load it with thirty of his closest personal friends and a keg of beer, and direct it from one Twin Cities drinking emporium to the next until the occupants collapsed out of pure exhaustion and overindulgence. I most certainly did *not* drive on any of those occasions.

Mr. Mosley allowed that these weren't necessarily the qualifications that he sought in an attorney.

"If you're going to hire a lawyer," I told him, "hire one who's prepared to do almost anything."

A secretary ushered us into Tilly's office. Introductions were made and greetings exchanged. I asked about Susan. Tilly showed me the picture he kept on his desk.

Tilly had never been particularly handsome. In fact, the less generous among us might call him downright homely. His wife, on the other hand, made Catherine Zeta-Jones look tired, and I wondered not for the first time how he had managed to woo her. I've been told that most women are attracted to power and money, that they're interested in a man's personality, his education, his occupation, his ability to make them laugh—but that physical appearance is way down on the list of requirements, somewhere around seventh or eighth. I decided it must be true. How else could Tilly get such an attractive woman to marry him? Why else would I be able to get dates?

"Have you seen this?" Tilly handed me a second photo. It was of a young girl with auburn hair and flashing green eyes.

"Sheila?"

Tilly nodded.

"My Lord, how old is she now?"

"Twelve."

Talk about feeling ancient. "The last time I saw her, she wasn't even in preschool."

"You should visit more often."

I handed back the photograph. "She's a very lucky girl. She looks like her mother instead of you."

"Tell me about it."

Mr. Mosley said, "Can we get to it? I have to meet my man working the hives near South Dakota."

I don't think Mr. Mosley meant to be rude. It was just that lawyers made him nervous.

Tilly sat behind his desk. We sat in front of it.

"So, gentlemen. What can I do for you?"

"We're looking for a little payback," I told him.

"Talk to me."

We told our story. Tilly didn't hesitate before giving us his recommendation.

"We can call the Carver County attorney—whom I play golf with, I might add—and have Crosetti charged with three counts of assault. Certainly there's a reasonable fear that he was going to cause bodily harm to both of you and Ms. Flynn. The fact he used a racial slur might also give us access to the hate crime statutes. There was no posting of trespass signs that you could see, correct?"

"Correct."

"That's enough for criminal charges. It's also enough to start civil proceedings for emotional distress. It's weak, but you could probably do it."

"I don't want to arrest him. I don't want to sue," Mr. Mosley said.

"Well, sir. What do you want?"

"I want him to know that he can't push me around."

"That's easy."

"How is that easy?" I asked.

"We'll send him a letter printed on my stationery in which we *threaten* to have him arrested and drag him into civil court unless he—unless he what? Unless he allows you to go anywhere on his property, at your convenience, and take soil samples without interference. What do you say, Mr. Mosley? Do you like the idea of Crosetti cussing you out from behind his window shades while you roam about his land doing exactly as you please?"

"I like that very much."

"We'll send the letter by messenger this afternoon."

Tilly smiled broadly, leaned back in his chair, and clasped his fingers behind his head.

"I love the law," he said. "It lets you get away with so much mischief."

Her name was Margot, and she was standing in the center of my pond. She was wearing a dazzling one-piece canary yellow swimsuit that barely contained her. I wore sunglasses when I approached so she wouldn't see where my eyes were roaming, although I'm sure she guessed.

Margot was five years older than I was, but she looked younger. Lately I've been thinking that everyone looks younger than I do. She was my neighbor. I inherited her when my father and I moved into the house shortly after I came into my money. The house was located on the wrong side of the street. I didn't know that until after I had made an offer on it. I thought it was located in St. Anthony Park, one of the more fashionable neighborhoods of St. Paul. But because I was on the north side of Hoyt Avenue instead of the south, I actually lived in Falcon Heights. I had inadvertently moved to the suburbs, a fact I still refuse to admit publicly. I'm a St. Paul boy at heart, and whenever anyone asks, I say that's where I live. Margot insists I should get over it. That's easy for her to say. She's from Minneapolis.

"I've been thinking," she said when I reached the edge of the pond.

"What have you been thinking?"

"Oh, many things," she cooed, arching her dark eyebrows at me. "But mostly I've been thinking that we need fish."

"Fish?"

"I think the ducks would like to eat fish when they return."

"What kind of fish?"

"I don't know. What kind of fish do ducks eat?"

"I don't even know that they eat fish."

"Call that guy you know, the one with the DNR."

"Why should I call? It's your idea."

"It's your pond."

"Since when?"

True, the pond was built in my backyard, but the far shore bordered Margot's property and she had long ago asserted at least partial ownership rights, especially after the ducks arrived. There were only two mallards at first. I called them Hepburn and Tracy. Only the thing about ducks is they breed. Soon there were five additional ducklings. I named them Bobby, Shelby, Victoria, and Katie after the Dunston family and Maureen after my mother and fed them dry corn from a plastic ice cream bucket. Margot fed them bread and crackers. Soon they would waddle up to each of us without fear, would even sit quietly next to us when we stretched out on lounge chairs, catching rays—but they liked me best.

All the mallards flew off in late September, and I was afraid that would be the last we'd see of them. My friend with the Minnesota Department of Natural Resources said not to worry. If they survived the trip south, the ducks would probably return in the spring to establish new nests. Only it was May and still no sign of them.

I used to hunt ducks with my dad. I can't imagine doing it now.

"Goldfish," Margot said.

"What about them?"

"At the Japanese garden exhibit at the Como Conservatory, they have goldfish."

"Do ducks eat goldfish?"

"I don't know if they eat goldfish. I'm just saying goldfish is something to think about. Big goldfish. They look good swimming around. They looked very good swimming around at the Japanese garden exhibit at the Como Conservatory."

"I've never been to the Japanese garden exhibit at the Como Conservatory."

"You should go. You should look at the goldfish."

"Margot, why are you standing in the pond?"

Margot tapped the top of the fountain that circulated the pond water. "When are you going to turn this on?"

"I don't know."

"You should turn it on. Make sure it works."

"I'll do that, but first—"

"When are you going to turn it on?"

"In a minute. Margot?"

"What?"

"Why are you standing . . ."

"In the pond? I wanted to see how deep the water was."

I had cleaned the pond and filled it with a garden hose two days earlier. It was now at its ideal level, which was midway between Margot's knees and the bright material of her swimsuit. Margot must have known I was admiring her thighs, because she splashed water at me.

"See anything you like?"

"That's a nice suit you're almost wearing."

"This old thing?"

"I have handkerchiefs that have more material."

"My ex-husband gave it to me."

"Which one?" There were three that I knew of.

"Who keeps track?"

"I'll turn on the fountain."

"McKenzie?"

"Yeah."

"I've been throwing myself at you at least twice a month since you moved in. How come you haven't caught me yet?"

"Do you want an honest answer?"

"I don't know. Will it hurt?"

I crouched at the edge of the pond and splashed gently. The water was surprisingly warm for May.

"It's my father," I told her.

"What about him?"

"Remember when he built the pond, dug it out, put in the fountain?"

"Yes."

"You helped him and brought him lemonade."

"Until I discovered he preferred Leinenkugel's."

"When he finished each day, he would come in and comment on how beautiful you were."

"He did?"

"Yes. And how smart and how sexy, too. And he'd say, 'If I was only twenty years younger . . .' After a day or two, it became fifteen years. Then ten, then five, then just a couple. And then . . ."

"And then he died."

"Yeah, he died."

"I miss him."

"The thing is, he really liked you. And when I see you looking resplendent in that canary yellow swimsuit you're almost wearing, I think—that's my dad's girl."

Margot stared for a few moments, then wrapped her arms around her chest and turned her back to me. She bowed her head and I saw her shoulders shudder. She plowed through the water to the edge of the pond bordering her property. She called to me over her shoulder. Her voice didn't sound quite right.

"That's either the sweetest thing I've ever heard or the biggest bucket of crap. I'll let you know what I decide."

I went into my garage and turned the switch that fired the circulating pump. A few moments later I was standing in my backyard and watching the water arching out of the fountain and back into the pond. Margot stood on the other side of the pond in her yard. She had pulled on a white robe and was also watching the fountain. I don't know what she was thinking. I was thinking of my dad.

I had a twelve-ounce prime rib and twice-baked potato at Rickie's, a jazz club located in St. Paul's Cathedral Hill neighborhood that was developing a nice reputation for showcasing gifted performers on their way up; both Diana Krall and Jane Monheit had performed there early in their careers. It also had a well-regarded dinner menu, a little pricey by my standards, but worth it, especially since they gave me the employee discount. I was dating the owner.

They served me at the downstairs bar. Rickie's had two levels. The first floor reminded me of a coffeehouse. It had a large number of comfortable sofas and stuffed chairs mixed in among the tables and booths. There was even an espresso machine behind the bar. The second floor featured a larger bar set against one wall and an elevated stage with a baby grand piano set against the opposite wall. Arranged between them were a couple dozen tables covered with white linen, elaborate place settings, and candles.

I saw Nina Truhler standing on the staircase midway between the two floors, menus under her arm. I enjoyed watching her—the way she moved so smoothly and effortlessly; her short black hair, high cheekbones, narrow nose, and generous mouth; her curves, which she refused to diet away. But mostly I enjoyed her eyes, the most arresting eyes I had ever seen in a woman. From a distance they gleamed like polished silver. Up close they were the most amazing pale blue.

"Luminous," I said quietly, pleased with the word, wondering if I had spoken it aloud before.

Nina waved when she saw me. I waved back. She blew me a kiss, and I pretended to catch it. She leaned against the railing, raised her leg, arched her back, tossed back her head, and gave me her Marilyn Monroe. I pointed to the couple watching her from the bottom of the staircase. She smiled and went to them without even a suggestion of embarrassment.

We're taught as children that everyone is special, but time and experience prove that to be a lie. It's true we're all different. But damn few of us are special. Nina was one of them. She always looked and behaved as though she had never had a moment of gloom or self-doubt. I knew this to be untrue. Her unplanned pregnancy and disastrous marriage, the early years raising Erica after her husband abandoned them both, and the frightening risk and punishing effort of making her club a success brought a great deal of misery into her life. Yet she survived. And how. Now it was smiles nearly all the time.

"Audacious," I said, another word I don't often use. Nina brought out the linguist in me.

Yet in the back of my mind I remembered what Mr. Mosley had said. *I notice you ain't never brought her around.* Why hadn't I? I wondered.

Rickie's had two dinner crowds. The first consisted mostly of people who arrived early, ate quickly, and ran to whatever event they had planned for that evening. The second arrived later, ate slowly, and usually stayed for the upstairs entertainment that always began at 9:00 P.M. Tonight it was local chanteuse Connie Evingson performing Beatles standards to a jazz rhythm. I had caught her act twice now and looked forward to a third helping.

Nina had other plans. After the first dinner crowd was seated, she occupied the stool next to mine at the bar.

"Rickie's on a weekend retreat sponsored by her high school," she told me, using the name that her daughter preferred. "A confidence-building retreat."

"Is she teaching it?"

"No, why would she be?"

"Because Rickie needs confidence like Tiger Woods needs confidence."

Nina looked like she was trying to identify the dialect I spoke.

"She already has plenty," I translated for her.

"McKenzie, as usual you're missing the point."

"What's the point?"

"Your place or mine?"

Hers. It was closer.

'Course, it's never simple with Nina. First we had to drive to the Black Sea, a Turkish restaurant located near Hamline University for a takeout order of what Nina claimed was the best baklava in the Twin Cities. Some people like a cigarette after sex. Nina prefers dessert.

She insisted on driving and slid behind the steering wheel of her brand-spanking-new Lexus while I rode shotgun. "It still has that new car smell," she insisted, inhaling deeply. I didn't agree but wasn't about to say so. People with new cars—especially people with new cars that are the same color as their eyes—you don't mess with them.

A few quick turns after we left Rickie's parking lot, we were on Dale heading north toward I-94. Almost immediately an SUV appeared on our back bumper. It rode higher than the Lexus, and its lights flooded the inside of the luxury car and reflected off the rearview into Nina's eyes. She adjusted the mirror without thinking about it.

"Did I tell you the salesman gave me a discount?" she asked.

"Yes, you did. Several times. If I had been the salesman, I would have given you a discount, too."

"You know why?"

"Because you're an extremely attractive woman?"

"No." Nina sounded offended. "It's because I know how to haggle."

"That, too."

"I'm not kidding. I'm a great haggler. Want me to prove it? If you expect to come to my place tonight, you have to pay for the baklava."

"I'd be happy to."

"See."

Nina slowed to make the right turn off Dale onto the service road that led to the I-94 entrance ramp. Apparently she was too slow for the SUV. It edged just inches from her bumper and leaned on the horn. Nina flinched. "What's he doing?" she wanted to know.

I turned in my seat to look out the rear window and got an eyeful of high beams.

"Probably afraid he'll miss the *Law & Order* reruns on TV tonight."

Nina accelerated faster than she normally would have to accommodate the tailgater. That's what we do now—we hit the gas and hope to avoid trouble. There was a time, if someone was riding my bumper, I would have deliberately slowed down and make the guy pass me or back off. But that was before growing population, urban sprawl, and an overworked traffic system turned road rage into a spectator sport. It's become so nasty out there that I, for one, refuse to use my horn for fear of setting off a confrontation—especially since the state legislature now permits any Clint Eastwood wannabe over the age of twenty-one who completes seven hours of classroom and firearms training to carry a concealed weapon.

Nina was five miles over the speed limit by the time she reached the bottom of the ramp. The SUV was still on her bumper, but it now had three freeway lanes on the left to pass us. Only it didn't swerve away. It accelerated. And rammed the back of Nina's Lexus.

The blow shoved Nina forward against the steering wheel. Yet she kept control of the car, kept it moving in a straight line. She righted herself and glanced in her rearview mirror and did what most of us would have done. She began to slow down.

The SUV hit us again. Harder.

The Lexus swerved abruptly to the left, but Nina brought it back.

I was looking out the rear window, but the headlights were in my eyes. I couldn't identify the vehicle or read its license plate.

The SUV made another run at the rear of the Lexus. This time Nina saw it coming and accelerated. The SUV just grazed her bumper before the Lexus leaped ahead, gaining speed, gobbling up freeway.

Nina was heading for the next exit, moving fast.

The driver of the SUV must have read her thoughts, because he pulled into the left lane and punched it. The SUV surged ahead, drawing next to us.

It could have been a Chevy Blazer, but I wasn't sure. I stared hard, but the freeway lights were reflecting off the SUV's windows and I couldn't see the driver.

The SUV and Lexus were side by side, going at least ninety, maybe faster. I was afraid to look at the speedometer.

And then I noticed the SUV's passenger-side window rolling down.

"Stop."

Nina stomped on her brakes.

The nose of the Lexus angled down toward the pavement and the rear seemed to lift upward as the car came to a sliding, shrieking halt.

Balloons of bright orange popped inside the SUV—one, two, three—followed by snapping sounds that reminded me of a kid's cap gun. The vehicle was well past us now. It traveled fifty yards before its red taillights flared and it rolled to a stop.

"If it goes into reverse, you fly past it," I said.

Nina didn't say if she would or wouldn't. As it turned out, the instruction proved unnecessary. After a few moments, the SUV resumed moving forward, driving toward Minneapolis.

"Was he shooting at us?" Nina asked. It was the first she had spoken since we entered the freeway, the first sound she had made at all.

"You handled the car very well," I told her.

"Was he shooting at us?"

"Yes."

"Why was he shooting at us?"

"Because he could, I guess."

She didn't like my answer.

Nina drove the Lexus at the posted speed limit until she reached the Lexington Avenue exit, left the freeway, and pulled into the gas station at the top of the ramp.

I checked the front of the car for bullet holes and found none while she examined the damage in back.

"Look what they did to my new car."

The taillight on the right was intact. The rest of the rear had been smashed in, including the trunk lid, and half of the bumper was missing.

"My car," Nina moaned.

"I'm so sorry," I told her.

"What have you gotten me into?"

"Me?"

"Yes, you. You're always pissing off somebody. Who was it this time?"

I assured her that what had taken place had nothing to do with me or Mr. Mosley's bees—why would it? It was only another example of road rage. It had been happening to a lot of people on Twin Cities freeways lately. It was just our turn.

After she calmed down, Nina accepted my explanation. Unfortunately, so did I.

Chapter Three

Nina usually went to work late in the morning, and because Erica wasn't there, she had no reason to get up early. And since I seldom had a reason to get up early, we slept in. When I finally arrived home at about 10:30 A.M., the blinking red light on my phone informed me that I had a message on my voice mail. It was from Billy Tillman. He had called at 8:36 A.M. from the Fairview Southdale Hospital in Edina. He wanted to see me right now.

The first thing Tilly did was punch me.

He was standing outside a closed door in the middle of a dazzling white hospital corridor and vehemently arguing in hushed tones with a man and a woman, both in their late twenties. Even from fifty feet away I knew they were plainclothes cops. As I approached, Tillman broke away from the detectives. There was something in his eyes, only I didn't see it until it was too late.

I said, "Tilly—"

And he punched me.

He hit me square in the jaw, snapping my head back.

He hit me so hard that I left my feet and sailed backward down the hospital corridor.

My first instinct was to return the favor. Only I was flat on my back and looking up at him, so it didn't seem like much of an option.

"Get up," he howled at me.

The two detectives clutched Tillman by the arms and shoulders, and he struggled to free himself.

"Get up," he shouted again.

I rose slowly to my feet, never taking my eyes from him even as I cautiously probed my jaw with my fingers. It wasn't broken, but it felt as if it were.

"What's going on, Tilly?"

He struggled with the cops some more. A moment later, he abruptly stopped struggling. "I'm all right. I'm all right now."

He didn't look or sound all right.

"What's wrong?" I asked.

The cops relaxed their grip. He pushed them away. I brought my hands up in self-defense, but Tilly didn't come for me. Instead he strode toward the small waiting room at the far end of the corridor.

"Come here," he shouted.

The female cop said, "He won't talk to us. Neither will Mrs. Tillman. You must convince them to talk to us."

"About what?"

"Come here," Tilly shouted again.

"What's going on?"

They didn't say. I moved toward Tilly. The two cops didn't follow, which made me nervous.

"Tilly?"

He grabbed my arm, spun me toward the entrance to the waiting room, and shoved me inside. He slammed the door behind us.

"You sonuvabitch."

His face was only inches from mine.

"You goddamn sonuvabitch."

I moved backward, putting distance between us.

"What did I do?"

"They raped her."

"What?"

"My Susan, they raped her."

Oh no, oh no, oh no, oh no, oh no . . .

"There were two of them. Susan was at the end of the driveway with Sheila, waiting for the 7:10 school bus. I had already left for a breakfast meeting. They waited until the bus came and went, and when Susan returned to the house they were on her. Two of them. They beat her and they raped her and then—and then when they finished they told her to tell me to forget about Crosetti. Forget all about Frank Crosetti, they said, or next time it'll be your daughter. Susan won't talk to the police, she won't let me . . . That's why . . . Our daughter, McKenzie. Sheila."

I heard Tilly's words, understood their meaning, yet

my mind wouldn't accept them. *You're kidding, right? This is one of your outrageous gags. Right?*

"I'm sorry," Tilly told me. "I'm sorry, okay? I shouldn't have hit you, but . . ."

But you need to hit someone. And I deserve it because I didn't warn you. It wasn't road rage, what happened last night. Those guys were trying to kill Nina and me, and I didn't warn you. Oh, God . . .

"I know . . . I know it's not your fault, but . . . Dammit, McKenzie. What did you get me into?"

It was the same question Nina had asked me, only this time I had no answer. The gears wouldn't mesh. My brain raced along in neutral, going nowhere fast.

"Say something," Tillman said.

My mouth moved. Words came out. Useless sounds.

"I'm so sorry, Tilly."

"Sorry?"

"I didn't know they were this dangerous."

"You didn't know?"

"I don't even know who they are."

"The depth and breadth of what you don't know is staggering."

"Tilly, you and Susan have to talk to the police. You have to tell them . . ."

"Susan won't—she won't even consider it. Maybe later, maybe when she's had some time . . . Right now all she can think of is Sheila."

"May I talk to Susan?"

"Hell no! She hates you. I hate you, McKenzie. What they did to her . . ."

"I'm sorry."

"Sorry?"

"Tilly, I'll take care of this."

"How the hell are you going to take care of this, McKenzie? Are you going to wish it away? You going to make it so it never happened?"

"It'll be all right."

"It will never be all right."

"I'm sorry."

"I know you're sorry. I know . . . Listen, just—just go away, all right? Just go."

He flung open the door and was out of the waiting room before I could reply. It was just as well. I had nothing more to say except "I'm sorry" another two or three hundred times. He brushed past the detectives without answering their questions and entered his wife's room, closing the door behind him. The cops asked me the same questions when I walked past. I didn't have any answers for them, either.

"A crime was committed," the male cop announced.

"No kidding, Barney," I said and instantly regretted it. I had despised being called Barney Fife when I was a policeman.

"Sorry," I told him.

"Sorry doesn't cut it," he said.

He had me there.

I went to the elevators, punched the down button, and thought about Susan. I had dealt with rape victims when I was on the job. Sometimes I told them, "I know how you feel." Only I didn't. I was taught how to behave, how to "chaperone" a victim. I was taught that rape was the ultimate violation, just one step short of homicide. I was taught about the fear, shame, anger, shock, and guilt that a woman experiences. I was taught about her inability to sleep and the nightmares she'll have when she does sleep, the erratic mood swings and the feelings of worthlessness that will come later. But *feel* what she feels? Who was I kidding?

And Tilly. I could only guess at what he felt, too. The humiliation. The powerlessness. The crushing knowledge that he failed to do what men are taught they must do—protect their families. I've seen it suck the heart right out of a guy.

That's why I wasn't upset that Tilly slugged me, and I certainly didn't hold it against him. Having failed the image he had of himself, he'd need to do something rough to restore his self-respect, something that'd absolve him of the sin of helplessness. It's one way some men cope, and better than the alternatives many choose—blaming the woman for the assault or ignoring it altogether, pretending the rape never happened, out of sight, out of mind. Besides, the way I figured it, he had a few more free shots coming. Yet what I wished most for my friend was that he'd find within himself the strength, courage, patience, humor, and depth of love necessary to help him and Susan heal. That's what I wished for them both.

As for me—I should have warned him. *Goddammit, what was I thinking?*

I told Tillman I'd take care of this, and I meant it. I couldn't make it all right, I knew that. *But I could make it better.* I could find Frank Crosetti. I could find his thugs.

I could grind them into dust. It's the least I could do for Tilly and Susan. I owed them now.

I took a slow elevator to the main floor and worked my way out of the hospital. It wasn't until I was in the parking lot that it dawned on me.

"Mr. Mosley."

I didn't warn him, either.

I punched his number into my cell phone. There was one ring followed by a voice mail message. "You've reached Mosley Honey Farms. We're sorry we can't take your call right now . . ."

Six cruisers from the Carver County Sheriff's Department and one black Buick Regal were parked every which way on Mr. Mosley's property. I parked behind the Regal and ran to the house. A female deputy opened the door. She wore pink lipstick, but most of it had been gnawed off where she chewed on her lips.

"Mr. Mosley," I called and tried to push past her. She was a little thing, but she understood leverage and kept me pinned against the door frame.

"Who are you?" she asked.

"McKenzie," a voice told her.

Reverend Winfield was sitting on Mr. Mosley's sofa next to another deputy. He was the minister of the King of Kings Baptist Church of Golden Valley. I had met him on those few occasions when I attended services with Mr. Mosley.

"McKenzie," he said again, shaking his head. "It's too late. He's gone. He's gone."

Gone? Gone? What does that mean, gone?

Another voice said, "Let him through." That got me past the door and as far as the kitchen, where I was stopped again. In the kitchen I found several more deputies, one of them working a camera. Mr. Mosley was on the floor. Suddenly he seemed so small, so fragile, so old. He was lying on his stomach, his face turned to the side. His eyes were open. He was still grasping the handle of the ancient percolator, the coffeemaker now on its side, its contents spilling out on the floor and mixing with his blood. There were two mugs on the counter above him. Mr. Mosley had been pouring a cup of coffee when someone shot him twice in the back of the head.

It was the same kind of day as before. The sky was blue and cloudless. Bees buzzed. Birds sang. People went about their business. Except they did it in slow motion and their voices were like sounds heard from the bottom of a pool. The reverend rose from the sofa and approached me. His arms opened. I could see him so clearly—the deep creases in his face, the gray in his mustache, the tiny specks of lint on his black suit jacket. Oddest of odd, I could see myself, too. A man with a comical expression on his face, tears in his eyes and on his cheeks and dripping from his chin, and no voice, only a strange guttural sound like a man makes when he's strangling . . .

"I'm sorry," the deputy sheriff said. He didn't look sorry. He looked like a man with questions to ask.

It had taken a while for me to shove the pieces back together. Most of them, I'm sure, were still lying on the floor where I collapsed. I had seen things, some of the worst sights humanity had to offer. Yet none of them—not even the savage murder of Jamie Carlson last fall—had rocked me in the same way as seeing Mr. Mosley zipped into a black vinyl bag. Until now I had managed to keep all those displays of brutality at a distance, even those I had committed myself. True, they had a way of sneaking up on me and messing with my head at the oddest moments—during a ball game, at a supermarket checkout, while doing yard work—but not often and never for long. Now I felt the weight of all of them at once.

Reverend Winfield had discovered the body. He had come by to drop off a turkey-sized deep fryer that Mr. Mosley had lent the church and found him on the kitchen floor. I know because he kept telling me over and over, even as I repeated my own story—I was helping Mr. Mosley with his bees. *We're not at fault, we don't deserve this,* we told each other, told ourselves. This went on, between wails and sobs, for what seemed like a long time.

Finally a sense of acceptance, and with it coherent thought, began to seep through the sorrow. Function returned. Eyes, ears, nose, mouth, arms, legs, hands, feet began working again. I breathed in and out.

"I'm sorry," the deputy repeated. His name tag read BREHMER. There were sergeant's stripes on his sleeves. His expression was neutral, and his voice was calm. "What was your relationship to the victim?"

No, no, don't ask that. Don't make me think about that. Not now. I took the question and quickly built a wall of brick and mortar around it.

"My name's McKenzie." I was speaking quickly. *Don't think, don't feel.* "Let's cut to the chase. I know who did this. His name is Frank Crosetti. He lives two and a half miles from here—"

"How do you know?"

Don't interrupt. Let me finish before the wall crumbles.

I spoke over the sergeant's questions, telling him the story in chronological order, telling him about the bees and Ivy Flynn and the meeting with Crosetti and Billy Tillman—making sure he knew that Tilly and Susan had no intention of cooperating with him but maybe would change their minds once they had time to digest what happened. I withheld nothing except one vital piece of information.

"I don't know the exact address," I said. "But I can take you there."

"That won't be necessary."

"I can identify Crosetti for you."

"Thank you, but—"

"I was eleven and a half years on the job. I know how to take care of myself. I know how not to get in the way."

"Mr. McKenzie—"

"Call Sergeant Robert Dunston of the St. Paul Police Department. He works homicide. He'll vouch for me."

"It's not procedure."

"I'll wait in the car."

Brehmer gave that a moment's thought. "Are you armed?"

"I am not armed." I removed the blue sports jacket I wore over my gray sweatshirt, held my arms away from my sides, and spun slowly.

"You'll sit in the back," Brehmer said. "You will not get out unless I tell you."

"Yes, sir."

"Don't do anything that'll make me regret this, McKenzie."

"I won't."

Sergeant Brehmer locked his eyes on mine and held them there without blinking. He said, "This is Minnesota. People here usually kill only their friends and loved ones. They usually do it in their kitchens, rec rooms, and bedrooms, occasionally in bars. They use guns when they're handy, otherwise knives, blunt objects, sometimes their hands. With gangs it's drive-bys. Mostly they hit other gangsters on the street, in clubs, in the parking lots of fast-food joints, sometimes with automatic weapons, more or less trying to avoid collateral damage. But this. A double tap behind the ear with .22 hollow points. That's professional. That's organized crime shit, and we don't do organized crime in Minnesota. Not since the early sixties. Not since they put Kid Cann away."

"I know."

"Is there something you're not telling me?"

"No, sergeant. There isn't."

"There better not be."

There was no opportunity to approach the house on the hill without being seen, which made me think that's why Crosetti rented it. So it became a raid. Four cars and an SUV from the Carver County Sheriff's

Department—no sirens, no light bars, driving fast—took the gravel driveway past the ditch, then fanned out and charged up the hill, tearing up the lawn. The cars surrounded the house—three in front, two in back. Deputies spilled out. No one shouted, no one slammed a door. Cover was taken behind the vehicles. Shotguns and Glocks were leveled at every window and door from across car hoods and trunks.

I was in a fifth car, Sergeant Brehmer at the wheel. He stopped at the top of the driveway and approached the front door like he had been invited. The door was flanked by deputies, guns drawn. They were wearing helmets and Kevlar suits and carrying shields. Their backup was wearing Kevlar vests. Only I went without. It was decided that I didn't need it. I was locked in the back of the cruiser behind wire mesh—I couldn't break my word to the sergeant if I wanted to.

Brehmer pounded on the door.

"Sheriff's Department. We have a warrant. Open up."

No answer.

He nodded to the deputy behind him. The deputy smashed the door open with a portable battering ram. Brehmer and his deputies dashed inside the house.

I heard no shots, only voices.

"Clear," the voices shouted. "Clear. Clear."

Then nothing.

I waited.

And waited some more.

It took only minutes, but it seemed much, much longer.

Finally Sergeant Brehmer emerged from the house. He walked directly to the cruiser and unlocked the back door. He held it open for me.

"It's empty," he said as I slid out.

"He might come back. You should position your men—"

"The house is empty, McKenzie. And don't tell me what I should do."

"I'm saying, if he's not here now—"

"You don't get it. The house is empty. No furniture. No clothes in the closets. No dishes in the cabinets. No food in the refrigerator. There are no paintings on the walls or toilet paper in the bathroom or trash under the sink. There's no sign that anyone lives here. There's no sign that anyone has ever lived here."

"I don't get it."

"Exactly," Brehmer said.

"He was here yesterday."

"But not today."

"I'm not making this up."

The thought that Crosetti might escape, that he might get away with the murder of my friend, engulfed me. I felt a seething anger then—like mist clinging to my skin. A rage so primitive, so elemental, that it didn't have a name. I slammed a clenched fist against the roof of the car. I did it several times. Sergeant Brehmer muttered something about destruction of county property, but I wasn't paying attention.

You're losing control, my inner voice chided.

I know. I hit the roof again.

Stop it. I leaned against the car.

You're taking it too personally.

It is personal. I should have warned Mr. Mosley and Tillman.

You didn't know.

I should have.

Maybe so, but it doesn't matter now. Now you have to suck it up. Either start thinking like a cop or go home.

"What about the garage?" I asked.

A deputy approaching the car overheard the question.

"Clean," he said. "Except"—he held up two stained fingers—"for fresh oil on the floor."

"That's something," I said.

"Is it?"

"It proves I'm not lying."

Brehmer was checking the roof of his car for dings. "No one said you were. In any case—" He pointed at the fine-trimmed lawn. "This grass was cut just a few days ago."

The deputy asked, "What do you want me to do, Sarge?"

"The messenger," I said.

"What messenger?" Brehmer asked.

"The messenger from Billy Tillman's law office. The man who delivered the letter."

"What will he tell us?"

"If nothing else, he'll tell us that Crosetti was here yesterday."

Brehmer put his arm around the deputy's shoulder and slowly walked him toward the house. I followed from far enough back to be respectful but close enough to monitor their conversation.

"Canvass the area. There aren't many houses, but you

never know, someone might have seen something. I also want you to get CID up here. I'm looking for fingerprints, something we can match to the Mosley scene, and anything else they can find."

"Yes, sir."

"I want you to contact all the moving companies in the area, all the truck rentals. Get the names of everyone they've done business with in the past forty-eight hours. I also want you to contact all the landscaping companies, anyone who cuts grass, including the kid down the street if there is a kid down the street. Understand?"

"Yes, sir."

"One more thing." Brehmer threw a glance at me over his shoulder. "Contact an attorney named William Tillman in Edina. Find out what messenger service he uses." He looked at me again. "Satisfied?"

"I just had a thought."

"Feel free to share."

"The second man. The one who showed up when Crosetti had the shotgun on us."

"What about him?"

"He was driving a new Mustang ragtop. I don't have a plate, but—"

"How many Mustangs do you think Ford sold in the past two years?"

"Not as many as they built, but—"

"But."

"It was yellow."

Brehmer grimaced. "What kind of guy drives a yellow Mustang convertible?"

My thought exactly.

Brehmer nodded at his deputy. The deputy said, "No one said the job would be easy," and went away.

I was questioned for nearly five hours inside the Justice Center Building in Chaska, the Carver County seat, but the deputies were pretty good about it. They kept the door to the interrogation room open and brought me cup after cup of surprisingly good coffee and takeout from a Chinese restaurant that served Peking chicken for white suburbanites. I answered all their questions in excruciating detail, explaining as best I could my relationship with Mr. Mosley and my efforts to learn what was killing his honeybees. I gave them Professor Buzicky's name and number, and Ivy Flynn's name and number, and told them about the meeting with Billy Tillman. I broke down only once. Fortunately, Sergeant Brehmer was well trained. He managed to both comfort me and get the answers he needed at the same time.

They interviewed Billy Tillman, too. For a short time we were in the same room together. He refused to speak to me, to even acknowledge my existence, until they were leading him to another location. Without looking back, he said, "I'm sorry about Mr. Mosley."

I stood in the center of the downstairs bar at Rickie's, not quite sure what I was doing there. A waitress carrying a tray of drinks stopped to ask if everything was all right. I could have told her a thing or two but didn't.

I asked for Nina.

The waitress pointed at a door marked EMPLOYEES ONLY. I went through the door and down a short corridor. I found Nina in her office. She looked up from her paperwork. She smiled. The smile turned into a frown.

"My God, McKenzie. Who died?"

I wept some more.

I drank bourbon—without ice—pouring it from a bottle Nina appropriated from a carton in a storage room. I had three before she cut me off. Then one more over her objections. I told her about Mr. Mosley and my father and me. Occasionally she'd ask a question, but mostly she listened. It took about an hour to talk myself out.

"I never met Mr. Mosley," Nina said. "I wish I had."

"I should have introduced you. I don't know why I didn't. You would have liked him. He was a good guy. In my neighborhood growing up, that was considered high praise, being a good guy."

"You're a good guy, too."

"If I am it's because my dad and Mr. Mosley showed me how."

"You're going after them, aren't you? The people who killed Mr. Mosley. Who raped Susan Tillman."

"Yes, I am."

"It's because you blame yourself for what happened."

"I should have done something after those guys shot at us last night. I should have warned them—Mr. Mosley and Tillman. I should have . . ."

"It's not your fault."

"I know. It's their fault—whoever they are. And I'm going to get them."

"May I offer you some advice, McKenzie—advice from someone who cares about you?"

"You're not going to lecture me, are you? About justice and vengeance and all that?"

"After all these months I think I'm starting to know you. I'm starting to understand who you are and why you do the things that you do, so no, I'm not going to lecture. I'm going to tell you this one thing and then let it go. Okay?"

"Okay."

"Whatever satisfaction you hope to gain, it won't be worth it if something bad happens to you."

I didn't understand her logic until she kissed me. And then I pretended not to.

The next day was Sunday. Here's what happened. I was alone. The phone rang, but I didn't answer it. Messages were left, but I didn't listen to them. Music spilled from nineteen speakers scattered through eight rooms and my basement, but I didn't really hear it. The TV was on—the Timberwolves were in the NBA playoffs and the Twins were playing the White Sox—but I wasn't paying attention. Food was cooked; most of it was left untouched. The sun rose. The sun arched across the sky. The sun set. That's what happened on Sunday.

Except late in the evening the phone rang. The caller ID said Brehmer. I answered it. I said, "Sarge?"

"McKenzie?"

"Right here."

"I checked you out. They told me you were solid. A good cop. I wouldn't call you otherwise."

"Okay."

"The reason I called, I wanted to give you a heads-up. I've been taken off the case. They gave it to a bureaucrat, Lieutenant Brian Dyke. He's head of the county's Criminal Investigation Division, but he doesn't belong there. He's not smart enough to find Mr. Mosley's killer."

"Okay."

"Do you hear what I'm telling you? He's not smart enough to find Mr. Mosley's killer."

"Yeah."

"There's more."

"More?"

"Frank Crosetti doesn't exist. At least not according to any records I could find."

"What do you mean, he doesn't exist?"

"There's no record of him—the Frank Crosetti you're looking for, anyway. No Social Security number. No driver's license. No birth certificate or passport. No credit cards. No health care. No subscription to *Sports Illustrated*."

"Lundgren-Kerber was renting to him."

"Lundgren-Kerber never heard of Crosetti, claim the property has been vacant for months."

"He was there."

"I believe you. But he's been erased."

"That's not possible."

"Of course it's possible."

"You can't erase a person's existence. There's always

something left behind. A cable bill, a name on a lottery ticket, an order for Girl Scout cookies . . ."

"You could do it if the person never existed in the first place."

"Identity theft? Crosetti stole someone's identity?"

"Try again."

"A entirely new identity. Crosetti created a new identity for himself. Fine. It's been done before. But he must have left a trail."

"Not this time."

"Listen, Sarge. I worked a couple of missing person cases like this, okay? If it's worth your time, effort, and expense, you can find anyone. People don't just disappear. They always, always, always leave behind a trace of themselves."

"He could pull it off if he had help."

"From who? Who has the resources for a gag like that?"

"Who do you think?"

The answer came to me quickly, but I didn't want to say it.

"Hey, McKenzie," Sergeant Brehmer said after a brief pause.

"Yeah."

"We didn't have this conversation."

Chapter Four

I was surprised by how calmly the news reader at MPR said, "Authorities are still seeking suspects in the apparent gangland slaying of an elderly Carver County beekeeper Saturday morning." But then Minnesota Public Radio always gave the news without hype or suspense or fury, and while you could detect a certain liberal sensibility, it sure beat hell out of the "nuke 'em 'til they glow" self-righteous fervor found on the so-called conservative radio stations.

Still, I had had enough bad news. I switched on the Jeep Cherokee's CD player and found the Badlees. They carried me west along I-394 and then north on Highway 100 into Golden Valley.

There were few African-Americans living in Carver County and no church that spoke to him, so Mr. Mosley drove all the way to King of Kings Baptist Church for services. It occurred to me that it took Mr. Mosley as much time to go to church as it took me to drive to his house, yet he had managed to visit the first-ring suburb of Minneapolis at least once a week while I couldn't visit him a half dozen times a year.

"I'm sorry, sir," I heard myself mutter. "I should have . . ."

Don't go there. Don't think about the many things you should have done for that good old man.

The parking lot was empty. I found a space near the front door and went inside. Churches make me uncomfortable. I haven't entered one in twenty-five years without feeling like a trespasser, and King of Kings was no exception. I had gone there with Mr. Mosley on a few occasions over the decades because he had insisted, and although the spirituals and gospel music were astounding, I found the free-flowing emotions of the parishioners embarrassing. And the spectacle of the normally reticent Mr. Mosley giving voice to his faith unnerved me. Perhaps it would have been different if my own relationship with God hadn't been so strained. Since my mother died, I've seen only glimpses of him.

Funny how tragedy brings some people closer to God while pushing others away. I figure it's because one group doesn't expect as much from him as the other.

King of Kings was built like an amphitheater. The sanctuary seated eighteen hundred, with all of the pews sloping gently down toward the pulpit and a thirty-seat choir. I found Reverend Winfield in the pulpit, reading silently to himself. He looked up when he heard me and quickly removed his glasses, concealing them in a pocket.

"McKenzie," he said. Reverend Winfield spoke in a musical baritone, and his voice wafted gently up to me.

"Reverend," I replied.

"I can't tell you how deeply sorry I am. Violence—so many black men die today of violence."

I sat in a middle pew. He descended from the pulpit and crossed to the railing in front of the first pew. His hands were at his side, his fingers tapping a rhythm against his thighs, a nervous habit, perhaps, that I hadn't noticed in our previous meetings.

"I've been trying to remember the last time I saw you in church," he told me.

"So have I."

"How can I help you?"

I asked about funeral arrangements.

"Since he was a Korean War veteran, Mr. Mosley will be interred at Fort Snelling with military honors."

Fort Snelling National Cemetery, I thought. They would add his bleached-white headstone to its 430 acres of monuments, all laid out in tidy military columns, some dating back to the Civil War. I had been there with my father, watched him salute long-ago comrades. Many fell in battle. Others from accident, disease, or just old age. *How many were murdered?* I wondered. And did it matter? Fort Snelling was very strict about the uniform dimensions and composition of the headstones. Most were marble or granite; a few were made of bronze. Yet after all was said and done, wasn't one stone as cold as any other? Wasn't death just as final?

"Mr. Mosley had no immediate family," Reverend Winfield said.

"I know. He was property of the state."

"Mr. Mosley was no one's property."

I couldn't argue with that.

"The church was his family," the reverend said.

"I know."

"He left all of his worldly possessions to the church."

"I know that, too. That's what I came to talk about. I'm concerned about his business, about Mosley Honey Farms. Are you going to sell it?"

"Do you want to buy it?"

"I might."

"You don't strike me as a beekeeper."

I had to laugh. "I'm not. Far from it."

"Why, then, are you interested?"

"A man should leave more behind than just the joyful memories of the people who knew him."

"I personally believe that's the best a man can leave behind. But no matter. The church is going to keep Mosley Honey Farms, McKenzie. We'll continue to operate it under Mr. Mosley's name, with the profits going to the church. Lorenzo Hernandez, Mr. Mosley's employee, has volunteered to run the business for us."

That didn't exactly fill me with confidence, remembering what Mr. Mosley had to say about Hernandez, but I let it slide.

"Obviously you cared for Mr. Mosley," Reverend Winfield said.

"I loved that old man. He helped raise me."

"You should speak of him at the memorial. The funeral can't take place until the county medical examiner releases the body. We don't know when that will be.

But the church is holding a memorial service for Mr. Mosley tonight."

"I don't like funerals."

"Who does? I expect to see you, McKenzie. At 7:00 P.M. sharp."

"I'll be there if I can."

"What could possibly keep you away?"

I didn't answer.

The reverend seemed to read my mind.

"Vengeance is mine, sayeth the Lord."

I headed for the doors. Reverend Winfield called my name. I answered with a wave.

I didn't tell him, but as far as I was concerned, the Lord could get in line.

Norwood Young America had two downtown areas, separated by Highway 212, and I searched them both. It didn't take long. Norwood and Young America had originally been two independent cities, but the single community that was created following their 1997 merger could still fit inside the Hubert H. Humphrey Metrodome with room left over for a few nonincorporated townships.

My plan, such as it was, was simple. Like bees, people tend to stay close to their hives, and judging by Crosetti's enormous stomach, he was a man who indulged his appetites. So it wasn't unreasonable to assume that he might have frequented a bar or restaurant within, say, a ten-mile radius of his house on the hill. Possibly he revealed something of himself to someone he met there. Possibly that someone might give me the information I needed to identify him, to find him and his thugs. Possibly.

The search began cheerfully enough. I even bought drinks and sandwiches and joked with the help at Richard's on Main, Kube's, Daboars Bar and Grill, the Flame Lounge, and Siggy's on 212. But I began losing patience by the time I reached the Elm Street Station. I had asked for Crosetti by name and described him to each manager, bartender, and waitress and all the patrons who would talk to me, yet no one admitted to knowing him. My frustration reached its peak when I stepped out of the Last Call to discover a parking ticket tucked beneath my windshield wiper. Murphy's Law. If I knew where the SOB lived, I'd go over there and kick his ass. I crumbled the ticket into a ball and tossed it in the direction of my backseat. "You'll never take me alive, coppers," I snarled in my best Edward G. Robinson. Sometimes I like to entertain myself.

A roadhouse near Braunworth Lake late in the afternoon showed promise, but only because the bartender was belligerent. It was cramped and dark and had sticky rubber tiles on the floor. The clientele was 90 percent male—not a gay bar, just a joint where you don't take women.

When I entered, the drone of conversation decreased in volume while the dirt and dairy farmers, creamery workers, construction workers, and county highway employees assembled there assessed my value. It took only a moment for them to decide that I wasn't worth noticing, and the volume quickly returned to normal.

The bartender was leaning against the stick. He

looked like a man whose idea of a mixed drink was water on the side.

"I'm looking for Frank Crosetti," I told him.

"Should I care?"

"I owe him a few bucks."

"Yeah?"

"I bet on the Wild to win the NHL title."

"Why'd you do a stupid thing like that?"

"Wishful thinking. So, has he been around?"

"Maybe."

I felt a flush of anger at his remark, as if the bartender were trying to cheat me out of my share of the lottery. I tried to keep it out of my voice.

"Look, pal. If you know Crosetti, you know he's not somebody you welsh on. Do you expect him around or not?"

"Who wants to know?"

"My name's McKenzie."

"Sometimes he comes in, sometimes he doesn't. He don't keep to no schedule."

"Have you seen him around lately?"

"Not for a couple of days."

"Know where I can find him when he's not here?"

"No."

I believed him. Crosetti had moved in only six weeks earlier, and I doubted that he would have become so valuable a customer that the bartender would protect him. Only what did I know? Maybe they had been Boy Scouts together.

I ordered a draft. The bartender poured it. I slid a

five across the stick, and he put it in his pocket. I knew there would be no change.

"If you want to talk to Crosetti so bad, why don'tcha call 'im?" he said.

"Do you know his number?"

"No."

"Neither do I."

The bartender folded his arms across his chest and watched me sip the beer. From his exaggerated sigh, I had the distinct impression I wasn't drinking fast enough. I drained the glass and set it down in front of me. He made no effort to refill it. I took that as a hint.

I was running out of possibilities. All the names on the list I had compiled from the Norwood Young America telephone directory had been scratched out except for the name of the roadhouse, which I had circled, and two others.

My next stop was the Norwood Inn. The folks there were pleasant enough, but no one had ever seen or heard of Crosetti. That left Carver Suites on Highway 212, just east of the city.

The lounge was light and airy, and so was the conversation of the women and men who gathered there—more women than men—all of them dressed for business that was conducted in an office. The happy-hour piano player was beating the daylights out of some very good Cole Porter, and for a moment I could imagine Nina Truhler beating the daylights out of him. She loved Porter, and Hoagie Carmichael and the Gershwins and anyone else who could put words to melody and create magic.

I sat at the bar. A table tent recommended a lite beer. I ignored it. The bartender smiled and welcomed me warmly—actually said, "Welcome"—and asked what I'd have. I ordered black coffee with a slug of bourbon in it and wondered if Mr. Mosley would approve. The bartender served it on a napkin that told me Carver Suites was a proud sponsor of Stiftungsfest, the annual founders festival, and then went off to welcome other guests. While he was gone I dragged the room with my eyes. There were a few couples, but mostly groups of four or more gathered at the tables. Against the wall, as far away from the piano player as she could get, sat a woman alone. She wore a thin dress and an expression that solicited company. I had the feeling that any company would do. There was a cast on her left hand.

When the bartender returned, I asked him, "Have you seen Frank Crosetti lately?"

"That fat pig?" Talk about taking the happy out of happy hour. "No, I haven't seen him, but if I do I'm going to kick his ass. Why? You a friend of his?"

He asked the question like he was inviting me to step outside.

"He's no friend of mine," I assured him. "And if you want to kick his ass I'll be happy to hold your coat."

The bartender's smile returned just as quickly as it had left. "Sorry 'bout that."

"No problem."

"Let me freshen that for you." He refilled my mug. "So you don't like Crosetti, either."

"What's to like?"

"Not much."

"I take it he was a customer."

"Briefly."

"But not anymore."

"If I ever see him again . . ." He shook his head bitterly.

"What did he do?"

"He broke a woman's hand."

"Why?"

"For the fun of it."

"Yeah, that sounds like my guy. When did you see him last?"

"About a week ago."

"Know where I can find him?"

"No, but—" His eyes wandered to the woman sitting alone. "Are you screwing with me?"

"What do you mean?"

"You say you're no friend of Crosetti. So why are you looking for him?"

"I want to hurt him just as badly as I can."

I regretted the words the moment I spoke them—I could already hear the bartender repeating them to various cops and county attorneys. But playing off his anger seemed like a good idea at the time.

The bartender nodded and looked again at the woman, who was looking back. "You should talk to Janel."

He gestured with his head. The woman smiled expectantly and rose from her chair. In her heels she ran to five-ten, most of it in her legs. I caught the blue in her eyes halfway across the room.

"Gentleman would like to speak with you," the bartender told her when she approached.

"What would the gentleman like to speak about?"

"Frank Crosetti."

The woman spun around neatly and, without a suggestion of haste, returned to her table.

"Guess she doesn't want to talk," said the bartender.

"What's she drinking?"

"Gimlets."

"Bring her one." I drained the coffee and bourbon. "And another one of these."

I left the bar and sauntered over to the woman's table.

"Hi, Janel. My name's McKenzie."

"Are you a cop?"

"Do I look like a cop?"

"Yes."

"Your instincts are good. I used to be one, but not anymore. May I join you?"

She didn't say I couldn't, so I took the chair opposite her. She watched me suspiciously.

"Like I said. I'm not a cop. I'm not a prosecutor. You have nothing to fear from me."

"What do you want?"

"I'm looking for Frank Crosetti."

"Why?"

I glanced down at her cast.

"So I can hurt him the way he hurt you."

Janel slipped the cast beneath the table as if she were suddenly embarrassed by it.

She said, "F-ing Frank."

"F-ing?"

"You know what I mean."

I did. But the fact that she couldn't bring herself to say the word was strangely endearing. When I first saw her, I guessed she was a prostitute. Now I wondered.

"Did you spend much time with Crosetti?"

"Some. He has a house on a hill not far from here. He would invite me to go to private parties over there. Finally, I did."

"Okay."

"Do you know what I mean by private parties?"

"I know."

"I thought we were—friends. I thought he cared about me. He said he did. He lied."

The bartender appeared, set the drinks on the table, and left. Janel picked up the fresh gimlet and drank half of it.

"Thank you for this."

"Sure. About Crosetti, why did he break your hand?"

"It was over a drink." She looked hard at the glass in front of her, turned it slowly, then gently slid it away, but not so far she couldn't reach it in a hurry. "He asked me to meet him here. I was late. Just a few minutes, but he was really upset about it. Said no one keeps him waiting. I said I was sorry. There was a drink in front of him, and I reached for it, to take a sip, you know, and he grabbed my hand."

She pulled the cast out from under the table and held it up.

"He didn't say anything. He just grabbed my hand and squeezed it as tightly as he could. Frank has strong hands. I heard the bones crack. Then he smashed it against the table—twice. Smashed it down hard. Broke a finger and three bones. Then he left. He never said a word. I never saw him again. We called the cops"—Janel gestured toward the bartender—"but they didn't do anything."

"I'm sorry." I seemed to be using that word a lot lately.

"All because I wanted a sip of his drink."

"Before this happened, did you spend much time talking?"

"Some, in the beginning. Not much after I started—you know, going to his parties. And never before the party. Frank wanted what he wanted when he wanted it. If there was any talking, it was always afterward."

"Did he ever use any other name besides Frank Crosetti?"

"What do you mean?"

"Did you hear anyone call him by a different name?"

"No."

"Did he ever ask you to call him by a different name?"

"Why would he?"

"I think he's using an alias."

"A phony name?"

"Frankie Crosetti was a ballplayer with the Yankees in the thirties and forties."

"I never checked his driver's license or anything, but I guess it makes sense."

"Why do you say that?"

"Frank was from New York."

"How do you know?"

"He said so. I figured that's why he broke my hand. You know how cultures are different, how something might be an okay thing in one place and terrible in another. Maybe in New York sipping someone's drink is like a supreme insult."

"I doubt that. But you're sure he's from New York."

"Yes. He said he was born in someplace called Hunts Point. He was very proud of it. And he kept insulting Minnesota, calling it flyover land, and Minneapolis, saying it was hickville, saying he couldn't wait to get back to New York—to a real city, he said."

I felt a twinge. *What if he was already back in New York? What would I do then?*

"He told me once he would take me with him, but . . ." Janel rested her cast on the table and took another sip of the gimlet. "I didn't really want to go, anyway."

"When was he going back to New York?"

"Soon as he took care of some business."

"What business?"

"I don't know. He just said he had business and when it was finished he could go back to New York."

"Could? He said could?"

"Uh-huh."

"Not would?"

Janel shrugged. "What difference does it make?"

"Maybe none," I told her. But in my head the wheels were spinning. "Would" meant that Crosetti was on a simple business trip—he'd return home once he finished his work. "Could" meant that he needed to complete a specific task in order to be *able* to return to New York. Yes, I know it was flimsy. But since I was grasping at straws, why not take the tiny ones, too?

"Did Crosetti have any friends?" I asked.

"I saw him talking to two men once. But he didn't introduce us."

"What did they look like?"

"The two men? One was small, kinda scrawny. The other was big. Very big. And solid, if you know what I mean. But I didn't pay that much attention."

"Crosetti never called them by name?"

"No. I only heard a name once. He was on the phone. I don't know who he was talking to or what was said—it was at his place, and he made me leave the room. But after he hung up, he said—he said, 'F-ing Granata.' "

"Granata."

"Yeah. Only I don't know if it had anything to do with those two guys."

I bought Janel another gimlet and asked several more questions, but it was just talking. As far as she knew, Crosetti still resided in his house on the hill, and she had no more idea of how to find him than I did. She made some noise about asking the authorities for help, only it didn't get past the table.

The bartender came to tidy up. I paid him and bid Janel good-bye. As I was leaving she said, "If you do find Frank, don't hurt him. He's really not a bad guy."

The bartender and I both glanced down at her cast. Janel quickly hid it beneath the table. The bartender shook his head and chuckled softly, but I didn't think there was anything funny about it.

* * *

Caution is a habit. Practice it long enough and it becomes muscle memory. Longer still and it becomes instinct. Unfortunately, I hadn't quite reached that place yet. The man who crept up silently behind me and rammed the business end of a handgun under my ribs caught me by complete surprise. He said so himself.

"Surprise, shithead."

I had just crossed from the motel entrance to the far rim of the parking lot where I had left my Jeep Cherokee. I had unlocked and opened the door and was about to get in when I felt the muzzle.

"Don't even think about moving."

I examined him over my shoulder. He was about five-six and thin—you could knock him down with a Ping-Pong ball. He was smiling at me with all thirty-two teeth. I lifted my arms in a pose of surrender and looked down at the gun still pressed against my ribs. It was a single-action 9 mm Browning Hi-Power—with the hammer down.

I looked him in the eyes. He kept blinking at me like he hadn't stepped out of the shadows in a long time. He didn't seem too bright nor too ambitious despite the gun. One of those guys who did only what he was told between eight and five and whose idea of excitement was challenging the slot machines at the Indian casinos.

"Let me guess. You're putting yourself through community college selling magazine subscriptions."

He jabbed me harder with the gun.

"Don't fuck with me. I'll put a hole in you the size of a basketball."

He could, too. The nine was more than enough to do the job. Yet even a small-caliber gun would have earned my respect. *Except the hammer was down.*

"What can I do for you?" I asked. I was still clutching my keys in my right hand. I manipulated them so that the blades stuck out between the fingers when I closed my fist.

"We hear you've been lookin' for my man."

"Does your man call himself Frank Crosetti?"

"Tha's right, and he ain't happy you lookin' for him."

"How antisocial."

"You think you're funny?"

"Yeah."

"Well, you ain't."

"Sure I am."

"You ain't."

"What are you arguing for? You're the one with the gun."

"Tha's, tha's right."

"Frank ever tell you his real name?"

"Huh?"

"Frank's real name—did he ever tell you?"

He didn't answer.

"Did he tell you he's from New York?"

"Yeah, I know that."

"What's your name."

"Danny—now wait a minute."

"Where is Frank, Danny?"

The question seemed to confuse him. After a couple of starts and stops, he finally said, "We're supposed to take you to him."

"I don't think so. But if you tell me where I can find him—"

"Whaddya mean? You're comin' with me."

He pushed the muzzle into my ribs again. Enough, I decided. I pivoted swiftly to my right and covered his gun hand with my left, gripping tightly. The Browning was now pointed at the interior of my Cherokee, yet Danny didn't seem to mind. He kept trying to pull the trigger just the same.

"The safety's on, you moron."

I punched him just below the ear. My keys gouged his flesh.

"Where's Frank?"

Danny tried to twist away. I hit him again. The pain caused by the key blades tearing his skin caught up with him and he screamed.

"Where's Frank, Danny?"

He brought his left arm up and tried to hide his head behind it, but it did him no good. I pounded his face twice more.

"Where is he, Danny? Where's Frank?"

He dropped the nine. It caromed off the Cherokee's rocker panel and clattered on the asphalt but didn't discharge—with Browning, it was safety first. I slid my grip from Danny's right hand up to his wrist. He tried to escape, but I jerked him back toward me. This time I hit him below his left eye. The force of the blow bounced him off the SUV. I released his hand and he fell. His face was bleeding profusely. I dropped my keys into my pocket and gripped Danny beneath both armpits. I lifted him up—he weighed about as much as a large box of laundry detergent—and leaned him against the Cherokee.

He spat the word "motherfucker" in my face. Somewhere inside me a switch clicked off. Suddenly there was nothing but darkness.

I backhanded him with a closed fist.

"Was it you, Danny? Did you rape Susan Tillman? You and Frank?" I hit him. "Did you threaten her daughter?" And hit him again. "Was it you?"

I drove my knee into his groin just as hard as I could. He cried out. He would have folded like an accordion, except I wouldn't let him.

"Was it you and Frank who shot my friend?"

I was like a dog when the leash breaks. I pounded my fist into his solar plexus. Once. Twice. Three times. Four times.

His body convulsed. He retched and gagged, and I pushed him away just as the vomit spewed from his mouth. He crumbled to the asphalt and rolled into a ball. I aimed the toe of my shoe at his stomach but paused while Danny threw up on himself.

"Hey, Danny." I was surprised by how relaxed my voice sounded. "Where's Frank, Danny?"

He coughed and sputtered, and I thought he might answer me. But a Chevy Blazer drove up fast and skidded to a stop next to his writhing body. There was a man behind the steering wheel. I couldn't tell how tall or wide he was, but he had brown hair, and his black eyes—I've skated on ice that was warmer.

And I remembered. *Danny had said, "We're." Plural. How could I have missed that?*

And something else. *The guys who shot at Nina and me were driving a Chevy Blazer.*

"Sonuvabitch," I yelled.

The driver reached across his body with his right hand. There was a gun in his hand. He pointed it out the window. I was already moving. I dove backward and rolled and crawled behind the Cherokee. I heard a single shot. Crouching low, I ran along the rim of the parking lot, keeping the other vehicles between me and the driver. I had a permit—it had been issued by a friend of mine, the Itasca County sheriff—but I wasn't carrying. Don't ask me why. Fortunately, the driver wasn't chasing me. I paused long enough to peer cautiously around a bumper. The driver was helping Danny into the SUV. He was as Janel had described him. Big. Solid. He saw me watching and pointed his gun in my direction. Only he didn't fire. Instead, he scrambled into the SUV and accelerated toward the exit from the parking lot. I caught only part of his license plate as he turned onto Highway 212. A moment later, he was gone.

They're after me, I told myself. *They missed the other night the night they got Mr. Mosley and the Tillmans, but they're still coming.*

"Who are these guys?" I said aloud.

I came out of hiding and walked back to my Jeep Cherokee. My door was still open. Danny's Browning was lying on the asphalt beneath it. I left both as they were.

I heard a noise that sounded like laughter but wasn't. I spun around. Two women dressed in business suits were standing on the other side of the parking lot. One had covered her mouth with her hand. The other had turned sideways as if she were preparing to run. Both were staring at me.

I used my own cell phone to call 911.

Lieutenant Brian Dyke seemed slight for a law enforcement officer, and I had no doubt he had barely met the minimum height and weight requirements. Yet he moved and spoke like he was twenty feet tall. A giant among men.

"The witnesses"—he jerked his head toward where the two businesswomen had been standing—"confirm your account of the incident."

"Swell."

Danny's gun was still lying on the asphalt beneath my car door. Dyke looked at it as if he were seeing it for the first time, even though I had shown it to him an hour earlier. He shut the door and picked up the gun by the butt.

"I guess you don't worry about things like fingerprints in the Carver County Sheriff's Department," I told him.

"You think you're funny?"

"Odd. That's exactly what Danny asked me."

"Danny, who you claim pulled the gun on you."

"Danny, who can no longer be identified by his fingerprints."

Dyke sniffed at me like there were forces at work in the Criminal Investigation Division that I was just too dim to grasp and stuck the gun in his belt. Behind him a young deputy was chatting with a teenaged girl wearing a revealing halter and jean shorts hanging low on her hips. The girl kept her ten-speed bike between them. All the other deputies had departed shortly after Lieutenant Dyke arrived. I began to think Sergeant Brehmer was right.

"I'm this close to running you in." Dyke held his thumb and index finger about a half inch apart.

"What charge?"

"Obstructing justice. What do you think you're doing, conducting your own personal investigation?"

"You don't seem to be doing it."

"I don't care for your attitude."

"Maybe I'll lose sleep over that. Whaddaya think the chances are?"

"All I can say is you had better stop sticking your nose into business that doesn't concern you."

"Doesn't concern me? My friend was killed. Another was raped."

"No complaint was filed on that."

"I was shot at, and you're doing jack about it."

"Yeah, get all indignant on me. Go 'head, see where that'll get you."

"Let me guess. Bullies stole your lunch money when you were a kid, and now you're using your badge to prove how tough you are."

"You want to see how tough I am?"

"Did you at least run the license plate?"

"It was a partial."

"First three letters—*F* as in Francis, *A* as in Albert, *S* as in Sinatra. How many Chevy Blazers can there be in Minnesota with those initials?"

Lieutenant Dyke didn't say.

"There's a security camera in the foyer of the motel. It might have caught something. Did you secure the videotape? Janel in the bar saw two men who were friends of Crosetti. Do her descriptions match the ones I gave you? Did you canvass for witnesses? The one called Danny was hurt. Are you contacting local hospital ERs and outpatient clinics to see if his partner brought him in?"

It was like conversing with an empty parking lot for all the attention Dyke paid me. He said, "You're too smart for your own good, you know that, McKenzie?"

"Do your job, for God's sake."

"That's enough. No more from you. You're done. No more investigation. You don't go anywhere. You don't talk to anyone. Not in my county. Better yet, get out of my county. Hear?"

I didn't say if I did or didn't. He moved close. His nose was inches from mine.

"Hear?"

"I hear."

Dyke backed off and smiled triumphantly. "I don't want to arrest you, McKenzie."

I didn't believe him.

I drove. An amazing thing. I accelerated, I braked, I turned corners, I even signaled my lane changes. It was amazing because I was so upset my hands trembled on the steering wheel.

It was very hot and very cold inside the Cherokee, and nothing seemed to make sense. Mr. Mosley. Frank Crosetti. Lieutenant Dyke. Especially me. What I had done to Danny. I had never hurt anyone like that before, yet I managed it without even a hint of pity or remorse. I had killed several men—once on the job, a few afterward. They were righteous shoots, meaning the grand jury refused to indict me. And each time I told myself, *Here's this guy trying to kill you, trying to kill someone else, don't go shedding any tears over him. Just be glad you're alive and move on.* Only it never worked that way. I always felt nauseous afterward, sometimes for days. I always felt ashamed. Only not with Danny.

As I drove, snippets of song lyrics inexplicably entered my head and departed with startling speed. *There's nothing you can know that can't be known, why do the birds go on singing, you can help yourself but don't take too much, I went out for a ride and never went back, the things that you're liable to hear in the Bible it ain't necessarily so, and the colored girls go doo, doo doo, doo doo, doo doo doo . . .* Maybe my subconscious wanted to tell me something, only it was like trying to find a coherent message in a bowl of alphabet soup.

Eventually I found myself outside the King of Kings Baptist Church of Golden Valley without having made a decision to drive there. I stopped the Cherokee in the middle of the street and lowered the window. Another song lyric reached out to me. *How sweet the sound that saved a wretch like me.*

I wasn't any good at funerals and hadn't been since my mother died when I was twelve. The fight-or-flee instinct kicked in, but I suppressed it. The lot was full, and I ended up parking on a side street a block away from the church. I entered through the rear door. Faces turned toward me, most of them African American. Some wore expressions of curiosity, others admonishment. *You're late. How could you be late?* I didn't tell them that I didn't want to be there at all, that I had tried to make myself too busy to be there and failed, as I had in so many other things. I didn't tell them that I was afraid to say good-bye to Mr. Mosley.

I was impressed by the number of people who had come to memorialize him, especially by the number of Asians, Hispanics, and Caucasians. Among the white mourners were Shelby and Bobby Dunston. I would have liked to sit in the back with them, but Reverend Winfield saw me enter and waved me toward the front. He found a seat close enough that he could stop me if I attempted to escape. Maybe I would have run off, too, if only I had someplace to go.

Most of the men and women who rose to eulogize Mr. Mosley were strangers to me, although I knew of some of the events they spoke of. Cornelius Jackson was there, and he told how Mr. Mosley had saved his life at the Minnesota State Public School for Dependent and Neglected Children. Another man rose to say how Mr. Mosley had saved his life during the Korean War. Lorenzo Hernandez testified that Mr. Mosley had saved his life, too, by giving him a job tending honeybees, a job that helped him escape the suffocating poverty of Guatemala, that allowed him to remain in the United States.

The speeches were all sweetened with choruses of amens and alleluias and easy laughter, for many of the stories were both funny and joyous, and there was raucous music that made a white boy from Minnesota think of Memphis and New Orleans. Although I had promised myself that I was done weeping, tears rolled down both cheeks.

Reverend Winfield gestured at me several times during the service, urging me to stand. I refused. He persisted, gesturing again, mouthing words that I refused to acknowledge. Finally he called my name loud enough for everyone to hear and pointed at me and said I wished to speak. There was nothing I could do but stand and turn and face the congregation, which suddenly seemed to be much quieter than it had been. This was not something I had planned to do—speak of my relationship with Mr. Mosley, a man whom I had known my entire life. Where would I begin? I was surprised when the words came out.

"I had two fathers . . ."

Someone in the back shouted, "Alleluia!"

Afterward, I shook the hands of a great many people that I didn't know. Many others hugged me. Two old women even kissed my cheek. They were the only ones who used Mr. Mosley's first name, and I wondered if after all these years there were a few things that he hadn't told me.

I noticed Lorenzo Hernandez waiting. When the crowd thinned he came up and said, "Ju look for killer of Mr. Mosley, Reverend say," in a thick accent.

"*Sí,*" I said.

"Ju find 'im, ju tell me."

I didn't reply.

"Por favor," he added.

"We'll see."

"Mr. Mosley, 'e good to me. I make 'im proud."

"Sí," I said.

A moment later, Reverend Winfield was hugging me. He hugged me several times.

"It went very well," he told me.

"It was almost enough to restore your faith in the Almighty."

He raised an eyebrow when I said that. Maybe he knew that during the service I had managed to say a prayer for Mr. Mosley. And Susan Tillman. And, God help me, for Danny. Maybe he could see it in my face. But I wouldn't give him the satisfaction.

"Almost," I added.

"You'll be back," he said.

Shelby and Bobby had waited for me. Shelby hugged me, too. Bobby looked as if he might also give me a squeeze.

"Don't even think about it," I told him.

They insisted I spend the night on their sofa. I didn't think that was necessary, and I gave them an argument. But the thing is, while I've debated successfully with each of them separately, I've never been able to stand up to both at the same time.

"McKenzie. Wake up."

Shelby was leaning over the sofa, shaking my arm. She was wearing a pink off-the-shoulder sleep shirt, and for a brief moment I thought one of my most fervent fantasies was about to come true.

"It's Bobby."

"Bobby?"

"Get up."

I followed Shelby into the kitchen. The clock on her wall read 6:15. She handed me the receiver of her wall phone.

"It's Bobby," she repeated.

"Bobby?" I said into the receiver.

"McKenzie. Are you awake?"

"I am now."

"You're in trouble."

"So what else is new? Where are you?"

"I'm at my desk. Listen. The FBI has just issued paper on you."

"What do you mean, paper?"

"A Seeking Information Alert."

"A what?"

"You know what a Seeking Information Alert is. It's just this side of Wanted, Dead or Alive."

"I don't get it."

"The FBI's looking for you. Are you sure you're awake?"

"I am awake. What are you talking about?"

Bobby sighed deeply. Here he was trying to help me, at no small risk to himself, and I was being dense.

"We just received it—a flash e-mail. The FBI has issued a Seeking Information Alert on McKenzie, Rushmore James."

"What's it say?"

"The Federal Bureau of Investigation is requesting the assistance of all city, county, and state law enforcement agencies in determining the whereabouts of Rushmore McKenzie, a United States citizen last seen in St. Paul, Minnesota. Although the FBI has no specific information that this individual is connected to any potential terrorist activities, based upon information developed in the course of ongoing investigations, the FBI would like to locate and question this person. It comes with a photograph. The photo was taken when you were younger. I hardly recognized you."

"Why? Why is the FBI doing this?"

"You tell me."

"I'm not a terrorist."

"You expect us to take your word for that?"

"That's not funny, Dunston."

"Did I say something funny?"

"Ahh, jeezus."

"It's like when Joe McCarthy was calling people reds. Once he dropped the label on a guy, you were pretty much colored for life."

I mixed a half dozen obscenities, profanities, and vulgarities into a long, complicated sentence.

"My words exactly," Bobby said.

"But it doesn't make sense."

"Doesn't it? Think about it."

I did, for about seven seconds. Finally I said, "The Carver County deputy who caught Mr. Mosley's murder—before he was taken off the case, he told me that not only had Crosetti disappeared, there was no record that he had ever existed. I asked him who had the resources to make someone vanish like that, and he said, 'Who do you think?' I guessed at the time it was the government. Now I know which branch."

"Bingo."

"That's why Dyke blew me off earlier. The FBI got to him—I bet the guy driving the yellow Mustang was FBI. They're protecting the man who killed Mr. Mosley. Now they want to pick me up because I'm trying to find him."

"That's what I'm thinking."

"But why? Why would they do this?"

"Ask them."

"What do you mean, ask them?"

"How long have we known each other?"

"Several lifetimes. We were legionnaires together under Marcus Aurelius."

"I need you to listen to me, McKenzie. Are you listening to me?"

"I'm listening."

"I want you to come in."

"Be serious."

"I am serious. Come in. Now. Before things get out of hand."

"No."

"Please."

"So the FBI can label me an enemy combatant? Drop me in a hole in Guantánamo Bay—no charge, no lawyer, no rights? I don't think so."

"That won't happen."

"Why not? What's going to stop them? The Constitution? C'mon. Bobby, a man was murdered and a woman was raped and the FBI is protecting the guys who did it.

Suddenly I'm in the way. What do you think is going to happen if I walk into the Federal Building with my hands up? Hey, guys. I hear you're looking for me."

"What's the alternative?"

"I keep doing what I'm doing now."

"Or"—Bobby's voice became softer, more cautious—"you could promise them you'll be a good little citizen and do exactly what they tell you."

"Someone has to pay for Susan and Mr. Mosley."

"I figured you'd say that. Only, Mac, you're trying to catch someone whose throat you can get your hands around. But it's not one person. It's a committee, an organization, a government."

"One man. You go high enough, you always find one man giving the orders."

"And what are your chances of finding that one man? What are your chances of getting to him if you do?"

"What happens to me if I don't? Besides, remember Bill Tierney, our history teacher in high school? Remember what he used to say about success?"

"Half the battle is showing up."

"I'll see you, Bobby."

"Wait."

"I can't wait. If they're looking hard for me, they're probably also watching my friends. You could get into a lot of trouble just for calling me."

"What are you talking about? I called home to wish my lovely wife a good morning."

"You'd better talk to her, then, in case they wire you to a polygraph."

I handed the phone to Shelby and went into the living room. I dressed quickly. Shelby had just hung up the phone when I returned to the kitchen. She was standing in bare feet. The bright morning sun streaming through the kitchen windows surrounded her like the golden aura Renaissance artists painted behind angels and saints. I cupped her face in my hands and kissed her forehead.

"I gotta go."

Chapter Five

Twenty-five minutes later, I was ringing Margot's doorbell.

Disappear, I told myself. *Take a page from Frank Crosetti's playbook and vanish.* The FBI couldn't find me—and neither could Danny and his partner—if I didn't exist, if I adopted a new identity, if I became someone else for a time. It's not that difficult if you know how, if you know the right people, and if you have the money. Problem was, all my cash was locked in a safe in my basement, and the people I needed to deal with didn't take checks. Which is what brought me to Margot's at 7:00 A.M.

I had worked my way around Falcon Heights, parked in the lot of the University of Minnesota golf course on Larpenteur Avenue about a quarter mile from my home, and strolled casually to Margot's—just a neighbor taking his morning constitutional.

Margot was wearing a short white terrycloth robe

when she opened the door. If she had anything else on, I didn't notice.

"What do you want?" she asked, then said, "Let me rephrase that. Good morning, McKenzie. What brings you by so early?"

"Remember that canary yellow swimsuit you wore the other day? I'd like you to put it on."

"Honestly, McKenzie, I wish you'd come back later. I'm much more fun after I've had a cup of coffee."

I gave Margot a head start, watching her carefully from her kitchen window, vowing not to leave her house until she disappeared around mine. She walked barefoot slowly across her lawn, careful not to spill a drop of coffee from her enormous mug. "C'mon, c'mon," I heard myself mutter, at the same time regretting that I had suggested she carry the innocuous prop in the first place.

Margot paused when she reached the pond and took a sip of coffee. She seemed fascinated first by the fountain and then by a silver 747 that arched across the cloudless sky, studying both as if they were new to her. She sipped her coffee some more.

"Now you're just trying to annoy me," I whispered.

Eventually she began moving again, slowly, leisurely, taking her own sweet time as she crossed my lawn and passed my garage. I had told her to behave casually, but for God's sake! Finally she turned the corner of my house and vanished from view.

I was off. I dashed from her back door and sprinted across the lawn. I rounded the pond and ran in a straight line toward my own back door, house key in hand—if I didn't beat my personal best time in the 200-meter, I came damn close. I let myself in quickly and quietly. Cautiously I closed the door, took a knee, and waited to regain my breath. The house was still—I heard no sound and felt nothing to indicate that it was occupied. After a moment, I crept through the kitchen to the hallway, where I had a view of the front porch. Through lace window curtains, I could see Margot. She was leaning against the railing and glancing at the headlines in the *St. Paul Pioneer Press* that she held with one hand while sipping coffee from the oversized mug in the other.

I heard his voice before I saw him.

"Miss?"

Margot looked startled. "May I help you?" she asked.

"Wilson," the man said. He appeared on the porch next to her. He was holding his credentials for Margot to see. "FBI."

Hey, I know this guy, I reminded myself. *He owes me a favor.* Trying to collect it at that moment didn't seem like the wisest of actions. Instead, I slid silently back into the kitchen, out of sight of the porch, opened the basement door, and descended the staircase. I was moving quickly. I figured Margot was sexy enough to distract anyone who might be watching my house—male or female—especially in that yellow swimsuit. Only I had no idea how much time I had before someone caught on and said, "Hey, wait a minute . . ." 'Course, knowing it was Wilson made me feel better about the ruse. Seven months earlier I had helped him and an ATF agent named Bullert bust a gunrunning operation. He liked attractive women.

I rolled back a rug and removed four reinforced tiles. Beneath the tiles was a safe. I spun the combination too quickly and had to try again before it would open. I started pulling out items. First my handguns. There were three—a Heckler & Koch 9 mm, a Beretta 9 mm, and a Beretta .380. Then I dug out all the paper I had stashed in there—my last three tax returns, investment reports, mortgage information on my house and lake property, titles to the Jeep Cherokee and my boat, a life insurance policy, my last will and testament, passport, birth certificate, and $19,200 in cash in twenties and fifties. The money was what was left of $25,000 I had hoarded after I collected the price on Teachwell—that was the name of the embezzler I had captured.

"Mad money," I had called it.

"If you don't put it in a bank, you are nuts," my dad told me.

Only I sometimes had expenses that didn't bear scrutiny.

I returned the weapons to the safe. If I was going to shoot an FBI agent, it sure as hell wasn't going to be with my own guns. I found a shoe box on a shelf in my workroom and stuffed the paper inside it. I also added my wallet and cell phone. It all fit easily, my entire life, I thought—past, present, and future. Cremate me, and you could probably also find room for my ashes. I flashed first on an old Peggy Lee tune—*Is that all there is?*—and then on a line my father used to recite.

You don't deserve to own anything that you can't take care of.

For no particular reason except habit, I checked my voice mail while I was in the basement. It had recorded a message from Ivy Flynn.

"Mr. McKenzie, I am so sorry about Mr. Mosley. If there is anything I can do . . . I'm calling because I presume you wanted me to continue checking soil samples. I discovered that the Sevin XLR Plus originated just west of the property where the man shot at me. It's being used to control crop pests in a grove of hybrid poplar trees. Apparently, wind currents carried it to some nearby flowers favored by honeybees. That is how Mr. Mosley's hives were contaminated. Please call me and I will tell you more. I hope this helps."

I couldn't believe it. *All this because of some poplar trees? Mr. Mosley dead, Susan Tillman raped, me on the run because some jerk was sloppy in spraying his goddamn poplar trees?* It seemed so pointless. *But it's not because of the trees, is it?* I told myself. *It's something else. Something worse.*

I erased the message and crept back upstairs.

"Officer," I heard Margot say.

"Special Agent," Wilson corrected her.

"Special Agent Wilson—I like the way that sounds." Wilson smiled as if he did, too. "Special Agent Wilson, I don't know how many ways I can tell you the same thing. McKenzie called early this morning. He said he was leaving town for a while. He asked me to collect his newspapers and mail until he came back. He didn't say where he was going, and he didn't say how long he would be away. That's all I can tell you."

I took one last look around. It was a big house. I had eight rooms not including bathrooms and the basement, but only four were furnished—my bedroom, my dad's old bedroom, the kitchen stocked with every culinary gadget available to civilized man, and what my father called "the family room." That's where I kept my PC, a big-screen TV, VHS and DVD players, my CD player, and about a thousand books, some of them even stacked on the shelves. Would I miss my house? I wondered. Would I be upset if I never saw it again? And the pond? And the ducks? And Nina and Margot and Bobby? What if I never saw Shelby again?

From the porch, I heard Wilson say, "If you hear from Mr. McKenzie, please contact me."

"Of course, Special Agent."

Get out, I screamed to myself. *Get out while you still can.*

I didn't linger at Margot's but kept fleeing north, moving quickly, cutting through yards the way I did when I was a kid. I was out of breath when I reached Larpenteur Avenue. I hung a right and reduced my pace to a purposeful stroll, pretending I wasn't a fugitive, refusing to glance at the vehicles that whizzed past, resisting the urge to look behind me. I knew where I needed to go and calculated the safest route to get there. It wasn't in a straight line, and it certainly wasn't from behind the steering wheel of my Jeep Cherokee—I was sure there was a stop-and-detain order on it. Smarter, I decided, to acquire new wheels when the time came and let the golf course tow the Cherokee to an impound lot. I continued to follow Larpenteur east.

Like me, the St. Paul campus of the University of Minnesota was actually located in Falcon Heights. No doubt it was just as embarrassed by the fact as I was, since it was never, ever referred to as the "Falcon Heights campus." It wasn't long before I reached the student center. That's where I caught the free shuttle, a full-sized MTC bus that carried students nonstop from the St. Paul campus the few miles to the Minneapolis campus. You're supposed to be enrolled or an employee at the U to ride the shuttle, but no one asked to see an ID when I boarded.

I found a seat and waited. The bus filled quickly with young men and women dressed as though they had just finished cleaning out the garage. And pretty. Unmarked by the changing seasons. Looking about as intense as a Sunday afternoon. Especially the women, the finest women in the United States. Normally I would have taken pleasure in being among them, but it's difficult to enjoy girl-watching when you're also on the lookout for men in dark suits carrying guns.

I didn't begin to relax—and then just barely—until the bus shuddered and shook as it accelerated from the curb and slowly followed a circuitous route through the campus, eventually crossing from St. Paul into Minneapolis. It rolled up to the edge of the East Bank of the campus; the West Bank was located on the far side of the Mississippi River.

I took my leave of the shuttle in front of Mariucci Arena, where the Gophers played hockey, walked past Williams Arena, where they played basketball, and found a seat on the bench at the bus stop on University Avenue. The MTC stopped for me and several other commuters. I couldn't remember the last time I rode a city bus and didn't know the correct fare. I dropped an extra quarter into the meter and probably would have paid more if the driver hadn't looked at me like I had the IQ of a salad bar. I quickly found a seat, the shoe box balanced on my knee.

The bus headed east, crossing back into St. Paul. It made frequent stops, but the number of passengers never seemed to grow or diminish. For every one that disembarked, someone else boarded. Still, I had a seat to myself until we reached Snelling Avenue and a man dressed for business joined me.

"How you doin'?" he said.

I nodded and looked out the window.

"Some weather." He spoke with the enthusiasm of a telemarketer, trying to engage me in conversation, trying to interest me in his product. Whatever it was, I wasn't buying.

"Where are you headed?"

I turned casually toward him. He smiled. His teeth were stained by grape juice, and when he brushed his hair off his forehead the way bad actors do, I noticed that it was very thin on top. I estimated he'd be bald by the end of the week.

"I don't mean to be rude, sir, but I'm in a very bad mood. You don't want any part of it."

"Oh." The purple smile faded quickly. "No problem. I was just trying to be friendly."

"Normally I'd appreciate it."

"Sure."

He wasn't a bad guy. A Minnesotan trying to be nice just for the sake of being nice. Outsiders—and a few of our more cynical natives—often ridicule us for this behavior. I can't imagine why. When he left the bus at Lexington Parkway, I said, "Have a good day." He said, "You, too."

After crossing Lexington, the bus began a two-mile stretch of University Avenue known as "Asian Main Street" because of the hundred-plus Asian businesses found there. As a nickname, "Asian Main Street" wasn't very catchy. Nor was "Asian Avenue." Some had attempted to tag the area "Chinatown," but the label hadn't stuck because there were hardly any Chinese there. The inhabitants were mostly Hmong refugees from Vietnam, Cambodia, and Laos, with a smattering of Japanese and Koreans mixed in. I read somewhere that St. Paul had the greatest concentration of urban Hmong in the world. Which puzzled me. I would have thought the culture shock if not the climate change—we have six months of snow and ice, man—would have sent them scurrying to the southern states.

I pulled the cord that signaled the driver to stop the bus at an intersection near Rice Street.

Phu Photography sold film cameras, digital cameras, camcorders, lenses, gadget bags, tripods, darkroom equipment, film, and binoculars. One corner of the store had been reserved for passport photos, and a door behind the cash register led to two studios where individual and family portraits were taken.

A tiny bell rang when I entered the store, although no bell hung above the door. A moment later a young woman asked if she could assist me. She spoke in the clear and precise English that only foreigners speak.

I asked to see Phu. I would have used the owner's first name, but I couldn't remember it. A few moments later, I was approached by an older woman who looked the way I imagined a Vietnamese librarian would look. She pointed and said, "I know you maybe."

"Yes."

"You friend of Colin Gernes." She pronounced the name "Olin Ernes."

I said, "Yes." Colin Gernes had been my supervising officer when I first broke in with the St. Paul Police Department.

"Kenzie?"

I nodded. Close enough.

"You cop no more."

"No more," I confirmed.

"You not come to roust poor Phu." She pronounced the word "oust."

"I wouldn't think of it."

"You come maybe buy camera?"

The shop assistant who met me at the door was now behind the glass counter. She scrunched up her nose and shook her head like a sudden chill had run up her spine.

"Cut it out, Phu," I said. "You're embarrassing the help."

Phu glanced over her shoulder at the young woman.

"Oh, nuts, McKenzie. She's my teenage niece. I embarrass her just by being in the same room."

"Kids."

"If they didn't work cheap, there'd be a bounty on them. So what can I do for you, McKenzie?"

I took Phu's arm and led her deeper into the store, away from her assistant.

"Let's say, just for argument's sake, that I wanted some paperwork done and didn't want to trouble the bureaucracy. What would that cost?"

"Didn't you try to arrest me for that once?"

"Nah. That was two guys who looked like me."

"Uh-huh."

"Seriously, Phu. Can you help me out?"

"I'm retired."

"So am I."

"Who are you kidding?"

"Phu . . ."

"Help you? You want me to help you?"

"Yes."

"Times have changed since you were last in my store."

"Tell me about it."

Phu gave it some thought, then said, "You're not going bad on me, are you, McKenzie?"

"I need to hide in plain sight for a while, just like your clients."

"Former clients."

"Uh-huh."

"What are we talking about, McKenzie? Not passports."

"Nothing that elaborate."

"That's good, because I don't do passports anymore. Not since 9/11."

That's my girl, I thought but didn't say.

"So," she added. "Driver's license? Credit cards?"

"Yes to both."

"From where?"

"Anyplace but Minnesota."

"Twenty-five hundred."

"I need it right now."

"Three thousand." And she didn't mean dong, the official currency of Vietnam.

I agreed to the price.

"You come."

Phu led me down a flight of stairs to her cellar. She unlocked one door, then another, and ushered me into a cramped room where a digital camera mounted on a tripod and a pair of strobe lights were aimed at a blue screen. The camera and lights were cabled to an Apple computer. There was a gray filing cabinet against the wall, a table, and three chairs. *Yeah, Phu. You're retired.*

I said, "Can I ask a question?"

"Hmm."

"What's a nice girl like you doing in a place like this?"

"Mostly I help immigrants and refugees. You know that."

"No, I mean, why do so many Southeast Asians live here?"

"Family."

"I don't understand."

"In the seventies, St. Paul became a kind of refuge for people fleeing the war. The population was small back then. But it grew because the refugees had family here. It's like the Swedes and Norwegians. They settled in Minnesota because there were already Swedes and Norwegians in Minnesota, which in turn encouraged even more Swedes and Norwegians to come to Minnesota."

"A lot of Southeast Asians live here because a lot of Southeast Asians live here."

"Exactly."

"Makes sense. When did you come to Minnesota?"

Phu chuckled.

"I was born in St. Joseph's Hospital on the Fourth of July 1948."

"Why, then, do you insist on speaking in that pidgin English of yours?"

"So many of my white customers expect it."

Phu shooed me in front of the blue screen. Noting my appearance—unshaved, unruly hair, creased black sports jacket over wrinkled maroon T-shirt, blue jeans, white Nikes—she asked, "Is that what you want to look like?"

"No. I want to look like Russell Crowe, but what are you going to do?"

The lights flashed, and a moment later my image appeared on a computer screen. I actually looked pretty good, all things considered, and urged Phu to take another photo. It took several more shots before we were able to duplicate the vacant-eyed, mug-shot expression that we've all come to expect from bureaucracy photography. Afterward, she filled in my height, weight, eye color, and hair color, then slid a card printed with the outline of a rectangle in front of me.

"Sign in the box."

"What's my name?"

"Jacob Greene." She spelled it carefully, and I signed slowly.

"Where am I from?"

She told me, "Rapid City, South Dakota. Have you ever been there?"

"No, but my parents have." Mount Rushmore is near Rapid City.

"You sit. You wait."

Phu left the room. I sat. I waited.

About ninety minutes later Phu set a driver's license in front of me with a blue header bar, a driver's license number printed in red, the South Dakota state seal, the words "South Dakota" written all over the face, and Mount Rushmore in the background. It also had Jacob Greene's name and address but my face and signature. Next to it, she placed Visa, Discover, and American Express credit cards.

"More," she said, handing me a Rapid City Public Library card, an American Red Cross Volunteer Blood Donor card—it indicated that I had given six pints—a Blue Cross Blue Shield health insurance card, and another card saying I was a proud member of the United States Golf Association—all of them in Jacob Greene's name.

"These no good," she said, sliding into her pidgin English. "Just for show. Don't use. These"—she picked up the credit cards—"good until end of month. Greene get statements then, know something wrong, call companies, companies trace cards. No good."

I nodded my understanding.

"Three thousand dollars." She said that clearly enough.

I paid her from my shoe box.

"Do you have a wallet?"

"No." I didn't want to use my own.

"Everyone forgets the wallet." A moment later she produced a worn, thin brown wallet and gave it to me. "No charge."

I filled it with Jacob Greene's life.

What did Thoreau write? Beware of enterprises that require new clothes?

Fifteen minutes after I left Phu Photography, I entered the Sears store across from the State Capitol Office Building. I was carrying the shoe box under my arm, which made me a figure of some suspicion to store security—how many people carry worn cardboard boxes into department stores, and why would they? A plainclothes guard was dispatched to follow my every move at a respectful distance, watching me while pretending not to. I made sure I did nothing to arouse his suspicion. The last thing I wanted was for him to inspect the shoe box for either a bomb or shoplifted merchandise.

I found a cart and began loading it up with a week's supply of socks and underwear, an electric razor, toothbrush and toothpaste, deodorant, and a hairbrush. Next, I rolled over to the men's department, where I carefully shopped for the most bland polo shirts, Dockers, Top-Siders, sweaters, and blue sports jacket I could find, working hard to choose clothes that would make me appear as colorful and distinct as a loaf of white bread. Finally I selected the ugliest soft-sided suitcase to cram it all into.

The security guard followed me to the checkout.

The cashier smiled without actually looking at me. She took each item and ran it past an electronic eye that made an annoying "bip" sound—I couldn't imagine listening to that eight hours a day. Instead of a bag, I had her pack each purchase into the suitcase. I added the shoe box last. The cashier rang up a total, and I gave her a wad of fifties. After accepting them, she scribbled across each bill with a counterfeit detector pen. The ink turned amber—instead of brown—proving that the fifties were all genuine.

It was distressing to know how untrusting people can be.

I drove the posted speed limit in the right-hand lane and was passed by nearly every car on I-94. Some of the drivers gave me a look that bordered on open hostility, while others demonstrated their disgust with hand gestures. Instead of responding, I found KBEM-FM on the radio and cranked the volume, soothing my savage breast with some mainstream jazz. Normally I'd be speeding, too, but I couldn't afford a ticket-happy patrolman taking a close look at Phu's handiwork.

I had no doubt that the driver's license was all right, especially after the rent-a-car folks checked it out, but why push my luck? It had been tense enough leaning on the counter while the agent accessed both Jacob Greene's driving record and his credit card account. There had been a computer glitch, and when the agent said, "Just a moment, Mr. Greene," I nearly grabbed the suitcase and made a break for it. As it was, I needed the agent to return the driver's license before I could fill out his forms—in all the excitement, I had forgotten Jake's address!

The agent had attempted to put me into an SUV, but I requested something smaller and less expensive. I wasn't concerned about the money. I wanted a vehicle that was nondescript, only I didn't want to say it aloud for fear of arousing suspicion or giving the agent something to remember should anyone ask about me. To meet my request, he rolled out a blue four-door Plymouth Neon with a tiny four-cylinder engine, five-speed manual transmission, and a tinny AM/FM radio. It only goes to show, you should be careful what you wish for.

It called itself a sporting goods store, yet it served only two sports—hunting and fishing. The store was small and old and located just off of I-35 north of Forest Lake, about thirty minutes from St. Paul. A sign near the cash register read GUNS DON'T KILL PEOPLE, ONLY PEOPLE INSTRUCTED IN THE PROPER USE OF FIREARMS KILL PEOPLE. JOIN OUR SEVEN-HOUR "CONCEAL AND CARRY" HANDGUN COURSE. BECOME QUALIFIED TODAY! The store seemed ideal for what I had in mind.

After a half hour of browsing, I selected two handguns, a Beretta double-action 9 mm with an eight-round magazine and a modest .25 Iver Johnson. I piled fifties on the glass counter next to the guns until I covered the nearly thousand-dollar cost plus tax. The store owner didn't seem surprised that I was paying cash until I added three more fifties to the stack.

"What's that for?"

"I'd like to buy a little convenience."

"What's that mean, convenience?"

"I want you to backdate the 4473 three days so I can take the guns with me."

The owner looked at the ATF firearms transaction form as if he were seeing it for the first time.

"You do, huh?"

"I live in South Dakota, and I'm going home soon. If I have to come back to the store, I might as well buy the guns in South Dakota."

The store owner looked at the stack of fifties and then at me.

"I can appreciate that," he said.

"So how 'bout it?"

"Do you have identification?"

"Of course."

The Holiday Inn on I-494 insisted on a credit card. I gave Greene's Visa to the desk clerk. It went through without any problem. After my experience with the car rental folks, I was certain that it would. Nor was I worried that Greene had reported his card stolen, because it hadn't been stolen. Somehow—and there are many ways, including mail theft—Phu had acquired Greene's name and account numbers and had essentially made a duplicate of his existing cards. The same with his driver's license. They were as real as the cards he carried in his own wallet. In a month or so, Greene would start getting unexplained charges on his account statements; he'd start getting confusing bills from companies that he didn't remember doing business with. If he was smart, he'd realize that he was a victim of identity theft and would take the necessary steps to protect himself. Until then, I could confidently pretend to be him.

Still, I didn't want to cause any more grief for the man than was necessary. That's why I was determined to pay for everything in cash when the bill came due—at the motel, at the car rental agency, and anywhere else. I would steal his name for a time, but I wouldn't take his money.

When the desk clerk pushed the registration form in front of me, I signed Jacob Greene's name carefully.

There were no lights burning inside the Dunston home. I had watched it carefully before making my way around to the back and across the brick patio Bobby and I had built over the Labor Day weekend. I gently rapped on the sliding glass door—Bobby and I had installed that, too. A moment later, I rapped again, this time louder. A light clicked on inside. Its beam stretched across the floor. Shelby followed the beam into the dining room. She stood at the far end of the table, staring at my image through the glass as she tied a thin robe about her.

She came forward, unlocked the door, and slid it open.

"McKenzie, what are you doing?"

She was whispering. I whispered back.

"Hi, Shel. Is Bobby here?"

"No, he's at work. What's going on?"

"Are the girls asleep?"

"Of course they're asleep. Do you know what time it is?"

"Yeah, sorry about that. Look, if Bobby's not here, I'm gonna have to ask you to take this."

I handed her the shoe box. It contained everything except the cash.

"What's this?" Shelby asked.

"My life."

"Your what? What are you—" Shelby set the box on the floor and stepped onto the patio, closing the door quietly behind her.

"What are you talking about, McKenzie?"

Her feet were bare, and she wrapped her arms around herself.

"You're cold," I told her. "Go back inside."

"Are you in trouble?"

"Did Bobby tell you . . ."

"He told me everything."

"Then you know I'm in trouble."

"This is crazy."

"No doubt about it."

"What's in the box?"

"All my financial records and my will. The girls get everything."

"No."

"There's also a life insurance policy. Fifty thousand dollars. You're the beneficiary. If anything happens to me, I expect you to buy an expensive sports car. A red one."

"Don't talk like that."

"No one lives forever."

"Don't talk like that," she repeated.

"I have to go."

"Where?"

"I'm not telling you."

"Why not? Do you think you're protecting me?"

"Yes."

"Stay here."

"Not a chance. I'll see you."

"Rushmore, wait."

I waited.

"I won't take it very well if something happens to you. I'll go all to pieces."

"I should hope so."

"You think that's funny?"

She turned her back to me and hugged herself tighter. I could see her reflection in the glass of the patio door. I took a few steps across the brick and rested my hands on her shoulders. She tilted her head back against my chest.

"You shouldn't love me." She was talking to my reflection.

"I know, but what's a guy to do?" I quickly added, "I love Bobby, too." I said it so she'd know she had nothing to fear from me, now or ever. It was a nice gesture, I thought. Made me seem less like a jerk. It also had the added virtue of being true. And another minor concession to let Shelby know I wasn't obsessed with her.

"Tell Nina I'll call her when I can."

"Sure."

"Now I really do have to go."

"I know."

"Tell Bobby I'll be in touch."

"I will."

I kissed the back of Shelby's head and smelled her strawberry shampoo.

"Good-bye, Shelby."

She didn't answer. I left her standing in bare feet on the cold patio brick.

Rushmore McKenzie no longer had anyplace to go. But Jake Greene had a motel room on the I-494 strip in Bloomington, so that's where I drove. I had a club sandwich in the bar and three beers. It was nearly 2:00 A.M. before I took the elevator to my room. I showered, brushed my teeth, and climbed into bed.

"Now what?" I said out loud.

The gray light of dawn was stretching across the ceiling before I came up with an answer.

Chapter Six

Dr. Jillian DeMarais had a suite in One Financial Plaza, which in the imagination might conjure grandness but was only two connecting rooms. The first measured eight by ten feet and contained two chairs and a sofa with a coffee table between them—a reception room without a receptionist. Jillian used to have a receptionist, someone to book appointments, answer the phone, make coffee, and ensure that patients were comfortable in the waiting room until Jillian was ready for them, only she quit. So did the one before that and the one before that. Now a machine answered Jillian's calls.

There were four paintings, one on each of the four windowless walls—a Degas, Matisse, Chagall, and Van Gogh. I had often wondered if Jillian used them to diagnose new patients, a kind of artistic Rorschach test. *Before we begin, tell me which painting you like best.* I preferred the Degas. I had meant to ask Jillian what that revealed about me but never did.

There was a connecting door that led to an inner office, but it was closed, and I didn't knock on it. Jillian might be with a patient, and she hated to be interrupted. Instead, I waited. Eventually the door opened. Jillian had been alone, after all.

"I'll be damned," she said when she saw me.

"Hi, Jill."

"I didn't think I'd ever see you again."

"I'm like a bad penny. I keep turning up."

"Come in."

I followed Jillian into her office. She sat behind a desk that had probably cost a considerable fortune when it was built by French craftsmen in the eighteenth century. I sat in front of it. Jillian studied me for a moment with dangerous blue-green eyes. Gazing into them made you forget to watch the road ahead.

"It hurt me when you stopped calling," she said. "It hurt me worse than—you could have told me almost anything and it would have been less painful."

"I'm sorry."

"Why did you stop calling?"

"That," I said, pointing at the medical degree hanging on the wall. "And that." Moving my finger toward the Ph.D. from Stanford. Jillian DeMarais was two times a doctor. "And that and that." Pointing at more diplomas, plaques, and board certifications. "You have more degrees than a thermometer."

"McKenzie . . ."

"You're intelligent, educated, accomplished, beautiful, rich, and who am I? Just a cop from the neighborhood."

"You have money now."

"Yes, but I'll always be just a cop from the neighborhood. You can do better. I realized it every time we went to the ballet, or the opera, or one of those charity things you're involved in. I realized it every time we met one of your friends."

"That's ridiculous."

"Maybe so."

"You should have called me."

"I know. I'm sorry."

"You're here now," Jillian reminded me.

"I need a favor."

"A favor? After all this time? How audacious."

"I didn't know who else I could trust."

"Trust." She tasted the word, decided she liked it. "I'll take that as a compliment. What kind of favor?"

"You sometimes use hypnotism in your work."

"Sometimes. Not often."

"I need you to hypnotize me."

"Why? Did you forget something?"

"A license plate number."

"You're serious."

"Very."

"Tell me about it."

I did, holding nothing back. I wanted her to have as much information as she needed.

Jillian sighed and rose from her chair. She walked slowly around the desk, picked up a long blue pen, and began twirling it slowly with the thumb and fingers of her right hand. She sat on the corner of the desk, just inches from where I was sitting.

"I don't know, McKenzie. Didn't you once tell me that I couldn't hypnotize you? That I couldn't hypnotize anyone who resists? That only weak-minded people could be hypnotized?"

I stared at the pen.

"Didn't you tell me it had nothing to do with intellect and everything to do with emotions?" I asked her. "That the people easiest to hypnotize were those whose emotions were near the surface?"

"That pretty much leaves you out, doesn't it, McKenzie?"

"Maybe."

"We tried this once before."

"I remember."

"Do you remember that we talked about the colors of the rainbow?"

"Yes."

"I asked you to say them out loud."

"Yes."

"Blue's a rainbow color, isn't it, McKenzie?"

"Yes."

"Like the blue of this pen."

"Yes."

"Close your eyes and tell me if you can still see the blue."

"I can see it."

"Does it make you feel relaxed?"

"Yes."

"Keep looking at the blue. Do you feel like you want to sleep?"

"Yes."

"To help you sleep, think of the rainbow. Name the colors to yourself one by one. Start with red. When you get to blue, you'll be fully asleep."

"Yes."

"Have you reached blue?"

"Yes."

"Do you want to remember something you've forgotten?"

"Yes."

"Do you want to remember going to Frank Crosetti's house?"

"Yes."

"Remember what happened when you went to Frank Crosetti's house. Remember it out loud. Start with Frank Crosetti pointing a shotgun at you."

"I was frightened."

"What happened next?"

"I heard a car. A man is driving a car up the driveway. He is driving very fast."

"Do you see the car clearly?"

"Yes."

"Describe the car."

"It's a Ford Mustang convertible. 2002 or 2003. The top is up."

"What color is the car?"

"Yellow."

"What is the license plate number?"

I rattled off six digits.

"Remember the rainbow, McKenzie?"

"Yes."

"Go through the colors again. When you get to the color blue, you will wake up feeling rested and you'll remember everything you told me."

"Yes."

"McKenzie?"

"Yes."

"What is the real reason you stopped seeing me?"

"You're not a nice person. You were kind to me, but you were rude to everyone else, to your receptionists, to waiters, parking lot attendants, ushers, to a lot of people."

"Start naming the rainbow colors to yourself."

When I reached blue, I opened my eyes and found Jillian hovering above me. She had written the license plate number of the yellow Mustang on a sheet of her stationery.

"Here."

I took the sheet.

I said, "I'm sorry, Jill."

She said, "Get out of my office, McKenzie."

In some cities—New York and New Orleans come to mind—a sizable percentage of civil servants figure they earn their paychecks just by showing up in the morning. Actually doing work, that costs extra. And if you expect service with a smile, *forgetaboutit.* But in Minnesota, there is no culture of baksheesh. Most government employees here are happy to assist you. Some will actually go beyond their job descriptions to be helpful and will ask for nothing in return except a simple thank-you, and even that's not required.

Take the woman at Minnesota Driver and Vehicles Services in the Town Square Building in downtown St. Paul, for example. She seemed delighted to furnish me with both a Record Request form and the requisite Intended Use of Driver License and Motor Vehicle Information form. She even helped me massage the language I used to complete the section labeled "Explain How You Intend to Use Record Information"—"Owner of vehicle with above license plate number caused damage to rental car; requester would like information to present to rental car company." When time came to pay for the service, she said, "I'm sorry," before requesting the $4.50 fee.

In return, she gave me the name Penelope Joan Glass, 839 47th Avenue, Hilltop, Minnesota, as well as Penelope's vital statistics—height 5' 8", weight 125, eyes blue, hair blonde—and her phone number, date of birth, vehicle identification number, and driver's license number. I could've requested Penelope's driving record, too, but that cost extra.

I felt a flush of accomplishment as I wrote down the information in my notebook. I was doing some real detecting and it felt good, like the tingle you get when you exercise seldom-used muscles. But I was left with a question.

"Where in hell is Hilltop?"

"I'm afraid I don't know," the woman said. "I have a map you can borrow . . ."

* * *

Forty-seventh Avenue came to an abrupt and unannounced dead end against a high chain-link fence. I muscled the Neon around with a series of tight Y-turns until I faced the open street again and silenced the engine.

"You live in an area your entire life and you think you know it," I said aloud.

The city of Hilltop was little more than a glorified trailer park measuring half a mile long and two-tenths of a mile wide and surrounded on all four sides by the city of Columbia Heights. It wasn't even on the map. I had to seek help from the St. Paul Public Library to find it.

"How is this possible?" I had asked the librarian after she showed me the tiny city's location. She directed me to an article that had appeared in a decade-old edition of *Trailer Park* magazine.

According to the article, in 1956 the residents of two independent trailer parks located on the edge of Columbia Heights asked that they be annexed into the city. Columbia Heights refused. So, the residents voted to incorporate and created their own city, called "Hilltop." Meanwhile, Columbia Heights, fearful that this "junkyard for people"—that was quote from the article—would spread, purchased all the property surrounding Hilltop, effectively stunting its growth.

"The things you learn in a library," I said when I read this.

"That's just magazines," the librarian told me. "Wait until you're introduced to books."

You gotta love a sarcastic librarian.

Hilltop wasn't easy to find. There were no signs announcing where it began and where it ended. Eventually, I located it on the west side of Central Avenue NE between 45th and 49th Avenues behind two strip malls. Like Columbia Heights, it was a working-class community, a place with more picnic tables than patios, where you're more apt to see kids running through sprinklers than swimming in pools.

I couldn't tell which trailer belonged to Penelope Glass from my vehicle, so I left the Neon and began walking along 47th. It seemed more like an alley than a street, barely wide enough for two cars to pass. I tried to match the addresses on the roadside mailboxes to the trailers. Many of the boxes were hand-decorated, and homemade signs bearing the names of the owners were hung next to some front doors along with American flags. The trailers themselves all seemed to be pretty much the same size but came in an assortment of colors, most of them pastel. The narrow gaps between them were filled with grills, plastic picnic tables, tiny sheds, children's playthings, carports, and small gardens guarded by trolls.

There was activity—a little girl played jacks, an old man walked a St. Bernard, a trio of women of a certain age performed tai chi exercises, a woman dressed in black chino shorts and a pink tank top carried a blue recyclables bin to the curb. The woman in the tank top waved at the man with the St. Bernard and disappeared into a sparkling white trailer with maroon trim and shutters. I was just passing it when she reappeared carrying a Cub Foods grocery bag filled with discarded newspapers and mail and set it next to the recyclables bin. Her legs were long and lithesome, and her hair was sun-drenched blonde. She reminded me a little of Shelby, and like Shelby she was nearing the age when she would be considered at the high end of *Cosmopolitan*'s target audience. She fit the description I bought from Driver and Vehicles Services, but I was still confused by the addresses and wasn't ready to identify her as Penelope Glass. I noticed an empty carport next to her trailer as I strolled past. If she was Penelope, where was her yellow Mustang? Where was the man who was driving it? I kept walking.

The system of addresses began to make sense to me, and I soon realized that the trailer belonging to Penelope Glass was behind me. I turned around. The three older women practicing tai chi had dispersed. One of them was now chatting with the woman in the pink tank—Penelope, I decided. It had to be.

How are you going to make this work? I wondered. *How are you going to get this woman to identify the man who was driving her car without tipping your hand?*

It seemed impossible. But like Mr. Tierney used to say, "Half the battle is showing up." Just as I started walking toward the two women, a rusted pickup truck accelerated down the street. It hit a massive speed bump, bounced up and down on worn springs, and drove past me without reducing speed. It came to a sudden and noisy stop in front of the two women. The driver's door flew open. A man, tall and thin, dressed in dirty jeans, jumped out from behind the steering wheel. He shoved the older woman to the ground and made a grab for Penelope.

I was already on my horse, sprinting toward them.

Penelope shouted, "Let go!" as the man dragged her toward the truck.

Another man in his early forties appeared on the doorstep of the trailer three down from Penelope's. He was my height with black hair and carried a wooden baseball bat. "Stop," he yelled.

The attacker stopped pulling Penelope and looked at him expectantly.

The older woman was on her feet. She was standing sideways, her legs far apart, her feet at forty-five-degree angles, her body weight evenly distributed—it was a horse stance, a karate stance popular in the '60s and '70s. She let loose with a loud shout, a *kiai*, and I have no doubt she would have inflicted serious damage to the attacker, except I got there first.

I came up fast behind him and swept his legs. He went down hard. His head slammed against the asphalt. But he was tough. He quickly rolled to one knee and looked up at me. The expression on his face was of pure astonishment. I was about to drive my own knee into his nose when the man with the baseball bat shoved me aside. I fell into the older woman, and we both went down. The man with the bat swung on the attacker and missed. Twice. The attacker got inside him and pushed hard. The man staggered backward, swung the bat again, and caught nothing but air. The attacker was in his truck now. He muscled it into gear and motored down the street without bothering to close his door. The man slugged the trailer bed with the bat as it moved away. I looked for a number, but the license plates had been removed.

"Are you all right?"

The man with the baseball bat was talking to Penelope, the bat resting on his shoulder. They had hung a label on me early in my baseball career that I was never able to shake—"good field, no hit"—but even at my worst I was better than this guy.

Penelope smiled. It was a happy, trusting smile.

Amazing, I thought.

"Yes, I'm all right," she said. Her voice had a breathless quality that had nothing to do with fear or exertion. She rubbed her wrist where Dirty Jeans had grabbed her. "But—what was he doing?"

"I think he was trying to kidnap you," said the man with the bat.

Nonsense, my inner voice announced. He had been alone. He had no weapons. The attempt was made in the open, in broad daylight, before plenty of witnesses. And he couldn't possibly have known that Penelope would be standing outside her trailer at that precise moment. *Kidnapping?* I couldn't get my head around it.

"Why would anyone want to kidnap me?" Penelope asked.

"Because you're pretty," the older woman said. I was helping her to her feet. She shook off my arm. "I had him," she told me.

"Sure."

"I was going to put my boot through his groin—change him from a rooster to a hen right there. Then I was going to stomp his head."

"You're awfully bloodthirsty, lady."

She was in my face, giving me the mad dog.

"Who are you calling lady?"

I liked her.

"Who are you?" she asked.

I took a step backward before answering.

"My name's Jake Greene."

"What are you doing here?" Batman wanted to know.

"You don't live in Hilltop," said the older woman. "I know all my neighbors."

"So what are you doing here?" Batman repeated.

"I'm a writer."

"Where are you from?"

"Rapid City."

"In South Dakota?"

"Yes."

"Who do you work for?"

"I work freelance."

"What are you writing about?" asked the older woman.

"I'm writing about Hilltop."

"For who?"

"*Trailer Park* magazine."

"I read that," said the older woman. "But why write about Hilltop?"

"You have to admit, it's an interesting community. An oasis of mobile homes in a hostile environment."

The thing about lying, the more of it you do, the better you get.

The older woman smiled. "I like that. 'An oasis of mobile homes.' That's good. Usually, we get names like redneck reservation, hee-haw Hilton, tornado trap . . ."

"Not from me."

"I'm Ruth Schramm." She offered her hand and I shook it. Her grip was firm.

"I'm Pen." Penelope Glass extended her hand.

"Pen?"

"Short for Penelope. Penelope Glass. Thank you for helping me."

"You should call the police," I told her.

"Oh, sure," said Ruth. "So you can report what a high crime rate we have."

"I don't know what we can tell them, anyway," said Batman. "There were no license plates on the truck."

"It was a gray 1988 Ford Ranger 150 4×4 with thick rust on all sides. The man driving it was five-ten, 170 pounds, brown hair, dark eyes, wearing dirty blue jeans with a pack of cigarettes rolled up in the sleeve of his white T-shirt."

"You see a lot," said Batman.

"Occupational habit."

"I think I should wait about the police," said Pen. "I want to speak to my husband first."

"Husband?"

"He's a special agent with the Federal Bureau of Investigation."

"Is he?" I said.

"Bet you thought trailer parks were filled with nothing but undereducated, minimum-wage hicks," said Ruth. "Isn't so."

"We should go inside," said Batman and nudged Pen toward her trailer.

"And you are?" I asked, extending my hand.

He looked first at my hand and then at me. He obviously didn't want to reveal his identity but couldn't think how to get out of it.

"Nick Horvath." He shook my hand as if he were afraid I was carrying monkey pox.

"Thank you again, Mr. Greene," Pen said.

"Jake."

"Jake," she repeated.

"Perhaps you'll allow me to interview you later—for the article."

"I'd be happy to."

"And you," I told Ruth.

"You ain't trying to make us look bad," she said.

"No, I promise I'm not."

"Well, then, you come by anytime. I'm always here."

"Thank you."

A moment later, Pen and Horvath entered Pen's trailer. In another moment, Ruth disappeared into her own mobile home. I bent slightly, picked up Pen's grocery bag by the handles, and carried it to the Neon.

The Starlite Motel had a wonderfully tacky sign out front—red and bright with neon, topped by a huge star. It reminded me of a marquee for a drive-in movie theater. I nearly stayed there just for the sign. But a half dozen people were loitering in the parking lot, and I didn't want to be noticed by any of them. Instead, I drove another five hundred feet to a second motel, the Hi–top Motel—the two *L*'s in its neon sign were burned out. I checked in using Jacob Greene's American Express card. The manager, an elderly gentleman working past his retirement age, seemed happy to have my business and didn't mind that I was vague about my checkout date.

"Let me know each morning if you want me to hold the room," he said.

I told him I would.

"My name's Victor. If you need anything, and I mean anything"—I swear he winked at me—"just call the desk. I'll be here."

I told him I found that comforting.

The Hilltop Motel was smaller and not nearly as boisterous as the Starlite. It had sixteen units arranged in two cell blocks of eight units each, the cell blocks set at a forty-five-degree angle from each other, the parking lot between them. There were four units on the ground floor and four on top in each block. My cell block was facing busy Central Avenue. The mobile homes of Hilltop were behind it, just beyond a Cyclone fence. I could see a small patch of trailer park from the second-floor landing outside unit 8A, but it didn't amount to much.

It took about two minutes to unpack my suitcase. I set the grocery bag on a small desk fronting the room's single window near the door—there were no back windows. There was a lamp on the desk, and I tried to move it to give myself room to work, only it was bolted down. Everything was bolted down—the lamp to the desk, the desk to the floor, the landscapes to the wall, the TV to the credenza, a small refrigerator to the floor, the radio to the shelf next to the bed. Only the TV remote was portable, that and the worn white towels in the tiny bathroom.

I set the grocery bag on the floor next to the bed and

began removing its contents one item at a time and arranging them into separate piles. The biggest pile consisted of cast-off *Tribunes* and a few back issues of *Down Beat* magazine. Next came carefully collapsed boxes of food items—pasta shells, pizza rolls, a jambalaya mix, and cherry Popsicles, plus a box that used to contain wind chimes. I ignored both piles. It was the discarded mail that interested me. A third had been addressed to Penelope Glass, a third to Resident, and a third to Steve Sykora, the husband, I presumed. It isn't unusual for women to keep their maiden names after marriage—about 20 percent do. But usually there's a reason for it. I wondered what Penelope's was.

Included in the mail was a solicitation for Twin Cities Public Television, a pledge envelope from the Nature Conservancy, and several opportunities for Pen and Sykora to enjoy preapproved, no-annual-fee, fixed-introductory-APR credit cards. There was also a detached portion of a mortgage statement listing Pen's and Sykora's account number, how much they owed on the mobile home, and the details of each monthly payment, a health care copay statement that included Steve's Social Security number, a bill from a local music store—Pen was leasing an electronic piano—and two credit card statements, one in Pen's name and one in Steve's. You'd think that being a law enforcement officer, Sykora would have been more careful. I could easily steal his identity with this information, make his life a living hell. Probably Phu had stolen Jacob Greene's in the same manner.

I studied the credit card statements. Each detailed

Pen's and Sykora's purchases over the past month. Sykora had used his card mostly to pay for meals. Over half of the restaurants were within walking distance of the Federal Building in downtown Minneapolis. Pen had done a lot of shopping, primarily at Target and Marshall Field's. Both statements were dated a week earlier and didn't help. However, at the bottom of the pile of recyclables was a receipt from a motel in Chanhassen, a city in Carver County just down the road from Norwood Young America. The room had been charged to Pen's credit card.

Why would she need a motel room? Was she cheating on her husband?

I checked the date. It was the same day that I had punched out Danny.

I had seen a lot of motels lately and had come to a conclusion: They're all pretty much alike. The Chanhassen Inn might have been bigger and pricier than some; it had both a restaurant and a swimming pool. But the rooms were still stacked side by side and one atop the other. Half faced the parking lot and half faced the swimming pool, and I was willing to wager that everything in them was bolted down.

I parked across the street from the motel and went into the lobby. I asked for Frank Crosetti's room and was informed that he hadn't checked in and there was no reservation in his name.

"Hmm. He might have checked out already." I asked the clerk if he had taken a room a few days earlier. She assured me that he had not.

I went to the restaurant next. I didn't see anyone I knew. My stomach was grumbling—"Hey, remember me?"—and I was tempted to get something to eat. The special of the day—chicken fried steak and gravy—looked a little too iffy for my taste, though, so I told my stomach to quiet down.

I wandered to the pool. It was a large blue rectangle about six feet at its deepest point. Several signs warned NO DIVING just above several others that proclaimed NO LIFEGUARD ON DUTY. USE POOL AT YOUR OWN RISK. About a dozen kids risked it, along with two adults who watched them like eagles protecting their young. A few more adults were sprawled out on lounge chairs getting a jump on their tans despite the spring chill in the air. From the look of their pale skin, they had plenty of work in front of them, but after all, it was May in Minnesota. I moved slowly among them, pausing to scrutinize a few of the women carefully. Nope, not Frank. Not Danny.

I returned to the parking lot and debated my options. They didn't amount to much. All I knew was that Pen had rented a room here the same day I had pummeled Danny. What did that prove? Not a damn thing. But it was the only clue I had, so I decided to stick with it. Sit, watch, and wait. What else could I do?

I returned to the Neon and turned on the radio. I had a good view of the front lobby and the parking lot, and I watched both intently. After a while, the radio began to bore me. It was "drive time," that period when working men and women were most likely to be driving home, and the DJs were all yukking it up. I'd like to have a short chat with the man who decided that people prefer talk and lame humor over music during morning and evening rush hours, but I didn't know where he lived. Instead, I switched off the radio. I fantasized briefly about sneaking home to recover my CDs. I had enough that I could listen to music continuously for at least twenty-one days straight and not play the same CD twice. But why stop there? Why not grab my books—one a day for how many years? Three? Four? And movies—at least a month's worth on videocassettes and DVDs. Better yet, I could just hang out there, eat sno-cones and mini-donuts, and watch Martin Scorsese films until the FBI dragged me away.

You think too much, McKenzie.

I pumped an additional half dozen quarters into the parking meter and waited some more. The chicken fried steak and gravy was just starting to look good to me when I saw him, Danny, walking with a pronounced limp, carrying a tan paper bag with the golden arches printed on it in one hand and a cardboard tray with two soft drinks in the other. He was just there, in the middle of the parking lot—I had no idea where he came from. I left the Neon and dodged several cars as I crossed the street. Danny was heading for a staircase that led to a dozen second-floor rooms. I ran toward him, even as my inner voice spoke to me.

Why would Pen rent a motel room for Danny?

She didn't, you moron. It was her husband, Steve Sykora, using her credit card.

Why would he do that? The FBI has its own financial resources.

It's not FBI. Sykora is running an illegal op.

Are you sure?

No.

Danny was already on the second-floor landing when I reached the block of rooms. I followed from below, matching his speed, waiting to see which room he entered. But something was speaking to Danny, some instinct. He halted abruptly and looked over the railing.

I tried to conceal myself between four parked cars, two side by side in one row and two directly behind them. I failed.

"You," he said.

"Hi, Danny."

Danny dropped the sack of food and tray of drinks. The lids popped off the drinks, and caramel-colored liquid flowed over the edge of the landing.

He looked right at me, yet his eyes didn't seem to focus. Maybe he thought if he pretended I wasn't there, I'd go away. That lasted only a second. Then came panic. When Danny realized I couldn't reach him, his battered face knotted into an expression of pure hatred, and I remembered: I didn't just take away Danny's gun in the parking lot, I took away the illusion that he was a tough guy, I took away his pride, and he'd hate me forever for it. My inner voice told me to kill him while I had the chance. Instead, I raised my hand and fluttered my fingers ever so slightly at him—"a microwave," Victoria Dunston called it.

"So how's it going?" I chirped.

"You motherfucking sonuvabitch."

"Hey, hey, hey—let's keep family out of this."

"You bastard."

"What did I say?"

Danny gripped the iron railing as if he wanted to throw it at me.

"Fuck you."

Profanity, obscenity, vulgarity—they have become the bedrock of the English language. Just ask the scriptwriters at Fox.

My rage at Danny wasn't nearly as great as it had been. Probably it had something to do with his puffy, scarred, and black-and-blue face. I still wanted to blow his brains out for what he had done to Susan Tillman and Mr. Mosley, but there was something I wanted more.

"Say, Dan-man"—Dan-man was what Bobby Dunston and I had called a kid we played hockey with—"have you seen Frank lately?"

When Danny didn't answer, I decided to go with the Big Bluff.

"Special Agent Sykora of the FBI sent me."

Danny's eyes grew wide.

"You're a liar."

He shoots, he scores.

"Come on down, Danny. I won't hurt you."

Danny didn't believe me. He looked right and left, I don't know what for—a place to run, perhaps. *Go 'head and run,* my inner voice urged. *Show me where you live.*

Danny didn't run. After a moment, he released his grip on the railing and stood up straight while continuing to look down at me. He smiled.

Why would he smile?

Why are you smiling, Danny?

Oh, shit!

I whirled just in time to see the blade slashing toward me. My arms came up as I dodged to my left, hitting a car door with my hip. The knife stabbed empty air beneath my right arm and chest. I danced backward.

There are two of them, man. When are you going to learn?

Danny's friend had been surprised when I turned so unexpectedly. That's why he had missed—I assumed. From the merriment in his eyes and the grin on his lips, he might have done it on purpose, choosing to toy with me a bit. A little boy with flies and no adult supervision.

He advanced on me in a crouch, holding the knife close to his body, probing the space between us with his free hand. I hate knives. Normally I would avoid them at all costs, especially his—a seven-inch stainless steel combat knife called a "Yarborough" by the Green Berets. But trapped in the narrow space between the four cars, I had nowhere to go but forward or back. Forward was out of the question. Backpedaling wasn't much better—I had no speed and I kept glancing off the cars. I didn't dare turn my back to him. I thought about the Beretta pressed between my belt and the small of my back. By the time I reached for it, he would drive the blade of his knife through my heart.

I let him get close.

He feinted with his shoulder.

I hopped into the air and drove my left foot into his chest. It bounced back like I had kicked a truck tire.

"Stick 'im, Brucie," Danny shouted from the balcony.

Brucie? His name is Brucie?

Brucie jabbed at my throat. I shifted my head away

and slapped his knife hand to the side. I grabbed his wrist with my left hand, and with my right I drove a four-knuckle punch into his throat.

Brucie staggered backward but didn't lose his balance. He pulled his wrist free with such ease I wondered why I had bothered grabbing it in the first place.

This is not good.

Brucie moved toward me again, crouching low as before.

I held my ground, braced myself. Parry and strike. What other choice did I have?

Brucie raised the knife.

"Stick 'im," Danny urged.

A woman began to scream in high, piercing, continuous shrieks. She was standing behind Brucie and to his left, holding the hand of a little girl, who in turn was holding toy fins and goggles—they were both dressed for the pool.

When Brucie saw them, he hid the knife behind his back. The expression on his face made me conclude that he was embarrassed.

That would have been a good time to hit him.

But it was an even better time to run away.

And so I did.

I escaped from between the four cars and sprinted along the lane, gobbling ground in a hurry, until I reached the perimeter of the parking lot. Instead of running directly to my car, I went up the street, crossed against the light, circled the block, and approached the Neon from behind. No shouts followed me, no "there he goes," no "get him."

The screaming from the parking lot had ceased by the time I reached the Neon. I heard no sirens and wondered if the woman had called the cops, or at least the lobby. I waited, the engine running, my gun resting on the seat next to me.

A few moments later, Brucie's big Chevy Blazer appeared at the entrance to the motel parking lot. He was driving; Danny was riding shotgun. They hit the street without bothering to slow down. I wasn't surprised. If I was them, I'd be on the run, too. Come to think of it, I was like them. That's why I didn't linger in the parking lot when the woman screamed.

I followed, but I wasn't careful about it. Brucie made me in a hurry. The Blazer accelerated hard. I tried to match its speed. Danny's head appeared outside the passenger window, followed by his elbow, his arm, and a hand with a gun in it. He pointed the gun in my general direction, and my stomach suddenly had that express-elevator-going-down feeling. Only he didn't fire. His head jerked toward the cab of the truck as if he were listening to something. A moment later, he disappeared inside.

A few quick turns and we were on Highway 5 heading east, weaving between cars just like in the movies. The sound of angry horns followed us, but there was no squealing of brakes, no smashed fenders. We had been lucky so far.

A couple miles down the road, Highway 5 merged with U.S. 212 and we were driving north toward Minneapolis. The Neon had more giddy-up than I had expected. I quickly and easily accelerated to 80 mph, but there wasn't much more that her four cylinders could give me. The Blazer pulled away. I tried to keep close, hoping I'd catch it when Brucie and Danny exited the freeway, only I couldn't see around the other SUVs and vans on the road. I gave it up after a half mile and coasted to the posted speed limit.

That's it, I promised myself. *If I ever get my life back, I'm going to buy the fastest car they'll let me drive on city streets.*

It was dusk by the time I returned to Hilltop. The streets were quiet. I could see the flickering light of TV sets through trailer windows, and somewhere someone was playing Bob Dylan. I cruised past Pen's mobile home. Her carport was still empty. I drove to the end of the street, turned around, and drove back again. One-on-one surveillance was impossible. There were too many people living in too confined an area. There was no place I could park and not be noticed, nowhere I could walk and not be seen.

"I know all my neighbors," Ruth had said. She probably wasn't the only one.

Yet I couldn't let Pen go. She was my only link to Sykora, and through him to Frank Crosetti. I had convinced myself that Sykora was conducting some kind of black bag job; otherwise he'd be using bureau resources to hide Danny and Brucie, not his wife. Besides, although I had been a devoted fan of *The X-Files,* I wasn't prepared to believe that the FBI as a whole would behave so poorly.

Having helped to save her from an assault—I still couldn't believe her attacker was a kidnapper—Jake

Greene had achieved a certain amount of trust and goodwill with Pen. That and his cover as a reporter might get some questions answered. But I needed more.

The Easy Cash pawnshop was located in a Minneapolis neighborhood of dopers, prostitutes, gangbangers, immigrants, working poor, and other unreliable credit risks that so far had remained untouched by attempts at gentrification and social tinkering. Yet there was nothing desperate about the shop itself. It was light and airy and clean and at first glance resembled any department store you've ever been in. If there was a difference, it was in the astonishing array of merchandise—over twelve thousand square feet of VCRs and DVDs, computers, electric guitars, jewelry, tools, bicycles, lawn mowers, even motorcycles and snowmobiles. If a product had financial value, Easy Cash traded in it. The only exception was guns. There was a large sign next to the front entrance that read EASY CASH DOES NOT BUY OR SELL GUNS OF ANY KIND. YOU ARE PROHIBITED FROM CARRYING A GUN ON THESE PREMISES.

I was met at the door by a young man who wore a blue tie; all employees of Easy Cash were required to wear ties and dress shirts. I asked for the owner, and he pointed at Marshall Lantry. Lantry, who was wearing a tan sports jacket to go with his shirt and tie, was standing behind a counter in the center of the store. The counter was on a foot-high platform. I had convinced Lantry to build the platform in order to discourage miscreants from attempting to come over the top of the counter for either the cash register or him and his employees. Above and behind his shoulder were mounted posters of Anna Kournikova, Taye Diggs, and Jennifer Lopez. Hanging right above the posters were security cameras. The way I had explained it to Lantry, the posters would encourage customers—male and female alike—to look up, which in turn would help the security cameras to get a good shot of their faces.

The corners of Lantry's mouth were curled upward into a smile. Since his mouth always curled that way, giving Lantry a pleasant grin that never disappeared, I didn't know if he was happy to see me or not.

"Damn, McKenzie," he said. "I was just talking about you with Chopper. You remember Chopper."

Chopper was a borderline sociopath who took a bullet in the spine and now conducts his many illicit enterprises from a wheelchair that he maneuvers with motorcycle-like speed and recklessness.

"Yeah, I know Chopper."

"He was just saying that everyone he knows is either a mean sonuvabitch or an asshole 'cept you."

"High praise indeed."

"He was sayin' how you saved his life."

"All I did was call EMS after finding his bullet-riddled butt on the sidewalk."

"That's not the way he says it."

"Chopper has always been prone to exaggeration."

"Yeah, well, I agree with him. You ain't a sonuvabitch or an asshole."

"Stop it, Marsh. You're giving me a swelled head."

"As compared to other things that inflate."

I glanced up at Anna, and Lantry chuckled.

"So, you buyin' or sellin'?"

"Buying."

"I just got in a couple of great speakers if you're lookin' to expand that sound system of yours."

"Actually, I have something a little more high-tech in mind."

"High-tech as in . . . oh." Lantry leaned over the counter. The sparkle in his eyes added to his permanent smile. "You want to talk *serious* business?"

I nodded.

A few moments later, Lantry led me to a tiny room in his basement. I thought of Phu. So many of today's entrepreneurs conduct business out of their cellars.

Metal shelves were pushed against each of the four walls. Electronic surveillance gear, both new and used, was stacked on the shelves: bugs made to resemble electrical outlets and phone jacks, audio recorders, video cameras in every shape and size including a fountain pen, microwave and satellite dishes, and a lot of stuff I couldn't identify. Seven years ago, city officials had shut Lantry down for running illegal poker tournaments. That's how I met him, playing Texas Hold 'Em. If they knew about this setup, they'd probably send him to prison.

Lantry said, "You realize that it's illegal to intercept and record conversations without the consent of the folks involved, right?"

"It's also illegal to sell bugs for the purpose of intercepting conversations."

"And it's illegal for you, the customer, to buy bugs for

the purpose of intercepting conversations. I have a copy of the statute around here somewhere."

"You're telling me this why?"

"I just want to make sure you know what you're doin'."

"That's a different question altogether."

"So it is." Lantry rested his hand on an office calculator. "I just got this in. It not only transmits conversations and video images for over two hundred meters, it actually calculates. Cool, huh?"

"Very."

"So what do you want to surveil? House? Apartment?"

"Trailer."

"Trailer?"

"A mobile home."

"A mobile . . . where?"

"City of Hilltop."

"Where the hell is that?"

I explained.

"Hell, I musta driven by that place a thousand times and didn't know it was there."

"You learn something new every day," I told him.

"Okay, so your average single-wide trailer runs about nine hundred to eleven hundred and fifty square feet"—I was always impressed that Lantry knew these things—"which is good cuz we can do the job with only two bugs." Lantry found one and bounced it in the palm of his hand. It was black, about the size of a wine cork, and had a tiny antenna on top. "Couple of these babies for the trailer and another for the telephone ought to do the trick. They'll pick up a whisper from fifty meters. What we'll do is, we'll stash a receiver in the trunk of a car, connect the receiver to a voice-activated tape recorder with four-hour cassettes. We'll park the car about a block away from the trailer. The recorder has a real-time indicator so you'll know what was said and when it was said. You just cruise by every couple of hours—"

"That's not going to work," I said. "There's no place to park the car. It's a very dense, very high-traffic area. The car would be spotted in ten minutes. People would be asking questions about it an hour later."

"That makes it tougher." Lantry set the bug back on the shelf and glanced over the rest of his equipment.

"Also, I want to be able to monitor what is being said in real time."

"Tougher still," Lantry said. "How close can you get?"

"I have a motel room nearby."

"How near?"

"Three hundred, maybe three hundred and fifty yards as the crow flies."

"Why didn't you say so? Piece of cake." Lantry snatched a bug off yet another shelf. Like the other listening device, it was black. It was about two-thirds the size of a business card and had the width of a ballpoint pen. There was a cable jack and two wires with clamps protruding from the top.

"The double-oh-six," he said. "It monitors telephone conversations when the phone is in use. It's a room transmitter at all other times. It transmits on UHF so no dork with a police scanner will intercept your conversations. Great range. Just one of these and you're covered. But it's expensive. It retails for about five hundred and seventy-five pounds in England."

"How much is that in real money?"

"A lot."

"How do I install it?"

"You don't. I'll do it."

I chewed on the inside of my cheek, thinking it over. "There's no reason for you to take a chance like that."

"Better me than you, McKenzie. You'll only screw it up."

He was probably right, and I told him so.

"I can let myself in," Lantry said. "Question is—can you make sure the trailer is empty?"

"Yes."

"For how long?"

"How much time do you need?"

"Ten minutes. Maybe fifteen."

"I can do that."

"Next question—how many times do you need to go in? Once to plant the bug, yeah. But do we need to remove it later?"

"Can it be traced back to you?"

"No way."

"Then leave it for the maid."

"Final question—who's the target?"

"A federal agent named Sykora."

"Federal agent?"

"FBI."

"Getting a little ambitious, aren't you, son?"

"He's bent."

"How bent?"

"Paper clip bent."

"Bent enough to take violent action should we be discovered?"

"Probably."

"Fun."

Lantry wasn't being sarcastic. He meant it.

"Know what's more fun?" I told him. "Not getting caught."

"Yeah, but it's the fear that makes it . . . Never mind."

"I need this done right away."

"Tomorrow soon enough?"

"Morning?"

"Fine."

"How much is this going to set me back?"

"Normally I'd give you a discount seein' how we go back some."

"Uh-huh."

"But for the FBI—the price is five large, McKenzie, including expenses. Nonnegotiable."

"A workman is worthy of his hire."

"And I want it in cash."

"Of course."

"You gonna tell me why you're doing this?"

"Marshall, my friend. We live in an age of confusion, mistrust, and deteriorating moral values."

"A terrible thing."

"I fear for the future of the Republic."

"Me, too."

"You want to get something to eat?"

"Why not?"

Chapter Seven

The carport next to Pen's trailer was still empty when I rapped on her aluminum door at 9:00 A.M. I waited a moment, listening to the wind chimes she had hung there, then knocked again. Pen swung open the door like she expected to see a loving friend on the other side.

"Jake Greene." She spoke my name as if I were that friend. "Good morning."

"Good morning to you."

"How are you this beautiful, sunshiny day?"

A simple question, yet the way she asked it made me feel as if the success of her own day depended on my answer.

"I'm fine. How are you after yesterday?"

"I am deluxe."

She smiled broadly, and her eyes half closed. They reminded me of cobalt thiocyanate, the chemical dealers use to test the purity of cocaine. The higher quality the drug, the brighter the blue. Pen's eyes were at least 90 percent pure.

"Did you speak to your husband about what happened yesterday?"

"I did. Steve thinks it was a case of mistaken identity, some hophead confusing me with his ex-girlfriend, but he says I should keep a cautious eye out for junky-looking pickup trucks."

That didn't sound any more logical to me than a kidnapping attempt, but I said, "Wise advice," and let it slide.

"Would you like to come in for a cup of coffee?"

"Thank you, but—actually, I was hoping you could come out with me, perhaps show me around Hilltop while we chat. For my story."

"I need to tell you, Jake, you really should speak to someone like Ruth Schramm. I haven't been here that long."

"I will talk to Ruth, but I wanted to chat with you *because* you haven't been here for that long."

"Let me get my bag."

I felt a sudden jolt of excitement then, like she had just agreed to an offer of dinner and a movie.

Pen appeared a moment later with a bag slung over her shoulder that was big enough to tote New Zealand. She didn't bother locking the door when she left the trailer, and I mentioned it to her.

"Isn't that cool?" she said.

I flashed on the kidnapping attempt but said nothing.

In the bright morning sunlight, Pen looked like a midwestern farm girl. She wore a white blouse knotted under her breasts, blue shorts, and sandals. She had golden hair, a smooth, outdoorsy complexion complete with freckles, and a healthy figure, and she smelled a little like the autumn leaves we used to burn in the backyard before the state made it illegal—a delicious scent, both arid and sweet. I felt as if I were committing four of the seven deadly sins just by walking with her.

We strolled along 47th Avenue, turned south, turned again. I was already lost, but Pen moved with the assurance of a native, swinging her arms buoyantly. I carried a Bic and a small spiral notebook that I pretended occasionally to write in.

Pen said, "None of my friends back home can believe I'm living in a trailer park." She laughed as if she also found the idea ridiculous. "I'm trailer trash." She laughed some more. "I nearly killed Steve when he installed us here. I wanted a house. I figured if they were going to make us move to Minnesota, at least we could live in a house. But Steve said it was only a temporary assignment, so . . . Anyway, I really like it now—trailer living. It's really not all that different from living in an apartment."

I edged Pen toward the side of the lane to make room for a white van with the name of a cable TV company emblazoned on the side. I pretended not to recognize the driver as the van moved slowly past, and he pretended not to recognize me.

"We used to live in New York, Steve and I, in a crowded apartment building in the middle of the city. Five years we were there and I didn't know any of the neighbors, which is both amazing and kind of disturbing, if you know what I mean. I've been here for just under five months and I know everyone. A more interesting and truly eccentric group you'll never find. I love them all." Laughter. "I fit in real well." Then more laughter. It made me want to laugh, too, even though I didn't get the joke.

Under Pen's laughter I could hear the music of Bob Dylan. She heard it, too.

"This guy." Pen gestured at a periwinkle-colored trailer as we passed. "His name is Jerry, and he loves, I mean loves, Bob Dylan. I love him, too, but c'mon. Jerry plays Dylan's music twenty-four/seven. I am not exaggerating. Walk by at four in the morning and you'll hear it. And this guy"—Pen found another trailer—"he says his name is Shaka, and he claims to be the hereditary king of the Zulu nation forced into exile by an evil uncle who usurped his father's throne."

"Really?"

"That's what he says, only he speaks with a Creole accent. I'll tell you something else. He makes a shrimp étouffée that's to die for."

We continued down the lane. The bicycle of a small child had fallen off its kickstand and was resting on the asphalt. Pen righted the bike and wheeled it out of harm's way as if it were the most natural thing in the world.

"Life is pretty much in the streets in a trailer park," Pen said. "A mobile home isn't very big. There's not much room for socializing, and sometimes the walls can get awfully close, so you spend a lot of time outside. And because we live just a few feet from each other, there's not much privacy. You have to be neighborly to get by. Steve's not. I suppose it's an occupational hazard, being suspicious all the time. But I like people. I didn't know how much I liked them until I moved here and really got to know a few.

"This is Jerry's place—a different Jerry," she said as we walked past a dark brown trailer. "This Jerry makes sculptures out of beer bottles and beer cans."

"Does he empty them himself?"

"Sometimes his neighbors help." Pen chuckled mischievously. "Sometimes we help way more than we should." Her fingers closed around my wrist. "I heard Jerry's starting a new project. If you're interested, we can drop by later and see if he could use some assistance."

She released my wrist and I wondered if she was flirting with me, decided she wasn't, but maybe she was, then again . . .

We came to a gentle hill. At the bottom of the hill was a small park with swings, slides, monkey bars, and teeter-totters.

Pen said, "Everyone in the city pitched in to build this."

She broke into a trot. When she reached the park, she dropped her bag, kicked off her sandals, and ran barefoot to the swing. She had it going pretty well by the time I reached her. I watched as Pen stretched her long legs toward the sky, tucked them under her seat as she swung back, then stretched them out again, gaining altitude and smiling at me. I wondered again if she was flirting, decided she was, and suddenly I wanted to swing, too. I wanted to be that kid again who hung out at Merriam Park and played hockey and baseball and trifled with high school girls and who didn't have a care in the world except passing advanced physics. I wanted to go to pep rallies and mixers and keggers down at the river. I wanted to take Pen to the prom . . .

Stop it, McKenzie, my inner voice admonished. *Get your head in the game.*

"You said your husband is with the FBI," I told Pen.

"Yes," she replied in full swing. "Steve was one of the lead agents on an organized crime task force. But since 9/11 the bureau has been dedicating more and more resources to fighting terrorism at the expense of everything else. Steve is really upset about it. I guess most of the field officers are, too. They want to keep solving traditional federal crimes—bank robberies, drug trafficking, kidnappings. But the politicians at the top, they want to reinvent the bureau to reflect the current political climate. At least that's how Steve sees it. Anyway, they shut down the task force and sent us to Minneapolis. Steve says it's temporary, that'll we'll be going back to New York any day now. If we don't . . ."

Pen slowed to a stop.

"Trailer life is okay. But I want a house. I want to live in a real, honest-to-God house, with a garden and a rope swing in the backyard for the kids and thick green grass that you can walk on without shoes. We couldn't have that in New York City, but we can have it here and that's what I want. You're not going to write that down, are you?"

I glanced at the notebook in my hand.

"Nah," I said.

Pen laughed again.

"Ruth wouldn't like it. She was one of the founding residents of Hilltop."

"She was living here in 1956?" I said, remembering the *Trailer Park* article I had read in the library.

"When the city incorporated, yes. You've been doing your homework."

"Of course. I'm a professional."

I wondered briefly if there really was such a thing as a born liar and if I fit that classification. But I summarily dismissed the question from my head. It took years of practice to reach my level of competence. I wasn't a *born* liar, I was a self-made man.

We left the park and continued walking. Pen smiled for no particular reason. Shelby often would smile like that, smile as though someone had told her the most amusing tale. I asked her about it once. "Why do you smile so?" She said, "McKenzie, you can be such a drip sometimes," which I later took to mean, "Why shouldn't I smile?" Shelby was a happy woman, and I decided Pen was, too.

"Something else I want," Pen said.

"What's that?"

"I want my car back. I have a Mustang convertible with a 193-horsepower, 3.8-liter V-6 engine and five-speed manual transmission. I love that car, only I never get to drive it. Steve's always taking it. In New York owning a car is a self-indulgence. Most of the money I earned went toward keeping it in a garage. But out here it's a necessity. Everything is so spread out. Mass transit is a joke. You can't hail a cab to save your life. I really miss Matilda."

"You named your car Matilda?"

"Yes."

"Matilda the Mustang."

"You don't name your cars?"

"Well, no."

She looked at me like she had just discovered a disturbing flaw in my character.

"Anyway, I want Matilda back. She's mine. I bought her."

"What do you do?"

"I'm a songwriter."

"No kidding."

"Amazing, isn't it?"

"I didn't mean it that way."

"I did. I am constantly amazed that I make money doing this. Not a lot of money, but all it takes is one hit and you're on your way."

"What kind of music do you write?"

"Ballads mostly. We haven't sold a lot in the past couple of years. Mostly we've sold to artists like Bonnie Raitt who wanted something a little different to help fill out an album. No one has ever released one of our songs as a single. But Tommy thinks—Tommy's my partner, Tommy Heyward. Glass and Heyward. I write music and he writes lyrics. Tommy thinks we're in exactly the right place at exactly the right time because good old-fashioned crooning is coming back into vogue. Think about it. Rod Stewart goes platinum with an album of standards. Boz Scaggs, B. B. King, Diana Krall, k. d. lang and Tony Bennett, Harry Connick, of course, Lizz Wright, Michael Buble, Brian Evans, Peter Cincotti—

they're all expanding the audience for the kind of music we like to write. And then Norah Jones comes along. I absolutely, unequivocally adore Norah Jones. Seven million copies of *Come Away With Me* and counting. A young woman introducing that sexy, smoky, jazzy balladry to a generation that didn't have anyone its own age performing grown-up music. So much is geared toward the teen market these days, Britney and Christina and Justin, puhleez, and rap, which is—ugghh!—that there's been a backlash from people in their twenties, people who feel abandoned by the record industry, and crooners are a part of it. It's a good backlash. Audiences are suddenly reaching out for a cooler, more sophisticated, more artfully arranged kind of music, which is what I write. Now, all of a sudden artists and producers and record companies who wouldn't answer our phone calls are calling us. Amazing. I'm going to stop talking now and take a deep breath. I hope you don't mind."

Now I was laughing.

A white van was parked in the Hilltop Motel lot just below my second-floor room. The colorful name and logo that was on its side earlier had been removed.

I entered my room without knocking. The drapes had been closed, and there was little light. Marshall Lantry was lying on my bed watching Oprah. He said, "Attractive woman. I don't blame you for taking your time."

"Did everything go all right?"

"Hey. It's me."

I cut the power to the TV with the remote. "I know it's you. Did everything go all right?"

"Yes. Fine. Perfect. Six minutes in and out. You know, the lady doesn't even bother to lock her door."

"I like that about her."

"Yeah, but c'mon. How foolish is that?"

I didn't have an answer.

Lantry rolled off the bed and moved to the desk. He switched on the lamp to reveal a receiver and a tape recorder. The receiver was pocket-sized, assuming your pockets were slightly larger than mine. The tape recorder was a standard-sized portable with a few extra dials and gauges that required explanation. They were united by two coaxial cables. The entire thing could easily fit inside a small desk drawer, so that's where I put it. There were no electrical cords. Lantry said the unit was operated by a battery with a thirty-day charge.

Lantry gave me a crash course, demonstrating how to use the voice-activated recording function and adjust the volume. The bug was already transmitting. I could hear Pen washing dishes and humming a tune that I couldn't identify. I guessed it was one of hers.

"Nice job," I told Lantry.

"Now for the bad news," he said.

"Bad news?"

"Someone else is also listening."

"What do you mean?"

"There are at least two other bugs—one in her living room, one in her bedroom—and the phones are tapped."

"What?"

"Someone is conducting an audio surveillance of your

girl. Someone close. The equipment is very short range. Kinda shoddy, too, if you ask me. Nearly obsolete."

"Who?"

"How should I know who? The bugs don't have labels on them, you know."

"Jeezus."

The news forced me backward until the backs of my knees hit the edge of the bed and I sat down.

"You know, it's always something," said Lantry.

"Isn't it, though. You left the bugs in? Didn't tamper with them?"

"Yes."

"What?"

"I mean no. I mean I didn't touch the bugs."

"Did they hear you?"

"They heard someone, but I doubt they knew what I was doing."

Lantry showed me his perpetual smile. "Nothing personal," he said, "but stay away from me for awhile."

After Lantry left, I adjusted the volume on the receiver and stretched out on the bed. There was a lump in my stomach that felt like an unexploded Scud—I didn't know why it was there, but it was.

I wondered who else was bugging Pen. It could be her suspicious husband, I supposed. He wouldn't be the first to go to such lengths out of mistrust for his wife. But having met Pen, having enjoyed her company so thoroughly, I just didn't see it. It could be the FBI—probably was the FBI. They could have found out about

Sykora's extracurricular activities and be in the process of reining him in. Certainly it made more sense. In any case, there was nothing to be done about it but wait and listen. I came off the bed, went to the window, and threw open the drapes, letting sunlight shine into the room through the white lace curtains.

If I was going to hang around all day, I decided, I needed supplies. I switched on the voice-activated recorder, left the room, and walked south to the Central Plaza strip mall. I bought a roll of masking tape and a few munchies in the supermarket—including a bag of Twizzlers strawberry licorice, my favorite—and picked up a six-pack of James Page in the municipal off-sale liquor store on the way back. I also bought two papers.

Mr. Mosley's murder was still featured in both the *St. Paul Pioneer Press* and *Minneapolis Tribune*, although not nearly as prominently as a few days ago. I wasn't surprised. Unlike in some communities—Los Angeles comes to mind—murder, any murder, was still news here. We don't have so many that we quickly forget them. A local guy who won the Pulitzer a few years back wrote thrillers set in Minnesota. I read a couple—they're not bad. But seriously, if there were nearly as many psychopaths here as appeared in his books, we'd be sending our kids to school in armored personnel carriers.

I checked the recorder the moment I returned. Pen had finished her dishes in my absence and left her trailer—the door closing was the last sound on the tape. "Life is in the streets," she had said.

After placing the beer inside the tiny refrigerator and stacking the rest of my supplies on top of it, I unrolled two six-inch strips of tape and pressed them firmly across the top of both the receiver and recorder. On the tape I wrote PROPERTY OF U.S. TREASURY DEPT.

I wasn't uncomfortable in the motel room. I spent most of my adult life living on the top floor of a duplex off of West Seventh Street in St. Paul that was owned by a guy I played hockey with. It was small, but it suited me just fine. After I came into my money, I bought my house with the expectation that my father and I would live in it; it was far too big for just me alone. I would have put it up for sale after he died except for the kitchen. I love to cook and often throw elaborate dinner parties just for the opportunity to show off. I suspect that's one of the reasons I have so many friends, because I feed them regularly.

I grabbed six sticks of licorice and sprawled out on the bed. The motel TV only received a dozen channels, but one of them was ESPN and another was CNN, so I was set. I watched the French Open with the volume off, so the noise wouldn't interfere with anything I might hear over the receiver. Images of tennis players swatting a fuzzy green ball at each other made perfect sense without commentary. More, actually.

After a few minutes, Pen returned.

There were puttering sounds and then the telephone. The ringing was loud enough to make my fake landscapes shake on the walls, and I rushed to the receiver to reduce the volume.

"Hello," Pen said.

"Hi, honey, it's me."

"It's me who? My secret lover or my husband who usually calls this time of day to tell me he's working late?"

"We're not going to do this again, are we?"

I could hear tension in their voices like the static on AM radio stations during thunderstorms.

"You didn't keep hours like this in New York."

"It's different here."

"Why is it different here?"

"I can't tell you."

"Why can't you tell me? You could tell me things before."

"I know . . ."

"I feel like I'm living a life I know nothing about. Do you understand that? Do you know how painful that is?"

"C'mon, Lucky . . ."

There was a long pause before Pen said, "That's something you haven't called me in a long time."

"You'll always be my Lucky Penny."

"Will I?"

"The reason I called was to tell you that I *won't* be working late for a change."

"Okay, now I feel stupid."

"Don't, don't . . . Let me take you out."

"I have an idea. Why don't I make beef Stroganoff?"

"Isn't that what you made the last time you seduced me?"

"You know me, Steve. When something works, I stick with it."

There was more like that, and listening to the conversation, I felt a shudder of excitement that I hadn't expected. There was something thrilling about eavesdropping on other people's lives, and in that instant I understood the popularity of reality TV. I also felt a certain revulsion. Clearly I was no gentleman.

After hanging up the phone, Pen made a list that she read out loud. "Sirloin, mushrooms, onions, garlic, sour cream, white wine, tomato paste. Do I have beef broth? Yes, I have beef broth." A moment later the trailer door opened and closed. I presumed she went to the nearby grocery store for ingredients.

I settled in, wondering what I would have for dinner.

Steve Sykora and his wife went to bed less than five minutes after Sykora returned home. I admit to a certain jealousy. And anger. I held Sykora partially responsible for the murder of Mr. Mosley and the rape of Susan Tillman—the bastard didn't deserve to be loved by Penelope Glass. But that's not why I switched off the receiver. I did it because I still believed I was a good guy, and there are certain things a good guy doesn't do. Spying on people's most intimate moments was one of them.

I wondered if the party or parties unknown who also were listening had switched off their receiver, too.

Victor, the elderly manager of the Hilltop Motel, was spraying water on the asphalt driveway with a hose when I left the room. I gave him a little wave and wandered north. The traffic on Central Avenue never stopped, never seemed to increase or decrease in volume. It remained constant, like a river polluted by exhaust, noise, and lights. I followed it until I found a Mediterranean restaurant that looked authentic. Unfortunately, the food had a North American taste to it, gyros, shawarma, and kabobs for a midwestern clientele, as bland as the suburbs. Still, it was a pleasant evening, and after dinner I went for a walk.

I walked for ten minutes with an odd feeling that something was wrong. I walked for another ten minutes before I realized what it was. I had no place to go and no one to talk to when I got there. Jake Greene didn't have any friends, at least none I was aware of. Rushmore McKenzie had plenty, and although he spent much of his time alone—for he had always been content in his own company—he was aware that they were out there and usually happy to hear from him. But Jake was worse than alone. He was lonely. And I wondered, did someone love him? Did he love them in return? Did he wish he could go home? Of course. But he had a job to do, so instead of returning to Rapid City, South Dakota, he walked back to the Hilltop Motel.

They were eating when I returned. The talk was small. Spring in Minnesota versus spring in New York. Was Sykora treating Pen's beloved Matilda with the proper respect and consideration? Songwriters Glass and Heyward were still waiting to hear about some tunes the Indigo Girls had shown interest in.

The phone rang, and again I was forced to reduce the volume on the receiver.

Pen said, "Don't answer it."

"I wish," said Sykora. "Yes?"

A voice said, "Goddammit, you said you were going to take care of McKenzie."

I leapt for the tape machine and pressed the record button. The spools on the cassette began spinning a half beat later.

"Just a minute." Sykora muffled the phone. "I need to take this in private."

"Big surprise," Pen said. "I'll be in the bedroom. Let me know when you can trust me enough to come out."

"Pen—"

There was movement followed by the slamming of a door.

"What did I tell you about calling here?"

"Did you want me to call you at the Federal Building?"

"What do you want, Frank?"

"Fuckin' McKenzie. He found my boys."

"The boys you sent to harass my wife? Those boys?"

"I told you I didn't have nothing to do with that."

"Yeah, and you had nothing to do with raping that woman, either."

"You know what happened. I sent 'em over there to scare 'er, to slap 'er around a bit, get 'er old man off my case. They just got excited."

"Did they get excited when you killed the old man, too?"

"How many times I gotta say it? I didn't do the fuckin' darky. He was gone when I got there."

"Yeah, right."

"If I'm lyin', I'm dyin'."

"Fuck you, Frank."

"Watch your mouth."

"How many times I need to say it? This isn't goddamn Brooklyn. This isn't Jersey. This is Minnesota. There's no culture of violence here. You can't hurt innocent people and expect everyone to forget about it in a few days, or when the next act of violence occurs. The cops just arrested a guy for killing a coworker eleven years ago who accused him of sexual harassment. Eleven years, Frank. Eleven years they kept after this guy. I tried to explain that to you when you broke the prostitute's hand."

"I made some mistakes, okay? I was wrong. When I'm wrong I say I'm wrong, okay? But that don't address the problem with my boys."

"You're not supposed to have boys, Frank. You're supposed to sit quietly in your house, not go running off to some goddamn roadhouse and recruit talent like you were a capo running a crew back home."

"That ain't the point, Fed. The point is McKenzie found 'em in that motel you stuck 'em in."

"How?"

"How the fuck should I know how. He found 'em, that's all."

"I told you he was smart."

"You told me you was gonna take care of him. Well, he ain't taken care of."

"Look, I issued a Seeking Information Alert on him. We're watching his house, we're watching his friends—"

"That ain't good enough. You gotta put his face on milk cartons or somethin'. Put 'im on the news."

"To do that I'd have to give my boss a better explanation for why we're looking for him. You want to do that? 'Well, sir, we lied before. The real reason we're looking for McKenzie is because we killed his pal and raped his lawyer's wife and now he wants revenge.' "

"We didn't kill—ahh, fuck it. Look. We had a deal, okay? Protection for information."

"That's right. When are you going to keep your end of it?"

"I told you, the shipment will be here in a few days."

"Where, Frank?"

"I told ya where."

"When, Frank?"

"When you gonna take care of McKenzie?"

"Soon."

"That's when the shipment is comin' in. Soon."

"Don't screw with me, Frank."

"Yeah, whaddaya gonna do, Fed? You gonna call your boss? You gonna tell 'im what you been doin'?"

"No, Frank. I'm gonna call your boss."

There was a long pause. Finally Frank said, "I know where you live, Fed."

"Yeah, and I know where you live. So let's be smart, huh, Frank? We'll both get what we want."

Frank hung up without saying good-bye. Sykora did the same a moment later. I turned off the recorder and removed the cassette. I wanted to make sure nothing happened to it. I wrapped it in a sock and locked it in my suitcase.

The sound of a door opening startled me. I spun to face the entrance to my room, but of course it was closed.

"May I come out now?" Pen asked.

"I'm sorry."

"What's wrong?"

"Nothing's wrong."

"You're wound so tight lately. Mysterious phone calls . . ."

"I used the phone for bureau business, what's mysterious about that?"

"You've never done it before. Not like this."

"Pen, please—"

"Steve, please. Tell me what's going on."

"It's nothing to worry about, Pen. Nothing at all. I'm going to take a shower."

"Sure."

At 3:22 A.M. according to the cheap digital clock radio next to the bed, I came suddenly awake. I listened, stared at the outline of the desk, heard nothing, saw nothing. I thought of Pen and Sykora in bed together, lying side by side, and the idea of it angered me.

I closed my eyes and went back to sleep.

Chapter Eight

I woke up with more aches and pains than I had when I went to bed.

"You're getting so old," I told my reflection in the mirror. Plus I hadn't worked out in days. No sports. No martial arts. Nothing. "You used to be an athlete."

My reflection stared at me like he didn't believe it.

I heard Sykora tell his wife, "I'll see you later," while I shaved.

She said, "You don't kiss me good-bye anymore?"

There was movement followed by Pen's voice.

"You can do better than that."

A few moments later I heard the smacking sound that sometimes follows a long kiss.

"Not bad," said Pen. "You could use more practice."

"I know. I'm sorry. I'm sorry about everything, Lucky. But it'll be all right soon. Soon we'll be back in New York."

"We could be just as happy here as we were in the city. I've met people. I've talked to them. They like Minnesota."

"It's not New York."

"That's one of the things they like about it."

"Good for you, Pen," I said out loud.

A moment later, Sykora was gone. I finished dressing and opened the drapes of my single window. I ate a few sticks of Twizzlers for breakfast and sat on the edge of the unmade bed.

"So what are we going to do today, Pen?"

I heard a long, not altogether unpleasant groan—a woman stretching—followed by a deep sigh.

"I gotta get to work," Pen said.

Sounds like a plan, my inner voice agreed.

It was a delightful spring morning. There were clouds in the sky, but not enough to worry about, and the air had a pleasant taste to it.

I parked in front of Ruth Schramm's trailer. It was considerably older than Pen's and smaller. It was dark brown with tan trim and narrow strips of rust extending from the edge of the V-shaped roof down the metal sides. There was a wooden porch leading to a door that had been built about twenty years ago and painted once.

From the porch I could see Pen's trailer. She came out the door carrying a worn black notebook in her hand. Her enormous bag hung from a strap on her shoulder. I waved to her, but she didn't see. I waved more frantically and received the same response. I thought of calling her name, but before I could the trailer door opened.

"I know you," Ruth said. "You're—what's your name again?"

"Jake Greene."

"The writer. You're writing about Hilltop."

"Yes."

"I suppose you want to interview me."

"If it's not too much of an imposition."

"Well, come in."

Ruth held open the door. I stepped through it. The trailer seemed cramped. There were a lot of plants that appeared to be thriving, family photos, and assorted bric-a-brac, including a painting of John Paul II. Most of the furniture was old, and Ruth employed subtle tricks to conceal its shabbiness—a crocheted bedspread covering the sofa, a lace doily on top of a TV tray employed as an end table, a carefully trimmed tablecloth as curtains. I pretended not to notice.

"The place is a mess, but I won't apologize." Ruth directed me to a white wicker chair with faded blue cushions. "Sit."

"Thank you."

"Would you care for something? Coffee?"

"That would be great."

Ruth passed from her tiny living room into an even smaller kitchen. "So what do you want to know?" she asked in a rich smoker's voice, although I noticed there were no ashtrays in the trailer.

"I've been told that you were one of the founding citizens of Hilltop."

Ruth returned to the living room without the coffee. She pressed her fists against her hips and said, "You know what gets me? It gets me that you hear people degrading trailer parks. People making jokes, and not just comedians. Politicians, too. People who do that, they've never lived in a trailer park, let me tell you. The people who live here—do you want to know about the people who live here?"

"Please."

"There's nothing trashy about them. That's what most people think, that we're trash. Trailer trash. They think that mobile homes are cheap, shoddy, and unattractive, and that the people who live in them are the same way.

"A lot of people live here because it's affordable, I'll give you that. A two-bedroom single-wide trailer costs about $30,000 and a double-wide maybe $50,000, and lots run $250 to $300. That's not much compared to the housing market. But the people who live here don't live here cuz they're poor white trash. No, sir. Median income isn't much less here than it is in Columbia Heights. Hilltop is not a ghetto. Are you writing this down?"

I had been holding the notebook unopened against my knee. For appearance's sake, I started jotting Ruth's comments.

"Hilltop's a good place for seniors and it's a good place for couples starting out. Young couple moved in last week, just married. And why not? Why not live in a trailer while you save for the big spread in the suburbs? Why not live in one after you raise your kids, after you retire? There's not much maintenance to worry about, that's for sure."

"Do you get much turnover?"

"We're getting younger, young families coming in to replace the seniors that go off to nursing homes." Ruth spoke like she was afraid she'd be next.

"Have many people been moving in lately?"

"The young couple, I forget their names, but I can find out for you."

"That's okay."

"Before that, let's see . . . There were two middle-aged men around forty just a few weeks ago." It distressed me to hear what Ruth thought was middle-aged. "They moved in together. I think they're gay."

"Why do you say that?"

"They're two middle-aged men in their early forties living together."

It's hard to argue with that kind of logic.

"And you never see them. They just sit in their trailer. Once in a while one of 'em goes for takeout. You try to be friendly and it's like 'Don't talk to me.' "

"Which trailer are they in?"

Ruth gave me an address on 47½ Avenue. "They're behind me," she said, "about a dozen trailers down."

Which placed them about a dozen trailers from Pen. I made a note of it.

"Who else is new?" Ruth said. "A teacher, new teacher at the middle school. There's Nick Horvath, you met him. Steve Sykora and Penelope Glass. She's such a sweetheart. Writes songs, I'm told. And he's with the FBI. Do they sound like trailer trash to you? I don't think so."

I agreed with her.

"Let me take you down to city hall."

"You have a city hall?"

"Of course we have a city hall. Hilltop's a city, isn't it?"

I followed Ruth out of her trailer—I never did get my coffee—and down the same lane that Pen and I had taken the day before. Ruth set a brisk pace, and I had to work to stay with her. Along the way, she pointed out a tree.

"We used to have our own police department. We even had a squad car with 'Hilltop' painted on the door. Unfortunately, one of our officers drove the car into that tree back in '72 and the city didn't have enough money to replace it, so there went the police department. Now we have a contract with Columbia Heights."

Ruth stopped and pointed a finger at me.

"That's another thing. We don't have a high crime rate. That's a myth. People don't do nothing here that they don't do everywhere else."

Farther along the road, Ruth began pointing out more trees—maples, butternuts, black walnuts, sycamores.

"When I first came here, Hilltop had all these magnificent Dutch elm trees forming this great canopy over us, over the parkways. It was like a fairyland it was so green and shaded. But we caught Dutch elm disease in the '70s, and they all had to come down. We planted these trees, trees with large leaves, to make up for them. They're just now starting to get real size."

As we admired the trees, Penelope Glass crossed in front of us, strolling along yet another narrow lane. Her head was down as if she were deep in thought. She walked with her hands behind her back clasping the black notebook. Her bag hung from her shoulder and bounced against her thigh with each step.

Ruth called, "Morning, sweetie."

Pen waved automatically, then saw me and waved with more enthusiasm.

"Good morning," she called. "Hard at work, I see."

"No rest for the wicked," I told her, then instantly regretted it. *What a stupid thing to say.*

I paused with the hope of continuing the conversation, but both women kept walking in separate directions. As much as I wanted to remain with Pen, I jogged a few steps to catch Ruth.

"You like her," she said when I reached her side.

"Ms. Glass? Yes. I suppose I do."

"She has that effect on people. Men especially fall instantly in love with her. It's because she has this kind of Audrey Hepburn charm. Or aura. I'm not sure what you'd call it. But Pen makes men feel like Humphrey Bogart playing one of those tough, romantic action guys, and they adore her for it. Ever see the movie *Sabrina*? The original, not the remake with Harrison Ford, although that was pretty good, too."

"I've seen it."

"Then you know what I'm talking about."

Remembering how I had felt when I was with Pen the day before, I decided there might be something to Ruth's theory, but I said, "It was only a movie," just the same.

Ruth smiled. "If you say so."

I continued to follow Ruth until we reached a small, squat structure made of decorative brick and ringed with bright orange flowers I couldn't identify. A blue and gold City of Hilltop flag flew alongside the Stars and Stripes. Written in gold on the red canopy above the door were the words HILLTOP CITY HALL.

"It used to be just an old, beat-up trailer, but look at it now," Ruth said proudly. "I was mayor of Hilltop, you know. Twice."

And just like that I realized that Ruth Schramm wasn't being defensive after all. She was a living, breathing infomercial touting trailer park life, and unlike most infomercial stars, she actually believed in the product she was hawking.

There were a couple of cramped offices and one large room inside the hall. The large room contained several cafeteria-style tables arranged in a quarter circle and facing about a dozen metal folding chairs. One table was pushed against the near wall. On it was an assortment of brochures and forms and two fat blue scrapbooks. The scrapbooks contained the entire history of Hilltop in newspaper clippings, vintage photographs, minutes of council meetings, and the recorded proceedings of the now defunct Hilltop Village court. Ruth turned the pages for me one at a time.

A hundred years ago, Hilltop had been a dairy farm. Later it became the Oak Grove Riding Academy and Stables. The first trailer settled there in 1940. There were photographs in the book showing trees and hills, a tiny lake, a skating rink, and a drive-in theater that had once been across the road.

"You know," Ruth said, "we've recorded the name of nearly every person who has ever lived in Hilltop. Do you know any other community that has such a grasp of its own history?"

I told her that I didn't.

"Do you want to see the pool?" she asked.

The pool had been built by Hilltop residents next to the city garage and was surrounded by a high Cyclone fence. It was about forty feet long and twenty-five feet wide, with a depth of three feet at one end and twelve feet at the other. Plastic tables with umbrellas, lounge chairs, and an oversized picnic table were scattered around it. The temperature was only about seventy-two degrees, but three kids were splashing at each other in the shallow end. Two others were attempting to inflate a rubber raft.

Pen sat at one of the tables, her bag resting against the chair leg. She was wearing white capri pants and a slate blue sweater set that was no match for her eyes. She didn't seem to be in a hurry, didn't seem to be waiting for anyone. Children played around her and neighbors came and went without her noticing. Her notebook was open in front of her, and she stared at it, picked up a pencil, waved it at the book like it was a baton, and set it down again. She never looked up, never glanced at her watch.

Ruth was speaking to me, but I didn't notice until she nudged me in the ribs.

"I said I need to be going," she repeated. "I have my tai chi exercises."

"Yes, yes. Thank you for everything."

"If you have any more questions, don't hesitate to call."

"I appreciate it."

Ruth's eyes went from me to Pen and back to me again. She shook her head and smiled.

"I told you," she said. "Audrey Hepburn."

Nonsense, I told myself.

After she left, I made my way across the pool deck to Pen's table. I wasn't in love with Pen despite what Ruth had to say. How could I be? But I desperately wanted to become friends with her, to get her on my side and keep her there. Question was, how? Years ago, a guy named Eric Weber wrote a tutorial filled with surefire lines designed to impress women called *How to Pick Up Girls!* I never read it. I was a college sophomore when I came across the book, and I already knew everything. Only now I wish I had memorized it cover-to-cover, because my mind was a complete blank. When I reached Pen's table I blurted the first thing that came into my head.

"Do you believe in destiny?"

Pen looked up at me, shielding her eyes with her hand, unafraid in such a public place. She smiled when she recognized me.

"I do," she said. "I do believe in destiny."

"I've been seeing you all day," I told her. "Outside your trailer, on the street, and now you're here. It's fate."

"I think it's wishful thinking on your part. But please, sit down."

She gestured at a chair across from her and closed her notebook. Her smile stayed on her face, as if she had forgotten it was there.

"If I'm not interrupting," I said.

"Not at all. I could use a break. The more I work on this melody, the more it sounds like 'Skylark.' "

"Hoagy Carmichael and Johnny Mercer."

"Very good. You know music."

"Yes, I do."

"Let's see. Try this one. 'Here's That Rainy Day.' " She sang the title.

"Johnny Burke and Jimmy Van Heusen."

"Nice. How about 'Autumn Leaves'?"

"Johnny Mercer wrote the lyrics. I don't know who did the melody."

"I'd be impressed if you did. Actually, the melody was written by the great French film composer Joseph Kosma. He wrote it for a film called *Les Portes de la Nuit*"—her French accent was a lot better than mine—"back in 1946. In '47, Jacques Prévert, who was a poet, wrote lyrics and the song became 'Les Feuilles Mortes,' which Yves Montand sang in 1947. So even though it's one of Mercer's best-known lyrics, he was actually late to the party, writing the English version in the early 50s. I'm boring you."

"Not even a little bit," I told her. "Okay, now I have a song for you."

"Shoot."

" 'I'm a Believer.' "

She looked at me like I had insulted her.

"Neil Diamond," she said.

"Yes."

"Pretty lame, Jake."

"How 'bout 'West Coast Blues?' "

She repeated the title several times. "I think you got me."

"Wes Montgomery."

"You go from a pop star like Neil Diamond to a jazz guy like Wes Montgomery? What do you listen to?"

"Everything."

"Everything?"

"Jazz mostly, but also blues, rock, some classical, even a little opera."

"Country-western?"

"Some."

"Who?"

"Johnny Cash, Hank Williams, Mary Chapin Carpenter."

Pen nodded her head in approval.

"Ever listen to Suzy Bogguss and Chely Wright?"

"They sound familiar, but I don't think I know them. Why?"

"No reason. Okay, I have one more for you. Something tough. Are you ready?"

"I am."

She sang, " 'Till You Come Back to Me.' "

I gave it some thought, realized I had never heard the song before, and took a chance.

"Penelope Glass and Tommy Heyward?"

Pen laughed boisterously enough to cause several heads to turn toward her.

"You guessed," she said.

"I did not."

"You did."

"It's one of my favorite songs."

"Oh yeah? Hum a few bars."

I hummed "As Time Goes By."

"That's what I thought."

"I so admire what you do," I told her.

"Anyone can write music."

"You think?"

"It's writing good music that's hard. I didn't realize just how difficult it was until I started trying to make money at it."

"Who's your favorite composer?"

"I don't know if I have one, I've been influenced by so many people. Sometimes I think Cole Porter is God. Then I change my mind and think it's Antonio Carlos Jobim. Next day I wake up and pray to Joni Mitchell."

"If you had to pick one."

"If I had to pick one."

"Only one."

"Edward Kennedy Ellington."

"The Duke."

"You could argue that he invented American music."

I decided I was in love with Penelope Glass after all. Only I held back. I said, "I like you," instead.

"I like you, too."

"Have lunch with me," I blurted.

"I don't think so."

"Are you afraid your husband will disapprove?"

"The man does carry a gun. But the truth is, Jake, I have to work. I promised Tommy I'd e-mail him something by the end of the week, and it's the end of the week."

"Some other time?" I was trying to get Pen to commit. It seemed like the most important thing in the world at the time.

She touched my hand. It was an unexpected gesture and made me flinch with a shock of electricity.

"We'll see," she said.

Pen rose, retrieved her notebook, and slipped it into her bag. I didn't want her to leave. I said, "Pen, the man who attacked you yesterday—I don't think that was a case of mistaken identity."

"Neither do I."

She looked at me with eyes that were quite bottomless.

"Honestly, Jake, I enjoy the attention. But I'm not a damsel in distress, and you don't look much like a Knight of the Round Table." She patted my hand again, this time without the electrical charge. "I thank you for the offer. Maybe next time."

I watched her leave. At the entrance to the pool area she turned and looked back at me. She smiled some more and shook her head.

"Smooth," I said quietly to no one in particular. "You are sooooo smooth."

I moved the Neon about two hundred feet and parked at the end of 47½ Avenue. I wanted to take a look at the mobile home owned by the "gay guys" Ruth had mentioned, for the simple reason that I didn't believe they were gay or that it was a coincidence that they had moved in so soon after Pen and Sykora. I was betting that they were the people who were at the other end of the bugs Marshall Lantry had found in Pen's trailer.

I hadn't expected to see much, and I didn't the first time I walked past the mobile home, except for the Toyota Camry parked in front. But on the return trip, I saw the trailer door open and a man wearing a blue sports jacket step out. He was about five-seven, with black hair, and despite the many extra pounds he carried, he walked to the Toyota as if he were trying to outrace a tornado. His progress was slowed by a second man wearing a white dress shirt and gray slacks. He seemed slightly crazed, like someone who had been struck by lightning and couldn't quite believe he had survived.

The second man said something to the first. Blue Jacket spun around and said something back. I was too far away to hear what was spoken, but the gestures and body language were undeniably angry. They glared at each other as if they couldn't bear to be in each other's company for another moment, and I thought maybe they were gay. Certainly I knew several straight couples married for years that behaved in exactly the same manner.

Either that or government employees stuck together for too long in a confined space.

Blue Jacket sat inside the Toyota and slammed the door behind him. Gray Slacks stood with his hands on his hips and watched him drive away.

I thought of Pen and Sykora.

Mostly I thought of Pen.

At the same time, I caressed the back of my hand where she had touched me.

Nuts, I told myself. *Ruth was right.*

I went for a sub sandwich. Unrequited love drove with me, leapt out of the car at the light, ran in circles, then hopped back in again. It was goofy and childish and distracted me from the task at hand—finding Mr. Mosley's killer—but there it was. I found myself hurrying back to the motel so I could listen to Pen on my monitor.

A voice called, "Agent Greene, Agent Greene," after I parked my car in the Hilltop lot. I turned toward the sound. Victor was standing just outside the office and waving at me. I glanced around—there was no one else in the lot—and walked immediately to him, still carrying my sandwich.

"What did you call me?" I made the question sound like an accusation.

Victor took a step backward. He cleared his throat and said, "Agent Greene?"

"Who told you I was an agent?"

"The maid."

"The maid?"

"What happened was"—Victor was stammering—"the maid was making your bed and, and . . ."

"And what?"

"She heard voices."

"Voices?"

"That's what she said. She said she heard voices. And, and . . ."

"Get on with it, Victor."

"She opened your desk drawer and found your tape recorder thingy."

"She did, huh?"

"She didn't mean no harm. She heard voices and . . . There was a tape recorder and written on the tape recorder, it read . . ."

"I know what it read."

"And she told me."

"Who else did she tell?"

"Who else? Ahh, no one. Just me."

"And who did you tell?"

"No one. I figured you were undercover so I, I . . ."

"So you yelled my name across the parking lot."

"Oh, dear. I did, didn't I? I'm sorry."

"Don't be sorry, Victor."

"But I am."

"Victor."

"Yes, sir."

"My name isn't Jacob Greene. I'm not with the U.S. Treasury Department. I am not working undercover. Do we understand each other?"

"Yes, sir."

"You and the maid will not tell a soul that I am here, right?"

"Yes, sir."

I patted Victor on the back. "Good man."

Victor smiled like I had just made him a co-conspirator. I turned to leave.

"Agent . . . Excuse me. *Mr.* Greene?"

"Yes, Victor?"

"Who are you after? Someone in Hilltop?"

"We're not allowed to tell."

"No, of course not."

"It could be you."

Victor went from pleased to terrified just that fast.

"Mr. Greene," he said, drawing out the words. "Anything you need, you let me know."

* * *

I heard odd noises over the receiver that didn't amount to much as I settled in with my sandwich, noises I could only guess at.

The sandwich wasn't bad, even though the store advertised that it was healthy for me. Healthy or not, it made me long for the submarine sandwiches that Clark's used to make. The first time I drove my dad's car alone after getting my license, I drove to Clark's Submarine on University and Dale, next to Steichen's Sporting Goods, where I bought all my hockey equipment.

"Why don't you pick up a couple of Atomics," my dad had said to me.

Ahh, an Atomic, with absolutely everything on it. Now, that was a submarine sandwich. Unfortunately, Clark's had disappeared years ago—along with my youth.

I had just finished eating when I heard the notes of a piano. I remembered the invoice I had stolen along with the rest of Pen's recyclables, the one that said she had leased an electronic piano.

Pen began playing, stopped, and started again, repeating the same few bars over and over, the notes changing slightly each time she played them.

"No, no, no," she said. Followed by, "Think about it."

She sounded out a melody a single note at a time. I could picture her pounding the piano keys with one finger. She paused, hummed, played the notes again, paused, hummed some more. She played a half dozen notes in quick succession, added another half dozen, then scrapped them all and began anew. After a while, she began experimenting with chords and a variety of rhythm patterns. This went on for nearly an hour, and if Pen was making progress, I didn't hear it.

I became bored listening. Then angry with her constant starting and stopping, repetitions, experiments, and incessant humming. Music is like sausages, I decided—it's better not to see how it's made.

Pen managed to put about twenty seconds of music together before pronouncing herself satisfied. Satisfied with what, I couldn't say. I had taken a year of music appreciation in college, yet today I'd heard none of the musical elements I was taught to listen for. I began to ask myself, *Does she really make money doing this?*

"All right," Pen told herself. "Let's see what we have."

She started playing, only not the notes she had been writing the past sixty minutes. She began instead with an unhurried introduction that lasted about ten seconds, lingering over a single note at the end of it that hung in the air like the call of a songbird summoning its mate.

Deftly, she slid into an upbeat tempo, and the song began to soar—a quarter note executed with the speed of an eighth, a sixteenth flashing by like a thirty-second. After the introduction, she played two verses and launched into a chorus with a catchy, hummable hook that repeated and expanded the note structure of her introduction. I found myself diagramming the song in my head. I A A B. I was expecting another verse, but she fooled me by gliding across a bridge—a middle eight—eight bars played in the same key but with a vastly different chord progression, taking the song in a different direction, adding texture. It was the same twenty seconds of music she had worked so hard on, and suddenly it made perfect sense.

The bridge brought me back to the chorus, led into another verse, then went back to the chorus again, which Pen repeated twice. C B A B B. Only she had built an extro into the final chorus so the song would end dramatically and not merely repeat itself monotonously until the studio technician faded it out.

I was actually applauding when Pen finished. Then I leapt for my tape recorder and switched it on.

"Play it again," I said to the recorder.

Pen began with the introduction, but when she hit that wondrous note before launching into the body of the song, the telephone rang.

"It's me," Sykora said.

"I was expecting your call," Pen told him.

"You were?"

Pen didn't answer.

Sykora said, "Yeah."

"Coming home at a decent hour two nights in a row—what are the odds?" Pen asked.

"I have a job to do."

"I understand. Gallivanting about the countryside like the Lone Ranger battling the forces of evil. Meanwhile, I'm stuck in Hilltop in a crummy mobile home."

"It's all about you, isn't it, Pen? What's good for you."

"No. It's about what's good for us."

"We were together last night."

"One night a week we pretend we're married. What fun."

"Stop it."

"We didn't live like this in New York."

"Yes, we did. Only you were too busy to notice."

"That's nonsense."

"You were never there for me, Lucky. You were always too busy hanging with your gay partner. Or you were busy hitting the clubs uptown because you needed to 'feel the pulse of the music scene' "—I heard the quotes in his voice—"or you were busy 'taking a meeting' with some record producer no one has ever heard of."

"That's part of my job—"

"What job? It's not a job. It's a hobby."

"It's not a hobby," I shouted at the receiver.

"It's not a hobby," Pen shouted a beat behind me. "I've sold eight songs."

"Eight songs in four years. And made just enough money to buy a car."

"Which you drive."

"Pen, this isn't getting us anywhere."

"No. It isn't."

"Pen . . . It'll get better. Once I get Granata, it'll get better."

"Granata? From New York? I thought you were done with organized crime. I thought it was all about terrorism now."

"Granata is a terrorist."

"He's a gangster. The last of the godfathers. You said so yourself."

"I'm going to tie him to terrorism and bring down his entire family. Wait and see."

"You're obsessed with him, obsessed just like you were in New York."

"I am not obsessed. I'm a cop and he's a crook. That's all there is to it."

"Steven, I thought we transferred here because . . . Does the FBI know you're still working on Granata?"

Sykora didn't say.

"You're doing it on your own time, aren't you? That's why you're always working late. That's why you take my car instead of using a company car."

"Pen—"

"This is why our marriage is suffering? Because of Granata?"

"It's my job."

"Granata isn't your job," Pen shouted. "He's your hobby."

"There's no talking to you."

"Steven—"

"I'll be home late."

Sykora broke the connection. A moment later, Pen set the telephone receiver back in its cradle.

What was it Tolstoy wrote about unhappy families being unhappy each in its own way? This seemed fairly common to me—a husband too busy to make time for his wife. I recalled how Pen and Sykora had treated each other the evening before. They were in love. For a time. But the relationship between them had become a slow war of attrition—one step forward, two steps back. Gradually it would wear away all the qualities that had once made them dear to one another, leaving only scorched earth behind. Who knew if anything would ever grow there again?

There was silence on the other end of the receiver. Followed eventually by a long, almost agonizing sigh. Followed by metallic sounds. Followed by Pen's voice.

"Tommy, this is for you. If it's not quite what we talked about . . . Tommy, I'm in a mood."

She began to play, only it wasn't the same as before. Pen slowed the tempo to four-four time, and suddenly her upbeat song was mournful, almost despairing.

Then Pen surprised me yet again. She added lyrics.

You wonder how it went so wrong.
So do I, so do I.
You wonder if we can carry on.
So do I, so do I.

A telephone call had done this, I told myself. The argument had altered Pen's happy disposition, turning it both pensive and blue. And the result was something extraordinary. A song that saddened the heart. Listening to her play, I thought I had discovered a painful truth about creativity and genius.

There was a long pause after Pen had finished.

"That's it for me, Tommy," she said at last. "Give me a call."

Instead of applauding, I found myself wishing I could give her a hug and tell her everything would be all right. A silly thing to wish, I suppose.

I could hear the sound of fingers tapping a computer keyboard as I swapped the cassette in the recorder for a fresh tape and hid it in my sock with the other cassette. The finger tapping ceased, followed by Pen's voice. "Isn't modern technology swell?" she said.

I've always loved libraries, loved the very idea of them. They're citadels of peace and quiet and intellectual freedom and civilization—commodities that are becoming increasingly difficult to come by. They are, in a word, the most "democratic" places on earth, although they've been finding it harder to remain that way. The sign on the circulation desk read: UNDER SECTION 215 OF THE USA PATRIOT ACT, THE JUSTICE DEPARTMENT MAY OBTAIN ANY RECORDS THIS LIBRARY MIGHT POSSESS PERTAINING TO A PATRON'S READING HABITS AND INTERNET USE WITHOUT INFORMING THE PATRON WHOSE RECORDS ARE BEING SEIZED.

I took it as a warning.

The fact that the library felt compelled to post such a missive alarmed me. I remembered as a kid hanging out at the Merriam Park Public Library on Marshall and Fairview in St. Paul, grabbing a book, any book, often at random, and reading whatever it said without worrying if the choice identified me as a terrorist. Or worse yet, a liberal. Now there are plenty of people who are quite happy to do my worrying for me, who spend much of their time looking for things to offend and frighten them, things that they can protect me from whether I want that protection or not. It's all about life, liberty, and the pursuit of *their* happiness. If they don't actually burn books, it's only because it looks bad on TV.

To use the Internet terminals, I needed a library card and a personal identification number. I showed the librarian Jacob Greene's counterfeit card and driver's license and said I only wanted to check my e-mail back home, which apparently happens all the time. The librarian happily logged me on with a temporary PIN and moved away.

I called up a search engine and typed in the name Granata. I received thousands of hits. I narrowed the list by adding the words "organized crime." Four articles appeared, three published in New York and one by the BBC news service.

The first two New York articles weren't very informative. One trumpeted the fact that the heads of all five New York City Mafia families were simultaneously behind bars for the first time. It listed the families:

Bonanno. Reputed boss Joseph Massino had been indicted in connection with a decades-old murder.

Colombo. Alphonse "Allie Boy" Persico cut a deal with federal prosecutors and was now ratting on everyone.

Gambino. Peter Gotti, brother to John Gotti, was locked up on charges of racketeering and extortion a short time after Gotti's heir, John Jr., was convicted of racketeering and gambling.

Genovese. Vincent "the Chin" Gigante remained jailed on a racketeering conviction.

Luchese. Vittorio "Vic" Amuso was doing life without parole on racketeering and murder charges.

The name Granata was mentioned only once, toward the end of the article. The sentence read: *The only major crime figure who is not incarcerated or under indictment is re-*

puted Bonanno acting boss Angelo "Little Al" Granata, a reclusive figure, who lives modestly in Queens.

The second article was a fluff piece. It suggested that while people living in the Big Apple applauded whenever a local prosecutor took down a wiseguy, they seemed to love having them in their midst and gloried in reports of the adventures and feuds. Readers were disappointed, so the article claimed, that *notoriously publicity-shy Angelo Granata, alleged acting head of the Bonanno family, didn't live up to the standards set by the flamboyant Gottis.*

The BBC story was all business. It stated that the health of the New York Mafia was in decline and that starting with the conviction of John Gotti, the pressure on the Mafia clans had been relentless. It reported that hundreds of soldiers were now behind bars, along with the five reputed family leaders, revenues had been cut in half, and membership in the Mafia was waning. The exception, according to the BBC, was the Bonanno clan, which, *under the leadership of Angelo Granata, is by far the strongest and most disciplined of the five families.*

The final item appeared in the column of a New York tabloid's self-styled "crime watcher." *Little Al's big pain seems to have been cured (take two .22s and don't call in the morning). Prime 'vine has it that an irate coconspirator began working for a regime change when his scheme for a Bonanno-imposed Mafia EU went PU. Yet with the capricious capo now doing his best Jimmy Hoffa impersonation, peace and tranquility has once again returned to Granata world.*

There was no mention of Frank Crosetti in any of the articles. When I typed his name into the search engine, I discovered that he had been one helluva shortstop.

Since I was there, I searched for the name Penelope Glass. It took me about five minutes to discover why she had asked if I had listened to Suzy Bogguss and Chely Wright. Both country-western songbirds had sung tunes written by Glass and Heyward. Bogguss had recorded "Something Like Love" and "Gone So Long" on an album of jazz music; apparently she was switching genres. Wright had sung "Table for Two" and "The Bottom of the Sea" on an album that was essentially C&W. And then there was Bonnie Raitt, one of my all-time favorites, singing "Fire and Smoke" on a blues CD I had listened to a half dozen times already.

I really ought to pay closer attention to the liner notes, I told myself.

On the way back to the motel, I stopped at a record store and bought Suzy Bogguss's and Chely Wright's CDs and a machine to play them on. I listened to the songs Pen had written enough times that I could recite some of the lyrics in my sleep.

Chapter Nine

The sun was shining and the birds were singing, but I spent most of Saturday inside my motel room. Time passed slowly. I don't know what Pen was doing alone in her trailer, but she did it quietly. Sykora had left at a little after 9:00 A.M. "I'm sure you understand," he told her. Pen didn't say if she did or didn't. Since then I'd heard very little over the receiver, just enough rustling sounds to convince me Pen was still there.

The morning stretched into afternoon. I watched the Baseball Game of the Week on Fox with the sound off and was astonished when they started doing the wave at Busch Stadium. Rogers Hornsby must've rolled over in his grave. I don't like the wave. Or playing loud music between innings and before every at bat. Or scoreboards that tell the crowd when to cheer. Or guys who wear suits and ties to the ballpark. Or the designated hitter, for that matter. But mostly I don't like the wave.

Early in the third inning, Pen's telephone rang. I hit the record button and listened.

"Hello," she said.

"Is your husband home?" The voice was definitely Frank's.

"Who's calling, please?"

"Never mind that. Is Sykora home?"

"I'm sorry. He's not in at the moment. May I take a message?"

"Shit," Frank said and hung up.

Pen did the same.

In the bottom of the eighth, the phone rang again. This time it was Sykora.

He said, "You have to stop being angry at me."

"I'm not angry."

"Yes, you are. And whenever you get angry at me I get this terrible, hollow feeling in my stomach that makes me think that something awful is going to happen."

"I'm not angry," Pen repeated.

"I'm trying, Pen. Honest to God, I am."

"I know."

"Let's go out for dinner tonight."

"Really?"

"You pick the restaurant."

"Ruth Schramm—you know Ruth—she told me about a northern Italian restaurant called Lido's in Roseville that's supposed to have a simply divine terrace. It's such a beautiful day—we could eat outside."

"Make a reservation."

"I will. Oh," added Pen. "Someone called asking for

you. He didn't leave a name or message, only an obscenity."

Sykora paused a moment, then said, "I'll see you in a little bit."

After Sykora hung up the phone, there was plenty to listen to on the receiver. Pen making a reservation for two at Lido's. Pen humming. Pen taking a shower. Pen getting dressed. Pen humming some more.

The phone rang again.

Pen stopped humming.

"I'm sorry," Sykora told her.

"You said—"

"I know what I said."

"This is ridiculous."

"It's the job."

"You work your damn job. I'm going to dinner."

Pen hung up the phone. I heard the opening and closing of a drawer followed by the rustling of pages—I guessed a telephone book. Pen picked up the phone again. She booked a cab.

The cabbie was knocking on her trailer door at about the time I finished dressing.

Pen was standing with her back to the door when I entered Lido's. She was having a heated discussion with the maître d'. Something about her reservation.

She looked carefully put together—hair swept back, light makeup expertly applied, wearing a rose-colored ruffled silk dress that conjured images of village greens and ice cream socials and soft summer nights. I found myself watching her like you might watch a slowly flowing river or clouds in the sky.

After a few moments I came up behind her.

"We have to stop meeting like this."

The scowl on her face for the maître d' was quickly transformed into a brilliant smile just for me.

"Jake. What are you doing here?"

"I thought I'd treat myself to something a few notches above fast food. Ruth Schramm put me onto this place."

"Me, too."

"Where's the main squeeze?"

"Steve." She said the name like she didn't like the sound of it. "He's too busy to have dinner with his wife."

"He's a moron."

Pen didn't say if she agreed or not.

"I'm so happy you're here," she said. "This young man"—she gestured at the maître d'—"insists they will only seat parties of two or more on the terrace, *regardless* of my reservation."

"If the lady and gentleman would care to dine together," said the kid.

"Just what I was thinking," Pen said.

"I don't want to intrude."

"Don't be silly. I'm glad for your company."

A few moments later a waiter sat us at a table beneath a huge oak tree whose branches spread out over the terrace. There were two dozen other tables, all filled except for three, and they stayed empty only for a few minutes. I didn't blame the restaurant for its restrictive seating policy. In Minnesota when the weather is good, an outdoor restaurant table is prime real estate.

"I looked you up on the Internet," I told Pen after we were seated.

"You did?"

"I learned the names of some of the artists who recorded your music and then went out and bought the CDs. The song that Bonnie Raitt sang, 'Fire and Smoke'—it's wonderful. 'Bottom of the Sea' that Chely Wright recorded—it gave me goose bumps."

"That is so kind of you to say."

"Honestly, Pen. Why aren't you rich and famous?"

"I'm working on it, I'm working on it."

"You make Carole King look like an amateur."

"'A Natural Woman,' 'I Feel The Earth Move,' 'You've Got a Friend'—that Carole King? Let's not get carried away, Jake."

"I mean it."

Pen leaned across the table. "You're sweet," she said, giving my hand a squeeze.

After my heart restarted, I gave her my Groucho Marx eyebrows and said, "Given a choice, I'd rather be sexy."

Pen let her hand rest on mine. Her touch was as light as a hummingbird perched on my finger.

"Trust me. Sweet is better."

We ordered drinks and then dinner. While we were waiting for the food, Pen said, "Do you know why I'm having dinner with you? I mean besides wanting the table?"

"I figured it was because of my charm and Russell Crowe-like good looks."

"It's because my husband wouldn't like it." She watched my face to see if her words registered. "You have no idea what I'm talking about, do you?"

I figured she was being brave, standing up to her husband without actually having to stand up to him, but said, "Not really," just the same.

"I'm not sure I know, either." She added quickly, "You're not married, are you?"

"No."

"Have you ever been married?"

I shook my head.

"Why not?"

"The usual reasons."

"Name one."

"I'm still waiting for the perfect woman to sweep me off my feet."

"There are no perfect women."

"Yes, there are."

I meant her, and Pen knew it. Her eyes brightened, and blood rushed to her face, making her freckles that much more noticeable. She shifted in her chair and toyed with her wineglass. A black and orange monarch butterfly flitted around the table and drifted behind the tree. Pen watched its flight carefully.

She said, "A song Tommy and I wrote, I wanted to call it 'Butterfly.' But Tommy changed the title, named it 'Dragonfly.' It's a better title, I have no complaints. Except I had worked on it for a couple weeks calling it

'Butterfly' and it stuck in my head. It has to do with the danger of staying in one place too long. 'Wings were made to fly, lovers born to say good-bye.' That's one of the lyrics. Only—I don't believe it. I never have. Anyway, we're trying to sell it to the Indigo Girls."

I had to admire the way she so deftly made her point and moved on.

We had just finished dessert when it began to rain.

The rain had come in a hurry, one of those fast-moving cloudbursts that took everyone by surprise. Customers began scurrying for cover, some laughing, others cursing, while the waitstaff cleared everything off the terrace except tables and chairs.

Pen and I hid beneath the great oak during the few minutes until the deluge passed. She looked marvelous, a happy grin on her face, hair wet with rain, and the bodice of her summery dress clinging to her curves. I removed my jacket and slipped it over her shoulders. She smiled at me with such an expression of gratitude that I flinched—*It's just a coat, lady*—and wondered at how she could find such value in a simple act of courtesy.

"I love rain," she said. "I love snow, too. And . . ."

I leaned in and kissed her softly. I had never kissed a married woman before—not like that—and was both surprised and thrilled by the way it made me feel. She didn't move away when I finished. Instead, her eyes shined with pleasure and excitement and anticipation. So I kissed her again. Longer this time. *It's was a little thing,* I told myself, *and her husband wouldn't mind.*

Pen began to tremble like a teardrop that hadn't fallen—*the chill,* I told myself. She set her hands on my chest and pushed me away. There was nothing urgent in her gesture, but it was determined just the same.

"I can't," she said. "I'd like to. More than you know. But I can't. There's just no way."

She slipped my coat off her shoulders and thrust it into my hands. A moment later she was gone, with only the faint scent of her herbal shampoo remaining behind.

I paid for the meal and wandered into the restaurant's lobby. I found Pen working the pay phone.

"You can't get a cab in this town," she said.

"I'll drive you home."

"I don't think that's a good idea."

"I can't be as bad as all that."

"No." She shook her head. "No, it's . . . Hilltop is a small community, and I don't want to be a target of gossip."

"Pen—"

"No."

That was plain enough. I turned to leave. I spun back when Pen called my name.

She said, "You're smart, Jake. You're funny, you're generous, considerate, cute, sweet, you're brave. Jake, you're the jackpot."

"Am I?"

"Yes. And I like you a lot. But I'm married. As it turns out, I love my husband. Yet even if I didn't love my husband, I'd still be married, and there are rules about that."

"Whose rules?"

"Mine."

That was plainer still.

* * *

It had stopped raining by the time I left Lido's, but the way the clouds gathered on the horizon, it didn't look as though it was through for the evening. I found my Neon in the back row and rested against the door. *Maybe I should insist on taking Pen home,* I told myself. *Yeah, and tuck her into bed, too.*

I glanced back at the front doors of the restaurant.

"You've done enough damage," I said aloud.

I climbed inside the car, started it up, and maneuvered it across the parking lot. I was approaching the street when I felt a cold prickling on the back of my neck, a familiar friend announcing his presence—fear. I sensed it even before my conscious mind could determine the cause. Parked near the entrance to the parking lot was a gray 1988 Ford Ranger 4×4 with rust on all four sides. Two men were sitting in the cab. The one behind the steering wheel looked exactly like the man who had attempted to grab Pen in Hilltop three days earlier.

There was no indication that Pen's attacker made me, but then I wasn't looking for one. Instead, I forced myself to stare straight ahead when I drove past, pretending the pickup didn't even exist. I headed up the street, hung a U-turn the moment I was out of sight, and parked next to the used car lot across the street from Lido's. The lot was closed for the evening, and no one challenged me as I weaved past the rows of cars. I came out of the lot behind and to the right of the Ranger. I walked in a straight line toward it while trying to stay in the driver's blind spot should he glance at his mirrors.

The windows to the truck were rolled down, and I could hear music as I approached. Rachmaninov's *Russian Rhapsody*. The sound startled me. Heavy metal I could understand. Or country-western. But how many thugs do you know who listen to classical music?

I crouched low and circled the truck until I reached the driver's window. I popped up and said, "Hi, fellas."

Pen's attacker—the driver—leapt back in his seat like I had caught him dozing. His hands were empty. The second man recovered more quickly and reached for something on the floor of the cab.

"Hey, dummy!"

My shout froze him in midreach. I rapped on the door frame with the business end of my Beretta. He looked at me. I pointed the Beretta at his head.

"Do you want to die?"

Unlike Danny's single-action Browning, my Beretta was a double-action semiautomatic. I didn't need to thumb back the hammer before I fired it. But I did so just the same—for dramatic effect. The second man leaned back against his seat.

"Hands up, guys. Palms against the ceiling. Do it now."

Both men pressed their hands against the roof of the cab. The driver looked at me like I was one of those big cats at the Minnesota Zoo and he was wondering how I had managed to slip through the bars. I liked the look. The second man stared straight ahead. His eyes had the unfocused quality of someone wandering through an art museum and not seeing anything that interested him. That expression changed when the driver said, "I'm going to kill you for this." The second man smiled, and suddenly he reminded me of the kind of dog that fetches dead animals and drops them at his master's feet.

I jabbed the muzzle of the Beretta into the driver's ear. "What did you say?"

He just looked at me.

"Go 'head. Repeat what you just said."

"He said . . ."

The driver's head swiveled toward the man sitting next to him as if he were terrified his most intimate secret was about to be revealed.

"Shut up, Michael."

"I was just saying—"

"Shut up."

"Don't tell me to shut up, Lawrence."

Michael and Lawrence. I needed this. I really did.

"Guys, guys—both of you quiet down." I felt like a mother separating a pair of bickering children on a long road trip. "You." I gestured at Lawrence with the Beretta. "Do you remember me?"

Lawrence's hand came off the roof of the cab and touched the back of his head where it had slammed against the asphalt.

"Yeah, I remember you."

"Put your hand back up."

He pressed his palm against the ceiling again.

"You're here to snatch the girl," I told him.

"You can't prove that."

"Why would I want to? I'm not a cop. I'm not FBI, DEA, ATF, BCA, state police, county deputy, or Boy Scout. I'm the guy who's going to blow your head off unless you answer my questions."

I wondered if he believed me. I wondered if *I* believed me. I poked him in the ear again with the muzzle of the gun to strengthen my argument.

"You're here to snatch the girl. Right?"

"Nah, man," said Michael. "We're here for her husband."

"Shut up," said Lawrence.

"Huh?" grunted Michael.

"You remember what he said, doncha?"

"Oh yeah, like I'm gonna be more afraid of fucking Andrew Jackson than I am this asshole"—Michael gestured at me with his chin—"who's pointing a gun at me."

"Who's Andrew Jackson?" I asked.

"Man we're workin' for," said Lawrence.

"He didn't give us a name," said Michael. "But he paid us in twenty-dollar bills."

"That's why we call him Andrew Jackson," said Lawrence.

"What did he look like?"

"I dunno," Michael answered. "Tall."

"How tall?"

" 'Bout six feet."

"With black hair," added Lawrence.

"Was he fat?"

"He could afford to lose a few pounds."

"Uh-huh. What was the job?"

Lawrence glanced at Michael and sighed. "He's going to be pissed, man."

"Yeah, but think how happy you're going to make me," I said.

"He said snatch Sykora," said Michael.

"But not the girl," added Lawrence.

"He said not to hurt the girl," said Michael. "He was pretty serious about that."

"You tried to hit the girl before," I reminded Lawrence.

"No, man. That was just a message. We were just sending a message, you know, to her old man."

"I wasn't there," Michael said.

"I know you weren't there," Lawrence told him.

"I'm just sayin'."

As if on cue, both men turned their gazes forward and stared out the windshield. Lawrence shook his head sadly. Michael smiled. "Damn," he said.

I moved so I could watch them and see what they were looking at at the same time. It was a pretty sight. Pen leaving the restaurant and striding purposely toward a yellow cab, looking splendid in her rose-colored silk. The cabbie held the back door open for her. She lifted her skirt slightly and slid inside. The cabbie closed the door. A moment later, the vehicle eased out of the lot and down the street.

"Damn," Michael repeated.

"We was told to snatch her old man, but he ain't even here." Lawrence looked me in the eye. "You're here, though. What's up with that?"

"Who told you her husband would be here?" I asked.

"Andrew Jackson."

"How did he know?"

"What? Do I look psychic?"

"What did he tell you?"

"I told ya. He said to grab Sykora."

"Then what?"

"Then we were supposed to take him to this place," Michael said.

"What place?"

"A motel. On I-35."

"Which one?" I asked, thinking, *God, I'm getting tired of motels.*

"Well, here. I have the—" Michael had taken his hands off the roof and was reaching for his pants pocket. He stopped when I turned the gun on him.

"I got a key," he said cautiously. "In my pocket."

"Fuck, Michael," said Lawrence. "Why don't you give 'im directions while you're at it?"

"Slowly," I told Michael.

The key had the name of a motel and a room number on it. I had Michael pass it to Lawrence and Lawrence pass it to me, always keeping the gun trained on them, yet just out of reach. I slipped the key into my jacket pocket.

"Then what?" I asked.

"He said he'd call with instructions," Michael said.

"Just sit in the room and wait for his call. Is that it?"

"Yeah, man."

"Do you know why you were supposed to grab Sykora?"

The two partners glanced at each other like each was expecting the other to answer.

"Do you even know who he is?"

No reply.

"He's FBI."

"A fed?" said Lawrence.

"No fucking way," Michael insisted.

"We don't like feds," said Lawrence.

"We don't mess with 'em, neither," Michael added.

"Not in this lifetime."

"Look at it this way, then," I told them. "I'm doing you both a favor. Have you got any idea what kind of shitstorm would drop on your heads if you kidnapped an FBI agent?"

"Gee, mister. Thanks a lot," Lawrence said, but I doubt he was being sincere.

I gestured toward the radio.

"I like your tunes."

"Public radio," said Michael. "It kinda soothes us."

"Would you please shut up," Lawrence told him.

I stepped away from the pickup.

"Gentlemen, you've been very helpful. But here's the thing. I never want to see either of you again. If I see you again, I'll figure it's because you're after me, and I'll kill you. Do we understand each other?"

Both men smiled.

Yeah, right.

I took another step backward and fired two shots.

The first shot exploded the front tire. The second shot destroyed the rear.

The pickup truck listed hard to the left like a ship that was sinking.

I wasn't afraid the noise would attract attention. Whoever heard the shots would listen for more. Only there would be no more, and after a few moments they'd stop listening. Meanwhile, I walked backward swiftly about fifteen paces, watching Lawrence and Michael watch me, until I hit the curb. I turned and ran across the street, hiding myself among the used cars until I was sure they weren't chasing me.

Even criminals prefer easy commutes and safe neighborhoods. That's why the twenty-two motels stretching along Interstate 35 from Lakeville to Burnsville and Eagan are so desirable. They're peaceful, quiet, and safe, offer quick access to the southern Twin Cities freeway system, and are conveniently located a mere twenty or thirty minutes from the biggest drug market in the Upper Midwest: Minneapolis and St. Paul. Plus, it's easy for drug runners coming up from Mexico and the southwestern states to hide among all those out-of-state license plates bound for the Mall of America.

The day was fading fast and rain threatened when I reached the motel identified on the key Michael had given me. The sign out front claimed that it had the lowest rates of any national chain in America, and from the look of the place, I believed it. The fort Victoria and Katie Dunston built out of cardboard boxes in their backyard had greater architectural integrity.

There were two levels to the motel. The doors of the rooms located on the bottom level opened to the gravel parking lot. The doors on the top opened to a landing that ran the length of the motel. There were two metal staircases, one on each side of the landing. The first was tucked next to the office; the second emptied into the parking lot. I parked at the bottom of the far staircase. The room I sought was in the center of the second-floor landing.

I climbed the metal stairs and slowly made my way to the room. The drapes were drawn over the only window. I rested my ear against the glass and listened. Nothing. My Beretta was in my hand, the safety off, as I edged to the door. This time I rested my ear against the cheap wood. Again, I heard nothing. I slipped the key into the lock and turned it cautiously. Satisfied that the door was unlocked, I turned the knob and swung it open. I entered the room in a crouch, the nine millimeter leading the way. A quick glance over and under the beds—there were two doubles—and a more careful examination of the bathroom proved the room was empty.

I returned to the door and closed it. The room looked gloomy in the gathering dusk. The overhead light didn't improve matters much, either. I locked the door and slipped the chain on. I nudged the drapes out of the way and glanced out of the window. There was no movement in the parking lot. It had begun to rain again—not hard, but steady.

The telephone was located on the table between the two double beds, but it had a long cord. I dragged the phone across the far bed, setting it on the floor between the bed and the wall. I turned off the light and sat on the floor in the corner next to the phone, the bed between me and the door. I activated the nine and set it within easy reach.

"Anytime now," I said to the phone.

I had to wait only a half hour, but it seemed longer. When the phone began to ring, I picked up the Beretta and held it steady on the door. I gave it a few beats before answering the phone.

"Yes," I said.

"Like the room?"

"I've been in better."

"Uh-huh. You're McKenzie, right?"

"Yeah. Is this Frank?"

"Fuck, are you kidding me?"

Nuts. The voice wasn't the same as the one I heard over Pen's phone. I was sure Michael and Lawrence had been working for Frank.

"Who are you?" I asked.

"Call me Ishmael."

"I bet you have a whale of a tale to tell, too."

"Hey, that's funny."

I took a chance. "Mr. Granata?" I asked.

After a slight pause, Ishmael said, "You think I'm Granata, huh?"

"The thought had crossed my mind, yeah."

"Little Al's too busy these days for wet work."

"So he sends his flunky."

"That's what flunkies are for." Ishmael chuckled. If he was insulted, I didn't hear it in his voice. "Speaking of which, my boys are mighty put out with you. Do you know how much new truck tires cost these days?"

"Probably more than their truck is worth."

"Probably you're right." Ishmael sighed dramatically. "You want to tell me, McKenzie, what the fuck you're doing messing in our business?"

"Funny, I was going to ask you the exact same question."

"I'll bite—what's your business?"

"Frank."

"Frank, huh?"

"Calls himself Frank Crosetti these days."

"After the Yankee shortstop. Yeah, Frank always was a baseball fan. So what do you want him for?"

"He murdered a friend and raped another."

"And you want payback for 'em."

"Something like that."

"Can't say I blame you. I'd probably want to whack 'im, too. Only the boss won't like it."

"No?"

"Boss has somethin' special planned for Frank."

"Is that right?"

"After we chat with him a bit first."

"They say Granata is the last of the godfathers."

"Not to his face, they don't."

"Why is Granata looking for Frank?"

"It's business."

"What business?"

"*Family* business."

"Uh-huh. Well, I called dibs."

"Dibs? What's this dibs shit?"

"It means—"

"I know what it means. And you can forgetaboutit. Dibs. *We'll* fucking take care of Frank."

"Meaning the Bonanno family."

"How come you know so much?"

"I pay attention."

"You one of those nerd types always had his hand raised in school?"

"Pretty much."

A deep sigh. "Whoever we are, McKenzie, you don't have to worry about it. Not even a little bit. Russo's gonna get what's coming to him. I personally guarantee it."

"Russo is his real name? Frank Russo?"

"You're starting to annoy me, McKenzie."

"We can't have that, can we?"

"No, we can't. What are you interfering for? Aren't you listening to me? I promise, we'll take care of Frank for ya. If it wasn't for you, we'd probably have him already."

"By kidnapping Sykora and doing what? Torturing him until he gives Frank up? What, are you kidding? An FBI agent?"

"A dirty FBI agent. Anyway, what do you give a fuck about Sykora?"

"I don't. But I don't want the girl hurt."

"Neither do I."

"I like the girl."

"She is likable."

"You need to come up with another plan."

"Another plan to do what?"

"To find Frank Russo."

"What, are people stupid out here? You get past the Hudson and people just go fucking brain dead? It's none of your fucking business how we get Frank. You stay out of it and maybe you don't get fucked up, too."

"You have a bad attitude, do you know that?"

Ishmael thought that was funny.

"McKenzie, you're just gonna fuck up everything, aren't you?"

"I might."

"Ahh, man. I was gonna cut you some slack cuz you have balls, but you're just too big a pain in the ass to live. Go look outside your window."

"My window?"

"Go 'head."

I crossed the room, dragging the telephone with me. When I reached the window, I used the muzzle of the Beretta to push the drape out of the way. It had become dark, but not so dark that I couldn't recognize Michael and Lawrence. They were standing in the rain in the parking lot just below my room, the Ford Ranger between them. Michael waved at me.

"Hey, McKenzie," Ishmael said.

"I'm here."

"You see 'em?"

"I see them."

"One last time—you gonna back off or what?"

"It's not that I don't trust you to get Frank. It's just that my dear old dad taught me, if you want something done right, you have to do it yourself."

"Uh-huh. Well, tell me this. Just out of curiosity. How are you going to get out of the room?"

The phone went dead before I could answer.

I set down the phone and checked my weapons. The Beretta had one round in the chamber and five in the magazine—I had wasted two shots on the Ford Ranger's tires. The .25 Iver Johnson taped to my ankle carried seven rounds, but it wasn't worth a damn beyond ten or fifteen feet. I had no idea what Michael and Lawrence were packing. I glanced at them through the window. They were engaged in an animated discussion. I guessed at the topic. *Do we wait for McKenzie to leave the room or do we go up there after him?*

I decided to hold the high ground and make them come to me. To emphasize the point, I unlocked the motel room door and let it swing open. A moment later I was in the corner, the bed between me and the door. I kept the Beretta steady on the opening with both hands.

The wind had picked up and blew rain through the doorway. I waited. And waited. The carpet around the door became soaked, and a chill filled the room. My hands began to tremble—I blamed the cold—and my neck and shoulder muscles began to ache. I heard Michael's voice.

"Hey, McKenzie," he shouted. "You gotta be fucking kidding."

They were going to wait on me. *Well, let them,* I decided.

I abandoned my position, crossed the room, and closed the door. Once again I pushed the drapes aside and glanced through the rain-streaked window. Once again Michael waved at me.

Fine, I told myself. *Stand in the rain. What do I care?*

I actually grabbed the remote and turned on the TV. I watched about thirty seconds of a rerun of *Cops* before reality sank in.

Are you nuts?

I turned off the TV and returned to the window. Night had fallen, yet I could still make out Michael and Lawrence. They were now sitting inside the Ford

Ranger, but beyond that they didn't appear to be going anywhere anytime soon.

You're going to have to go out there.

I checked the load in the Beretta a second time. It hadn't improved any. I tore the Iver Johnson off my ankle and dropped it into my pocket, ignoring the pain caused by the duct tape. *Let's hope that's all you feel.*

I worked the calculations in my head, figuring I could open the door and run half the length of the second-floor landing before Michael and Lawrence opened their truck doors. I'd cover the second half, reaching the staircase just as they got out of the truck. I'd descend to the bottom of the staircase before they could cross the length of the parking lot. And I'd reach the Neon at just about the time they'd blow me to hell and gone, especially if they were carrying any kind of ordnance to speak of. 'Course, I might get them first because, as everyone knows, I'm a helluva shot. I once won a trophy.

Yeah, go 'head and bet your life on that. Maybe you should call Vegas and get odds.

I glanced at the telephone.

"Oh, for cryin' out loud."

Occam's razor, named after the fourteenth-century philosopher William of Ockham—the simpler an explanation, the better. If it isn't necessary to introduce complexities into an argument, don't do it. Maybe if I had paid better attention in Philosophy 101, I'd have come to it sooner.

I picked up the phone and called the motel office.

"This is room 23B," I told the man who answered.

"Yes, Mr. Cassidy."

My last name was Cassidy, I registered. I wondered if my first name was Hopalong.

"Listen, I don't want to make trouble for your motel . . ."

"Yes, sir."

"But there are these guys in a Ford Ranger pickup in your parking lot. I think they're dealing drugs."

"Why do you think that?"

"They're just sitting there in the rain, and people keep driving up and getting out of their cars and talking to them and then driving away. I mean . . ."

"I understand. It's nothing to worry about. This happens all the time because we're located so close to the freeway. I'll take care of it."

"Okay."

"I'd appreciate it, Mr. Cassidy, if you stay in your room for a little bit."

"Sure."

I stayed in my room for exactly six minutes. That's how long it took for three Burnsville police cruisers to surround the Ford Ranger, blinding the truck's occupants with their high beams. Guns were drawn and commands were shouted as I covered half the length of the second-floor landing. Michael and Lawrence were pulled from the cab, pushed up against the truck, and handcuffed by the time I walked the second half. A fourth car arrived, a K-9 unit, and a German shepherd held by a short leash began sniffing around the Ford Ranger as I descended the metal staircase. I was inside the Neon and starting the engine when a Burnsville police officer held up a Mac-10 and a Tec-9 with one hand and a baggie filled with what looked like marijuana with the other. The shepherd jumped at the grass like it was a chew toy.

People drove past the motel. Some slowed their vehicles when they saw the flashing lights on top of the cruisers—a gawker's slowdown, the traffic people call it—yet none stopped. I was willing to bet that they all lived quiet, normal lives and this was exciting to them. I admit I was a little excited myself as I drove across the gravel parking lot. I didn't look at the cops and they didn't look at me. A couple of left turns later, I was cruising down the entrance ramp to I-35. One of my great fears growing up was that one morning I'd discover that, like most people, I was leading a quiet, normal life, that I had become boring. So far I had managed to avoid that fate. Still . . .

Bob Seger and the Silver Bullet Band were singing "Hollywood Nights" on the Cities 97—*He was a midwestern boy on his own . . . He knew right then he was too far from home.* I had a feeling they were singing to me.

I had beers in the tiny refrigerator, and I drank two of them while I listened to the voice-activated tape recording. Someone had been moving around in Pen's trailer. I heard the sound of her door opening and closing and then the tape went silent. I guessed Pen was taking a walk, and for a moment I feared for her safety. Then I dismissed my concerns. Ishmael's co-conspirators had been incarcerated, and I doubted that he'd make a move on his own.

It had stopped raining. I decided to walk, too. Clear my head. Shake off Pen. Shake off the fear Lawrence and Michael had instilled in me less than an hour earlier. I got only as far as the coffeehouse up the street. Jellies and Beans. The girl who served me was small and overworked, with a face that had been nowhere and had done nothing. *Lucky her,* I thought. She held a large paper cup beneath a stainless steel spigot. There followed a hissing, gurgling, gulump. Voilà, a twenty-ounce café mocha.

"You want whipped cream? It's better with whipped cream."

"Absolutely."

She smiled at me when I told her to keep the change, and I thought, *I almost said it at the restaurant.* I had nearly told Pen, "I love you." A few more long kisses under the great oak tree and I might have. I had prided myself on not using those three words without meaning it. Prided myself on not being one of those guys. I could count on one hand the times I had actually told a woman "I love you" and the one time when I woulda, coulda, shoulda said it and didn't. I wondered if this was going to be another one of those times as I sipped my coffee. I had not seen Pen for several hours, and so much had happened since then. Yet I was still thinking about her. I could still feel her presence.

I flashed on Nina. Had I told her that I loved her? I didn't think so, but maybe I had. I couldn't recall. I adored Nina, yet I hadn't made any promises to her, nor had she made any to me. My impression: She didn't want promises, she didn't want a committment. She had been married. She had been in a long-term relationship. Both had ended ugly, and she was determined to avoid a three-peat. Which meant we were just friends, right? Which meant we were both free agents. Right? I decided not to think about it.

I liked the mocha so much I bought another and took it back to my room. Listening to the tape again, I heard Sykora arrive home. "Pen? Penelope?" He called her name like he was both surprised and disappointed that she hadn't answered. Movement followed. I heard the sound of clinking glass, a refrigerator door opening, ice in a glass, liquid being poured. I wondered what Sykora was drinking. Whatever it was, he had two of them.

Later, lightheaded from the alcohol and caffeine, I thought I could make it work. I could live out my days as Jake Greene. Pen would leave Sykora and we would go away together. It would be a good life, an exemplary life. We'd be kind to each other. Loving. I'd find a way to reclaim my money and we'd buy a house, a cottage. She'd write Grammy-winning songs and I'd—I'd do what? Go into business. Buy a Subway franchise and hire some kids to run it for me. Or a bookstore. Or a music store. Maybe I could just keep doing what I was doing now. Favors for friends. Only Jake had no friends. At least none that I knew of. No Bobby, no Shelby, no backyard neighbors to flirt with. No Nina. And Shelby's girls. Who was going to teach them the value of junk food and frivolous behavior? And what about the ducks?

That's where it broke down, the fantasy, the wide-awake dream as phony as the driver's license and credit cards I carried in my borrowed wallet. I wouldn't be McKenzie anymore. And I liked McKenzie. He'd had his ups and downs over the years, but he was a good guy—like his father and Mr. Mosley had been good guys. Jacob Greene wasn't a good guy. He was a liar. A fake. A fraud. He was willing to go to bed with another man's wife.

I was getting drifty when a loud noise snapped me back to full consciousness. It came from the receiver. Pen's door opening and closing loudly.

"Where have you been?"

"Steve! You startled me. What are you doing sitting in the dark?"

"I'm sorry. It's just when I came home and found that you weren't here—my stomach is killing me. Where were you?"

"I went to dinner like I said I would. After I came back, I went for a long walk."

"I'm sorry about dinner."

"It's okay."

"Can I get you anything? A drink . . ."

"No."

"Pen?"

"Steve, I've been thinking."

"You have? Umm, what have you been thinking?"

"You and I should go back to New York. We should leave right away."

"Oh, God . . ."

"Are you okay?"

"Oh, God . . ."

"Steve?"

"I'm all right. Let me, let me—I have to sit down. Oh, man—my stomach just did a somersault."

"What is it?"

"It's all right. I was—I was just frightened for a minute."

"What about?"

"I thought you were going to leave me. I thought you were going to ask for a divorce."

"A divorce?"

"After we spoke on the phone and you hung up I started thinking, 'She's going to leave me. I've been treating her like crap for six months and now she's going to leave me.' And when you said you'd been thinking—I've never been so frightened in my life. I've had guys shoot at me and I haven't been so scared."

"I wouldn't leave you, Steve. I love you."

"Thank you. Thank you, yes. I love you, too. I love you more than anything. I forgot that for a while, and I'm sorry. I really am."

"It's all right."

"No, it's not. Pen, it isn't all right. I'll take you back to New York. I promise I will. I've made a mess of some things out here and I have to clean it up before I go, but I'll take you home, I promise. I'll write my letter of resignation right now, if you want. I'll tell the FBI, transfer me back to New York or I quit. There's a lot of other things I can do. I could make a lot more money, too."

"Money's not important. What's important is that we're together. That we love each other."

I went to the desk and switched off the receiver.

"Bullshit."

I didn't believe a word that Sykora had said, and I was amazed that Pen did. She seemed smarter than that.

I left the room, left the motel, and crossed Central Avenue. The air was cold, and the wind blowing in my face had an edge to it. Lights reflected off the wet pavement, and I deliberately walked down residential streets that were darker and quieter to avoid them. I traveled twenty minutes in one direction, then fifteen in another before stopping. I rested my hands on my hips and stared straight up at the night sky. A solitary dot of light moved in a straight line among the bright stars, and I thought of the International Space Station, flashed on all those glorious photographs taken of Earth from space. The world looked quite spectacular when seen from a distance. It's only when you get up close that it loses its appeal, and I was way too close. I had lost perspective.

"Step back," I said aloud. "Step back and look at the big picture."

And I did, literally, stepping backward three paces while looking up at the night sky.

Now what do you see?

"Steve Sykora's future. He messed up my life. Now I'm going to mess up his."

Of course, jealousy had nothing to do with it.

Chapter Ten

Sunday morning. I slid open the window of the motel room, and the wind stirred the lace curtains like a skirt. I flashed on Pen's rose-colored dress. I could feel the warm pressure of her body against mine, taste her lips and smell the fragrance of her rain-soaked hair.

It occurred to me that I might be insane, and I wondered briefly what Dr. Jillian deMarais would say.

You're obsessing over a woman you barely know, who's made it clear she doesn't want to know you. What are you, nuts?

Good question. What would you advise, Doctor?

McKenzie, you need to get out more.

Sounds like a plan to me.

Sykora had vowed to spend the day fulfilling each and every one of Pen's whims, which mostly involved cultural pursuits—the Walker Sculpture Garden, the Minneapolis Institute of Arts, the Minnesota Historical

Society. Meanwhile, I sought enlightenment of a different sort.

I drove to a gas station that had one of those drive-up pay telephones you can operate from your car and pumped two quarters into the slot. I called Jeannie Shipman, Bobby Dunston's "young, beautiful, smart-as-hell partner" at the St. Paul Police Department, although I don't think he calls her that anymore. For the briefest period of time, Bobby had contemplated having an affair with her, but cooler heads prevailed.

"McKenzie," she said after I identified myself. "There are people looking for you."

"Are they looking hard?"

"I couldn't say about anyone else, but we're not."

"I appreciate that."

"Why are you calling me?"

"I forgot Bobby Dunston's extension number."

"Uh-huh. Well, why don't I wave him over. Just in case his phone is tapped."

"You're wonderful."

"If I'm so wonderful, how come you never ask me out?"

"Because you're way too good for the likes of me."

Jeannie snickered. "One day I hope to have a friend as close as you and Bobby are. Hang on."

A moment later, Bobby was on the phone.

"You sonuvabitch," he said.

Yeah, me and Bobby were like *this.*

"Don't call me that," I told him.

"You bastard."

"Much better."

"I could kill you."

"What did I do?"

"How 'bout that scene you played on my patio the other night?"

"What scene?"

"The scene where you gave my wife all of your worldly possessions—your fucking last will and testament—and said good-bye."

"I didn't say good-bye. I said good night."

"You said good-bye."

"I didn't say—did I really?"

"Yes, you did, really, and now Shelby's all shook up wondering what's happened to you. 'Is McKenzie all right?' 'Have you heard from McKenzie?' And another thing, pal—where do you get off buying my wife a sports car?"

"Are you kidding? The only way she gets a sports car is if I'm dead."

"Yeah? So?"

"You jealous bastard. How 'bout if I amend the policy so you both get sports cars? And the kids, too?"

"That would be much better, thank you."

"Fine. I'll take care of it when I get back."

"So you are coming back."

"That's the plan."

"Where are you now?"

"Bobby, you don't want to know where I am now."

"That's true. But where are you?"

"Close."

"How close?"

"Bobby . . ."

"All right, all right." I heard the exertion Bobby put into sitting down. He said, "So, how's it going?"

"Not bad. Could be better."

"Are you playing nice with the other children?"

"They're all being mean to me."

"Poor baby."

"I did meet a nice girl, though."

"Don't tell me that."

"What?"

"Nina."

"What about Nina?"

"If Shelby isn't asking about you, Nina is."

"Nina's worried, too?"

"Yes, she is."

"That's nice."

"You think so?"

"It's nice to know people care."

"McKenzie—oh, never mind."

"Bobby, I need a favor."

"I figured."

"Remember that woman, about four years ago, she worked for the *New York Times*—she did the story about crime in the Twin Cities."

"Yeah, the reporter, back when we had all those killings, the one with the big—"

"Glasses. She wore glasses."

"I remember those, too."

"What was her name?"

"Rose, Rosemary, Roseanne . . ."

"Roseanne Esmae."

"No. Esjay. Roseanne Esjay."

"She's the one who labeled Minneapolis 'Murderoplis.' "

"What about her?"

"Nothing. I was just trying to remember her name."

"That's the only reason you called?"

"Well, you could do me another favor."

"What?"

"Look up the phone number of the *New York Times.*"

I bought a fifteen-minute phone card at the drugstore and wasted six of them first trying to get through to Roseanne Esjay and then reminding her who I was.

"The St. Paul cop with the goofy name, I remember now. How's your cute friend?"

"My married cute friend?"

"Yeah, him."

"He's good."

I was surprised that Esjay was in the office on a Sunday morning and told her so.

"Trust me," she said. "It wasn't my idea. So, what can I do for you?"

"I'm looking for information."

"About what?"

"Some big fat slob named Frank Russo might've been a capo in the Bonanno family. My take is that he's hiding from Angelo Granata. I don't know why."

"Are you still with the St. Paul cops?"

"No."

"Are you with the FBI now, or some other . . ."

"Not at all. Why do you ask?"

"I'm trying to figure out what you have to do with Frank Russo."

"I'm looking for him."

"So is most of the New York Mafia. Why do you want him?"

"Are we on the record?"

"Hell, yes, we're on the record. McKenzie, why are you looking for Frank Russo?"

"If we're on the record, I can't tell you."

"C'mon . . ."

"Sorry."

"All right—look, off the record, then."

"Russo murdered a friend of mine."

"In Minnesota? Frank Russo's in Minnesota?"

"Yes."

"Where?"

"I don't know. The FBI is hiding him."

"The FBI is hiding—they must have turned him. They're using Russo to get to Granata."

"That's my understanding, too."

"Oh, man, this is great."

"I wouldn't go so far as to say that."

"In Minnesota, you say. I'll be damned. McKenzie, you need to go on the record. You need to—"

"Roseanne, Roseanne . . ."

"McKenzie."

"Roseanne, I don't care what you write, as long as you don't mention my name or why I'm looking for Russo. Is that a deal?"

"What do I get in exchange?"

"You get the name of the special agent who's holding Russo's hand."

"That's a deal."

"Just tell me, first—why is Granata looking for Russo?"

"It's complicated."

I glanced at my watch. I still had a few minutes left on my phone card.

"I have time," I said.

"Granata became acting boss of the Bonanno family when they busted Joseph Massino. He's very good at what he does. Very disciplined. Under him the Bonannos have become the strongest of the five Mafia families. Frank Russo was one of Granata's most dependable and ruthless capos. He wanted to use the Bonanno muscle to force the other families into a kind of European Union, five independent families but all of them under a single leadership umbrella—Granata's umbrella. From a strictly business standpoint, it wasn't a bad idea, only Russo's plan probably would have led to all-out war, and Granata wouldn't go along with it. Russo decided to take over the family and impose his union anyway. He tried to hit Granata. He missed. Now a hundred and fifty Bonanno soldiers are searching for him, plus God knows how many freelancers."

"That's not complicated at all," I told Roseanne.

"It is if Russo cut a deal with the FBI. You say he's in Minnesota?"

"He was the last time I saw him."

"You saw him?"

"I stood about two yards away from him."

"When?"

"Last Friday afternoon. The day before he killed my friend."

"He killed your friend, but the FBI's still protecting him?"

"That's right. Or at least some agents of the FBI are."

"Same thing happened in Boston. In exchange for information on the Patriarca Mafia family, a handful of maverick agents protected members of the Winter Hill Gang from prosecution. Eventually the Patriarca family was devastated by federal prosecutions, and the Winter Hill Gang took control of the Boston-area rackets. Now about a billion dollars' worth of lawsuits have been brought against the government by victims of crimes committed by the informants while they were under FBI protection."

"Same thing might be happening here."

"Your friend who was killed . . ."

"His name is Mr. Mosley. He was a beekeeper. You can probably pick up everything you need from back issues of the St. Paul and Minneapolis newspapers."

"You promised me a name."

"Steven Sykora."

"Sykora?"

"He's Frank Russo's babysitter."

"Sykora used to be with the organized crime task force that was investigating the Bonanno family. I heard he was transferred a few months ago."

"Guess where."

"The Minneapolis field office."

"What a coincidence."

"If I write this story—who am I kidding—*when* I write this story, probably tomorrow if I can get any kind of confirmation, all hell is going to break loose, you know that, don't you? Along with the FBI freaking out, a hundred hitters are going to descend on the Land of 10,000 Lakes looking for Russo."

"There's something you should know, Roseanne."

"What's that?"

"It's actually closer to fifteen thousand lakes."

Special Agent Brian Wilson wasn't in his office. I had to track him down at home.

He said, "Hello."

I said, "Hi, Harry."

"McKenzie."

"You recognized my voice."

"That, plus you're the only one who calls me Harry."

"That's because you look just like the actor Harry Dean Stanton, and that's how I came to think of you before I learned what your real name was."

"Yeah, you told me."

"Besides, I hear Brian Wilson and I think of the Beach Boys."

"Then you're the only one. What do you want, McKenzie? You know the bureau's been looking for you."

"So I understand."

"Tell me you're going to give yourself up."

"About that—how's my credit?"

"Do you think I owe you a favor because you helped us bust those gunrunners a while back?"

"Maybe a small one."

"McKenzie, we're talking our nation's security here."

"C'mon, Harry. You know that so-called Seeking Information Alert is b.s."

"I don't know. I've had your andouille and chicken jambalaya. If that's not a weapon of mass destruction . . ."

"You said you loved my jambalaya."

"I was being polite."

"Harry . . ."

"Okay, okay. A small favor. What is it?"

"Meet me at home plate of Metropolitan Stadium."

He thought about that for a moment before asking, "When?"

I gave him a time. "Do I have to tell you to come alone?" I added.

"I'll be alone."

"You won't be sorry."

"Hell, McKenzie, I'm already sorry."

After saying good-bye to Harry, I drove to an audio-video store and had a dozen copies made of the two cassettes I had recorded. Afterward, I found a sporting goods store. I bought a pair of Bushnell binoculars that were on sale and a set of palm-sized two-way radios. I also purchased a box of shells and a spare magazine for my Beretta.

A middle-aged white man in his fifties—my definition of middle age is considerably more conservative than Ruth Schramm's—stood on the corner of First Avenue and Sixth Street in downtown Minneapolis, across the street from the Target Center. He was dressed in the colors of the Minnesota Timberwolves and holding up a handmade sign: I NEED 4.

I watched Chopper roll up to him.

"My man," he said. "You want four? I got four. Where you want to sit?"

The man put down his sign and leaned over Chopper, examining the seating chart of Target Center that Chopper rested on the arm of his wheelchair.

"I can get you into blue, my man. You want four right here?"

"What do you want for those?"

"One and a half."

"For all four?"

Chopper started laughing. So did the buyer.

"I know, I know," said the buyer. He reached into his jeans and pulled out a roll of bills. He peeled off the correct amount of cash while Chopper reached into the saddlebag of his wheelchair and produced the four tickets.

"Listen," said the buyer. "If the T-Wolves win, they get the Lakers next week. Can you help me out?"

"Tough series," said Chopper. "All I got left, I got two. You want two? I can get you two in the upper deck."

"How high?"

"Second row midcourt." Chopper produced his chart again. "No way you're gonna get better seats this late."

"I don't have the cash on hand," said the buyer. Apparently he knew the rules. "You going to be around?"

"I be here, my man. I be here. But don't you wait too long. First come, first serve."

"I hear you."

The white buyer and the black scalper shook hands in that funky way hip guys do—I was never able to master it myself—and parted company. A moment later, Chopper was gliding down the avenue asking each and every stationary individual he passed, "You lookin' for tickets?"

It's a misdemeanor to scalp tickets in Minnesota, but mostly the law goes unenforced. As for building security, if you conduct your business off arena and stadium property, they usually leave you alone. Chopper had never been arrested or rousted; I doubt anyone wanted to be seen hassling a thin black man in a wheelchair. On the other hand, this was still a new enterprise for Chopper, the latest in a long list of profitmaking ventures, and he hadn't been at it long enough to get busted.

Game time was 2:00 P.M., but Chopper continued to sell until nearly 2:30. Once the sidewalks around Target Center became empty, Chopper spun his chair around and started wheeling north on First Avenue. I waited for him. He was only a few yards away when he saw me.

"Fuckinay, McKenzie. How you doin', man?"

"Hanging in, hanging in," I told him and shook his hand.

"I was just talkin' 'bout you."

"I know. Lantry told me. What are you doing, telling people I saved your life? I didn't save your life."

"You did." He seemed distressed that I would deny it.

"All I did was call the paramedics. They saved your life."

"That ain't the way I 'member it."

"Chopper . . ."

"You way too modest, McKenzie. That's one of your problems. You don't never take credit."

"Have it your own way."

Chopper had never been what fashion magazines might called "full bodied," even during his days running girls in Frogtown, but up close he seemed distressingly thin. I had to ask him, "You're not on the pipe, are you?"

"Fuck. You know I don't do that shit."

"You look awfully skinny, Chopper. Have you been eating regularly?"

"We talkin' food or pussy?" Chopper laughed at his own joke. When he finished, he said, "This is the new me. Mean and lean, baby."

"Maybe so, but you should come over one of these days. I'll give you a meal, fix you right up."

"You gonna make that Texas chili you had that one time?"

"It's possible."

"Cuz that was the best shit I ever had."

"Compliments are always appreciated, Chopper. In the meantime, you're making me nervous. I've seen anorexic models with more meat on their bones. Let's get something to eat."

"I ain't hungry, man. You hungry?"

"As a matter of fact, I am."

* * *

The hostess at the Loon Cafe sat us at a table by a window, giving us a good view of the traffic on Fifth Street. Chopper decided to order a little something. Just to be polite, he said. He ate quickly, devouring an order of calamari in jalapeño tartar sauce, a Chinese chicken salad, a ten-ounce rib-eye, coleslaw, a sixteen-ounce Leinenkugel Honey Weiss, and half my fries like famine was imminent and the old axiom "He who eats the fastest eats the mostest" was now the first law of survival.

Again I worried about him. He saw it in my eyes and laughed out loud.

"Man, you like the Chinese. Think you save a brother's life, you're responsible for 'im. I'm fine. Lost a little weight is all, rollin' up and down the avenues, engagin' in free trade. Man, I'm a free trader."

"How is business?" I asked.

"Now that I'm online, man, it's like printin' Washingtons."

"Online?"

"Got's my own Web site—ticketchopper.com. I sell through eBay sometimes, too. You lookin' for Dixie Chicks in Vancouver, the Boss in Chi-town, Mavericks in Dallas, I'm your man."

"Seriously?"

"I'm global. Got brothers all over waitin' in line at ticket offices, pay 'em fifty dollars, whatever, for a couple hours of work buyin' for me—that's where I get most of my tickets. Also get from TicketMaster, get from a pool of brokers I'm tight with—I resell 'em. Serious money, man. Got three-fifty for a pair to see the Stones last week cost me sixty-six-fifty each."

"What are you doing outside Target Center, then?"

"Same-day tickets, man, Internet ain't worth shit. You gotta be out there with the people. Gotta have the product in hand. Team like the Minnesota Wild in the playoffs, man, wait 'til thirty minutes before game time, I get one-eighty for a sixty-two-fifty ticket. More if they playin' good."

Chopper carelessly took a long pull of beer.

"Fillin' a need," he added, beer dribbling down his chin. "Givin' the people what they want."

"Chopper, you're a true entrepreneur. Bill Gates would be proud."

"Damn straight. Hey, man, you lookin' for tickets? I'll take care of you. You like them jazz guys, like that Wynton Marsalis, like that Harry Connor—"

"Connick. Harry Connick."

"They come to town, I'll get ya tickets. Best seats in the house. Face value, man. Give 'em to ya for face value."

"You're my hero, Chopper."

"You know it."

Chopper finished his meal and shoved the plate away.

"Dessert?" I asked.

"Nah. Spoil my dinner. So, you workin'?"

"What do you mean, working?"

"Doin' one of your Robin Hood things, you know."

"In a manner of speaking."

"I figured. Only, you gotta say, man. If you workin', you gotta speak up. Otherwise, a brother think you're just shootin' the shit to be polite, just trying to be, whatchacallit, politically correct—see a cripple and figure you gotta feed 'im a meal."

"Don't you mean 'differently abled'? And when have you ever known me to be politically correct just for the sake of being politically correct about anything?"

"What I'm sayin' is, you wanna know shit, just ask."

"Okay. What I want to know is this—what's new?"

Chopper looked at me like I had just asked him if it was raining outside.

"Fuck, McKenzie, whaddaya mean, what's new? I got Queen Latifah on DVD yesterday. That's what's new."

"I mean, is there anything happening out there that's disrupting the status quo?"

Chopper stared out the window as if he were searching for something.

"Gangs fighting over turf, but that is status quo."

"I heard a big shipment is coming in."

"A big shipment of what?"

"Hell, Chopper, I don't know."

"Drugs?"

"Could be."

"There's always pharmaceuticals changin' hands, but nothin' big. Nothin' bigger than usual, anyway. You're lookin' for what's unusual, right?"

"Yes."

"I ain't heard of nothin' that's unusual."

"Nothing at all?"

"Only thing I heard about that's different is cigarettes."

"Cigarettes?"

"Guys bringin' in a load of cigarettes. Supposed to be a big load of name brands."

"That can't be right," I said.

"Only big shipment I know of."

"Smuggling cigarettes?"

"Big business in cigarettes," Chopper said. "Gettin' bigger. 'Specially with cigarette taxes goin' up to pay for all them state deficits. Buy smokes in Kentucky where it's three cents a pack, sell 'em in New York where it's a buck-fifty, pocket the difference."

"What is the cigarette tax in Minnesota?"

"Forty-eight cents a pack."

"Doesn't seem worth it. All that trouble to make a lousy half buck."

"Do the math, man. Four-eighty a carton multiplied by say, a hundred thousand cartons. Maybe three days work drivin' 'em up here. I'd like a taste of that. And if you do it, like, say, every week . . ."

"I see your point. Tell me more."

"I don't know any more, man. I ain't in that line of work."

"What about the guys bring them in?"

"I heard wiseguys from New York."

I must have looked like an idiot, sitting there with my mouth hanging open. Chopper waved his hand in front of my eyes and called my name.

"Okay, Chopper," I said. "Just so you know, 'wiseguys from New York' is what you call a significant detail. Do you have any more? Details, I mean."

Chopper laughed out loud.

"I think the cupboard is bare, man."

"You don't know when they're coming in or where?"

"No. But I know a guy."

"And this guy is who?"

Chopper reached into his saddlebag and retrieved a cell phone.

"Chill, man," he said. "I'll take care of your ass."

Chopper punched in a series of numbers, put the phone to his ear, and waited while it rang.

"Yo, my man . . . Yeah, it's me. Hey, you get those tickets, man? Were them good seats? Wha' did I tell ya? . . . Fuck yeah, man. Anytime. You know my number . . . Hey, listen, listen. What you were talkin' about the other day, about them smokes . . . Yeah, man, but I was thinkin', I wouldn't mind a taste of that . . . Whaddaya mean, do I have a store? . . . That's just wrong, man. I can move volume. You don't need no fuckin' store to move volume . . . I got my own Web site. I could use the Internet . . . Fuckin' wiseguys, they ain't never heard of the new economy, man? . . . Let me negotiate with 'em . . . No, no, no, no, no man, no, no, man, that ain't . . . Fuck, like I'm gonna put you on the spot over fuckin' cigarettes? . . . I don't give a fuck if they're name brands . . . No, you're right, you're right, when you're right you're right, man . . . Where? Where we . . . Yeah, I know it . . . No, I ain't never been there, I mean, fuck . . . You got a location but no time . . . I hear that, I hear that . . . Yeah, yeah . . . No shit, man. You call me now. You gonna call me? . . . All right, my man. Yeah . . . Be cool."

Chopper packed his cell phone away and took a last sip of beer, draining his glass.

He said, "He don't know when the shipment is comin' in. Guess it depends on traffic or some shit. This is like the first trip, okay, and everyone is still workin' out the whaddaya call it, logistics."

"But he has a location?"

"McKenzie, have you ever been to Elk River?"

Special Agent Brian Wilson entered the Mall of America from the east parking ramp. He looked just the way I remembered him, maybe a little heavier. He even wore the same dark suit; I was willing to wager that he was the only one in the shopping mall who did wear one. I watched him carefully as he passed the shops and restaurants and the Bloomington Police Department substation. I didn't see anyone lurking in shop doorways or peering from behind potted plants or speaking into their sleeves as he passed, but then that'd be the point, wouldn't it?

He seemed to be doing the same thing I was, inspecting everyone around him as he walked, looking for tails. His eyes were steady, watchful, with a hint of curiosity. I doubted he missed much.

The Mall of America was the largest fully enclosed retail complex in the United States, with over 520 specialty shops and fifty restaurants. At the center of it was a Camp Snoopy theme park, built entirely beneath a glass-and-girder sky. Harry took the stairs, descending from the retail shops to the floor of the park. Sound followed him as he made his way toward the northwest corner—the laughter of children and the shouts of parents, the cries of young men and women on the Screaming Yellow Eagle and Mighty Axe thrill rides, the Hank Williams standard "Jambalaya" broadcast from merry-go-round speakers, the rock song "Wild Thing" played for all it was worth by the Hill-Murray Parish Schools jazz band, and beneath it all a low, incessant rumble of human and mechanical noise that neither abated nor increased in volume.

Harry halted abruptly, and I thought he might have made me, but he paused only long enough to allow a young woman wearing a green Camp Snoopy polo shirt and leading three dark brown llamas to pass before him. A few moments later, he was standing in front of the Northwoods Stage. A preteen I had paid twenty bucks earlier handed him a palm-sized walkie-talkie and disappeared. Harry pressed the talk button.

"McKenzie?"

"How you doin', Harry?" I asked as I worked myself into position.

"Getting a little paranoid, aren't you, McKenzie? Over."

"Haven't you heard? The FBI is after me. Over."

"I said I'd come alone. Over."

"But you didn't say you wouldn't arrest me. Over."

"Details, details."

I leaned against the second-level railing outside the Tall Girl shop near the west entrance to Camp Snoopy, next to Joe Cool's Hot Shop. I trained my binoculars on the Northwoods Stage.

"Why don't you come here and we'll talk about it. Over," Harry said.

"I'll tell you what, Harry. Why don't you stand on home plate. Over."

"Come again? Over."

"Actually stand on home plate. Over."

The Mall of America had been built on the former site of Metropolitan Stadium, where the Minnesota Twins once played baseball. As a tribute to the grand old lady, the mall embedded the stadium's original home plate in its concrete floor. It was identified in gold: METROPOLITAN STADIUM HOME PLATE 1956–1981. From where I was perched, I could clearly see Harry, but only if he stood on home plate. Two steps in any direction and he would have been obscured from view by indoor trees, the umbrella of a snack bar, and the pillars supporting the Northwoods Stage.

Harry stood on the plate, looking in the opposite direction from where I stood.

"You look like you've been putting on weight, Harry. Over."

"Thanks for noticing. Okay, I'm here. Over."

"I appreciate you coming, Brian. Seriously."

Harry hesitated, turned right and left, brought the walkie-talkie to his lips. "Brian makes me nervous. What's going on? Over."

"I'm going to tell you a few things, Brian. They're not going to make you happy. Over."

"I'm listening. Over."

"It begins with Steven Sykora. Do you know him? Over."

"From New York. What about him? Over."

"He's the one who issued the Seeking Information Alert on me. Over."

"I know. Over."

"Here's why . . ."

I gave Harry everything I knew, mixing in what Roseanne Esjay had told me. Harry recapped my remarks when I had finished.

"Sykora is protecting a New York gangster named Russo—who murdered your friend—so Russo can help him build a case against a Mafia underboss named Little Al Granata. Does that pretty much cover it? Over."

"Pretty much. Over."

"And you expect me—and the bureau—to take your word for this? Over."

"Of course not, Brian. Over."

"I'm still listening. Over."

"Look to your right. There's a green metal trash container that looks like a mailbox with the words 'waste paper' stamped in gold on the side. See it? Over."

"I see it. Over."

"There's an envelope taped to the bottom. Why don't you get it, then come back to home plate. Over."

Harry disappeared from view as he moved toward the trash container. He returned a few moments later. He had already opened the envelope and was holding two black cassette tapes in his hand.

"I got 'em. Over," he said into the walkie-talkie.

"The tapes contain conversations between Sykora and Russo and Sykora and his wife that substantiate everything I've told you. Over."

"Why do I have a feeling these were obtained illegally and are therefore inadmissible in a court of law? Over."

"If things go badly for me, Brian, I won't be playing the tapes in a court of law. Over."

"McKenzie, what have you done? Over."

"Tomorrow or the next day, the *New York Times* will be printing a story that says the FBI has Frank Russo in custody, that Russo is helping the bureau build a case against Granata, that the operation is similar to the one you guys ran in Boston against the Patriarca family a few years ago, and that Special Agent Steven Sykora is in charge. Over."

"Sonuvabitch, McKenzie—"

I broke in on him before he could finish.

"The FBI will deny everything, of course. Over."

"You can count on it. Over."

"And because the bureau will then quietly discipline Sykora and arrest Russo and his thugs and make sure they're tried for the murder of Mr. Mosley, nothing more will come of it. Over."

Harry let that sink in for a moment. Finally he said, "Let me guess. *If* these things happen, then the copies that you made of these tapes"—he was examining the cassettes as he spoke—"will be destroyed. Over."

"That's exactly what will happen. Over."

"That's my boy. Over."

"If not . . ."

"You'll be happy to share with CNN, Fox, National Public Radio, *Time* magazine," Harry said over my transmission. "I get the picture. Over."

"There's nothing like the threat of bad publicity to get people to do the right thing. Over."

"And there's nothing like the threat of bad publicity to get people to do the absolutely wrong thing, either. Have you thought of that? Over."

"I have. Over."

"I bet. Over."

"Something else, Brian. I want the Seeking Information Alert lifted. Over."

"I can do that. Over."

"I'd appreciate it. Over."

"This whole thing pisses me off. Sykora pisses me off. Russo. You piss me off, McKenzie. Over."

"Yeah? Look at it from my point of view. Besides," I added before he could speak, "they're both dirty, Brian—Sykora and Russo. I can't believe you don't want them, too. Over."

"If they're dirty, I do want them. But I haven't heard the tapes yet. Over."

"They're exactly what I say they are. Over."

"I'll listen to them when I get home. Then I'll talk to my boss. In the meantime, please, please, please, McKenzie, don't do anything rash, not until we get this thing figured out. Okay? Over."

"Brian, I promise you, on my word of honor, all I want to do is make this go away. All I want is to go home. Over."

"Just don't do anything foolish. Last thing we need is some amateur running around out of control. Over."

"Who are you calling an amateur, Brian? Over."

"It's all right, McKenzie. You can call me Harry."

The Mall of America took traffic flow seriously. I was able to get out of the ramp and onto the freeway in only a couple of minutes. I hated the idea of returning to the Hilltop Motel. But I didn't have much choice. I was still a wanted man.

Maybe in a couple of days, I told myself. *Yeah, maybe.*

Victor was watering his parking lot again when I reached the motel, using his hose to push dirt onto the narrow boulevard. I always thought that was a peculiar thing to do, wash sidewalks and driveways with a hose, but a lot of Minnesotans do it. I was tempted to ask Victor why, but what was the point? Some things will never make sense. Like the scoring system used in tennis.

I settled into my room with ESPN. It had been a good day. Minnesota won and Seattle beat Chicago. I'm not a big fan of the Mariners, although I like Ichiro. When it comes to baseball, I always root for the Twins and whoever's playing the White Sox.

After a couple of hours the phone began ringing in Sykora's trailer. It rang four times within a half hour, but there was no one home to answer it. It rang twice more and then didn't ring for nearly an hour. At about 9:00 P.M. it rang again as Pen and Sykora were entering their trailer. Sykora said, "I'll get it."

The woman on the other end spoke in the flat, monotonous tone of a telemarketer who wasn't having much luck selling aluminum siding. She identified herself as the assistant to the special agent in charge of the Minneapolis field office of the Federal Bureau of Investigation. She addressed Sykora as "Mister," not "Agent." She told Sykora that the AIC would be out of the office Monday morning but that Sykora was scheduled to meet with him at 1:15 P.M. or when the AIC arrived, whichever came first.

I would have liked to see Sykora's face. Pen did and

said, "What's wrong?" the moment he hung up the phone.

"Hmm? Nothing."

"Don't tell me that, Steve. What's wrong? Who was on the phone?"

"That was the assistant to the AIC. I think I'm in serious trouble."

Pen asked him what he was talking about. Sykora danced around the answer as best he could, giving her a glimpse of his predicament without revealing the grisly details. As for me, I was so happy I drank my last James Page.

By this time tomorrow, I'll be off the hook, I told myself.

My only regret was Pen.

By this time tomorrow, her whole world will be changed.

I wondered briefly what that might mean. Would Pen leave her husband? If she did, was it possible for me to become part of her new life? How would she react if I revealed myself to her? Would she forgive me for destroying her husband's career? Would she understand?

The phone rang again.

"Hello," said Sykora.

"It's me."

"Frank? What do you want?"

"It's on."

"When?"

"Nine tomorrow morning."

"Where?"

"In Elk River, like I told you before."

"Are you sure?"

"I'm sure."

"You're sure."

"How many times do I have to say it? It'll happen at nine tomorrow at the quarry. They'll be driving one of those rental trucks."

"You're sure?"

"Fuck."

"I'm gambling a lot on this."

"Yeah. Me, too. What about McKenzie?"

"Fuck McKenzie."

Sykora hung up the phone.

"Now what?" asked Pen.

"An opportunity."

"What are you talking about? Where are you going?"

"Back to the office. I need to set up an operation."

"I don't understand. I thought you were in trouble."

"I am, but . . . You give them a solid, high-profile bust, something big with a lot of PR value, the FBI will forgive almost anything."

The door to the trailer opened and closed.

Pen said, "Damn."

My reaction was considerably more colorful.

Later that night, I lay on my back in the dark, watching surprisingly crisp images floating around me. Mr. Mosley, Susan Tillman, Danny—what I had done to Danny. And others. Jamie Carlson. Two black kids named Young and Benjamn. A man I had killed with a shotgun. Still another man I had killed with a hand grenade. Jeezus, a hand grenade. Even now I shuddered at the thought of it.

We all have loops of videotape that rerun themselves on our bedroom ceilings late at night, movies we wish we would never see again. Maybe I owned a bigger archive than most. Maybe the films were more violent. The result of living an NC-17 life. At least it used to be NC-17. The way ratings are being deflated these days, what with crashing towers and a never-ending war against terrorism, it was probably only an R now.

The thing was, the only sure way to escape them was to stop going to the movies altogether. And that was what I did best, going to movies for people, a kind of freelance critic trying to help my friends avoid the bombs. It was pretentious as hell, of course. Like most films, the life I chose didn't stand up to serious scrutiny. Best not to think too much about it, I decided and rolled on my side. Best to just sit back and see what happens next.

Chapter Eleven

I followed Highway 169 north into Elk River. Traffic flowed smoothly, even during the early morning rush hour. Of course, most of the traffic was heading into the Cities and I was driving out.

People who don't live here tend to think of the Twin Cities as only St. Paul and Minneapolis. But according to the U.S. Census Bureau, the Greater Twin Cities Metropolitan Area actually consists of 191 cities and towns, some of them with even smaller populations than Hilltop. Elk River, population, 16,447, was located about forty minutes north of Minneapolis. Like most third-, fourth-, and fifth-ring suburbs, its businesses—mostly retail—were built along the freeways and highways, while its homes, schools, and churches were tucked more or less out of sight behind them.

The address Chopper gave me belonged to Spivak Stone, a failed quarry that was apparently abandoned.

There were two signs out front. The first was old and weathered and advertised sand, gravel, and crushed stone. The second listed the name and phone number of a finance company.

I turned off 169 and drove slowly past the quarry over a worn and gravel-strewn service road. I noted two large buildings, both tightly sealed, just inside a high Cyclone fence topped with barbed wire. The gate was open, allowing access to a dirt road that veered into the opening of the quarry itself. Beyond the opening I could just make out what resembled a huge bowl carved out of an immense five-story-high bluff. The second time I drove past I noticed an SUV parked alongside a mound of sand midway between the fence and the quarry. There were two men sitting in the SUV. They watched me carefully. I didn't dare make a return trip.

Instead, I followed the service road until it abruptly ended about a half mile from the quarry. There were no other businesses along the road, and I figured a parked car would look mighty suspicious, so I edged the Neon off the hard-packed gravel into a shallow ditch surrounded by waist-high brown grass, shrubs, and weed trees. You could still see it, but only if you were looking.

I left the Neon and made my way up the bluff, more or less climbing at a forty-five-degree angle to the summit. It was tough going, and I had to stop twice to regain my breath. I was covered with a fine tan-colored dirt by the time I reached the top. The bluff itself was flat and thick with the same kind of grass, brush, and trees as below. Birds sang somewhere, but I didn't see them, and there was a low buzzing sound that I guessed was wind blowing through the tall grass.

I pushed east toward the quarry. Along the way I discovered a broken and rotting rail fence. After another tenth of a mile I came across an ancient road not used for years, perhaps decades. I wondered if someone had farmed the top of the bluff at one time and had been bought or driven off. I kept on until I came to within a stone's throw of the quarry. That's where my acrophobia kicked in. I sank to my hands and knees and crawled forward. I was lying flat on my stomach, screened from sight by the scrub growth that hung above the quarry, by the time I reached the edge.

The walls were sheer and descended fifty feet to the sand-and-gravel floor of an irregular oval about the size of a professional baseball field. There was only one way in, the single dirt road I had seen earlier. It was cut wide enough for heavy earth movers, steam shovels, and dump trucks, although there were now none to be seen. From my perch I could just barely make out the back end of the SUV stationed at the mouth of the road with my binoculars.

I challenged my fear of heights by looking straight down. That lasted about three seconds before I squirmed backward away from the edge. *Never look down,* I told myself. It seemed like wise advice.

A few moments later, a small van drove into the quarry and parked along the north wall. It was followed a half minute later by a battered Ford Taurus. I glanced at my watch. 7:53.

During the next hour, the quarry filled up with assorted vans, SUVs, pickups, cars, and even a few ancient station wagons, the vehicles forming an irregular circle along the sand-and-gravel walls. Some of the drivers sat inside their vehicles. Others sprawled on their hoods or leaned against bumpers. Still others moved about with hands in their pockets. There was scant conversation as far as I could see. All in all, the gathering reminded me of an unhappy family reunion.

I examined the drivers with my binoculars. There was a mixture of Caucasians, African Americans, Native Americans, Hispanics, Hmong, Pakistanis, Indians—*what is this, the United Nations?* I recalled Chopper's telephone conversation. He had said, "Whaddaya mean, do I have a store?" I guessed these guys were all owners and operators of neighborhood convenience stores. Who else could sell a high volume of illegal cigarettes? It fit the stereotype, anyway.

Finally my binoculars rested on a decidedly white, European face. It belonged to a man who seemed to wander aimlessly among the other drivers while surreptitiously jotting down license plate numbers in a tiny notebook he hid in the palm of his hand.

Sykora.

I followed his movements. Eventually he led me to more than a dozen men standing in separate clusters of two and three near two vans parked on opposite sides of the road near the entrance to the quarry. Some of the men looked intense, like athletes waiting for the game to commence. Others were smiling like a pride of hungry lions that had happened upon a herd of sleeping wildebeests.

Sykora looked at his watch. I looked at mine. 9:16.

At 9:22, a semitractor and trailer chugged over the dirt road, passing Sykora and his colleagues and crossing the quarry to the west wall, where it halted. The drivers of the assorted vehicles seemed to hesitate, then moved forward en masse. Soon a single well-behaved, unhurried line formed at the back of the trailer. I seemed to be the only one who noticed Sykora's vans close with each other, forming a roadblock at the mouth of the quarry, or a dozen men suddenly pulling on blue windbreakers with large bright yellow letters on the front and back spelling FBI.

Sykora began shouting through a handheld electronic megaphone. I couldn't hear him from my perch, but the drivers did.

There was a moment of confusion, followed by panic, followed quickly by angry shouts and running. Lots of running. Most of the drivers dashed to their vehicles. They drove forward at first toward the barricade, then backward, then in circles looking for an exit from the quarry that wasn't there. The circle of vehicles expanded and collapsed upon itself, the attempted evacuation quickly becoming an unwieldy traffic jam.

A few SUV drivers—maybe they actually believed the TV commercials—attempted to scale the walls of the quarry, but the slopes were too steep and the sand and gravel too soft, and they slid backward. One SUV managed to climb almost vertically before it tipped over and rolled to the quarry floor. Other drivers abandoned their vehicles and tried to climb the walls, but they had no more luck than the SUVs.

In an effort to gain control of the chaos, an FBI agent discharged his weapon into the air. A driver turned and fired at the FBI agent. One of the agent's colleagues shot at the driver.

"Oh, Jeezus," I muttered, expecting a bloodbath. But there were no more shots, and soon the FBI restored order.

I found Sykora with my glasses. He was smiling while he and another agent made their way across the quarry to the semitrailer, smiling when they flung open the trailer doors.

The trailer was empty.

Sykora's smile disappeared.

He seemed shocked at first. Then visibly angry. An agent said something to him. He snapped back. The agent spoke again, and Sykora turned on him, shouting and waving his hands. The agent smiled benignly.

"Steven, Steven, Steven," I chuckled from my perch above and behind the FBI agent. "Put a fork in it, buddy. You're done."

Sykora knew it, too. Other agents tried to speak to him, but he brushed them off. He turned and managed a dozen steps away from the truck and his fellow agents before stopping, his hands gripping the top of his head as if he were afraid it would explode. Suddenly he looked up. I followed his gaze to the rim of the quarry. Something metallic flashed against the morning sun.

I brought my binoculars up but saw nothing. I trained the glasses back on Sykora, who continued to look upward. I couldn't hear him, of course, but his efficient mouth movements were easily readable.

"Fuck you," he said.

Frank.

I trained the glasses back on the rim. I saw nothing, but I knew he was there.

I have you now, you bastard.

I crawled backward until I was a good fifteen yards from the edge of the quarry, climbed to my feet, and started jogging along the rim toward the metallic flash. I was determined to get Frank once and for all for what he had done to my friends. Only I wasn't thinking clearly. For example, I was carrying the binoculars in my hand but not my Beretta. Careless. And I was running full bore, not even thinking about cover. That was worse than careless. It was suicidal. I realized it the moment I saw Frank and Danny standing away from the edge of the quarry, about 150 yards from my original position.

They were both armed, Frank with his shotgun and Danny with a pistol.

They saw me coming.

Danny raised his hand.

I shied like a horse; stopped running.

He shot at me with the small-caliber handgun. It would have been dumb luck if he had hit me from that distance, but it'd been done before. Fortunately for me, Danny's aim wasn't helped any by Frank, who shoved him toward me, jostling his arm as Danny squeezed the trigger.

I dove to the ground as Danny fired. The brown grass and shrubs were waist high, and I disappeared into them.

"Get him!" Frank said.

I lifted my head. Danny was gazing in my direction, but I don't think he saw me. Frank was waddling quickly away in the opposite direction—with his weight, he was lucky he could run at all. I moved toward my left to cut him off. Danny saw me and threw another shot my way. I went to ground again, paused for a moment, then circled hard to my right, staying low. When I came up again I saw Frank. He was about fifty yards away, opening the door of a Chevy Blazer. Apparently he had also discovered the abandoned road and used it.

Danny saw me and fired. Again I sank behind the grass and shrubs. I kept circling to my right until I heard the Chevy's engine catch.

Danny was now standing directly in front of the Blazer, studying the terrain. Frank put the Blazer in gear. Danny gave up his search and moved toward the passenger door. Only Frank wasn't waiting. He leaned on the accelerator. The Blazer's wheels spun, gained purchase, and propelled the vehicle forward. Danny leapt out of the way. Frank steered a tight circle across the grass, picked up the road again, and drove off. Danny chased after him, roaring epithets you won't find in Shakespeare.

"Don't leave me!" he shouted as the Chevy Blazer reached the far side of the bluff and dipped out of sight. Danny watched for a moment, then spun around, gripping his gun with both hands. I ducked out of sight. I wasn't worried about Danny. But where was Brucie? I couldn't find him anywhere, and not knowing his location frightened me. Twice he had managed to get behind me, and I doubted my chances of surviving a third encounter.

Danny left the road and took refuge in the tall grass and shrubs near a weed tree.

"McKenzie! Hey, McKenzie," he called.

I didn't answer. Where was Brucie? I gave it a few moments and decided he wasn't on the bluff.

"McKenzie," Danny called again. His back was to the tree, and he was glancing frantically from side to side. I moved toward him. By now I had discarded the binoculars and had activated my Beretta.

"We can work this out, McKenzie. Whaddaya say?"

Danny drifted a few steps away from the tree and crouched out of sight. I cautiously worked my way to his location, only when I reached it, he was gone. I lifted my eyes above the grass, did a quick 360. I couldn't see him. But I could hear him.

"We can talk. Can't we talk?"

I crept toward his voice, only he had moved again.

I was sweating, and the duckwalk through the grass was causing my back to cramp. I fought the impulse to stand and stretch it out.

"I can 'preciate you bein' pissed about the woman, okay? But that wasn't me, man. That's all Frank. Frank's the boss. You gotta know what I'm saying."

I found a large stone and decided to try the old movie trick, see if I could get Danny to reveal his position. I heaved the stone far to my right, listened for the thud. It came and went without Danny reacting to it. *I knew it wouldn't work. Stupid movies.*

I moved forward again, cautiously parting the grass

with the barrel of the Beretta, listening. I heard wind. And the pounding of my heart.

"McKenzie! I didn't do nothin' to you."

I veered slightly to my right. After a few yards the grass thinned just enough for me to see Danny squatting about twenty paces ahead. I brought up the Beretta.

"McKenzie, where are you?"

"Here," I said.

Danny spun on his heels and fired two quick shots at me from the hip.

I returned fire at the same instant.

Danny dove backward into the grass.

I waited for him to attempt another shot. When he didn't I rushed forward.

Only there was no need to hurry.

Danny had crawled about fifteen feet across the hard ground before curling into a fetal position, both hands clutching his stomach. His gun was lying in the dirt just out of his reach. I left it there. Maybe he'd go for it, I told myself, and I could shoot him again and pretend it was self-defense. A quick glance at his wound told me that wasn't going to happen. Danny was already dead, or would be within moments. Even if I wanted to save him, there was no way I could get him off the bluff and find medical attention before he bled out.

"I don't want to die," he told me.

I was pretty sure Mr. Mosley didn't want to die, either, but I didn't say so. What was the point?

Danny raised a bloody hand toward me.

"This ain't right."

He dropped his hand over his stomach. And he died.

As his last breath escaped his lungs, a thought flared deep inside my head.

This ain't right.

I thought I would feel satisfaction, if not outright pleasure, from killing one of the men who had killed Mr. Mosley and raped Susan Tillman. Yet I didn't. I felt instead like I sometimes did when I left the house, as though there was something important I had forgotten but couldn't quite place it.

I crouched next to the body and rested two fingers against the carotid artery. There was no pulse.

Why was he different?

I had killed men before. Sometimes I felt sick and ashamed. Sometimes I felt exhilarated. Sometimes I felt overwhelming relief. But with Danny there was—what? Indifference? Apathy? I didn't have a word to cover it. That, more than Danny's death, made me think there was something terribly wrong.

What's happened to me?

Me? No, no, no—not me. *Think about it. I didn't do anything wrong. It wasn't me. It was Jake. Jake Greene killed Danny. McKenzie wasn't responsible. McKenzie wasn't even here. He's in a shoe box in Merriam Park. It was the other guy. It was Jake—that crazy bastard.*

Yes, I know it was a lie. Yet I believed it for as long as I could.

I left Danny where he fell—not a particularly noble thing to do, but there was no way I could explain him to a county attorney and expect to escape jail. *Later,* I told myself, *I'll make an anonymous call to the Elk River Police Department.*

It took me a while to find my car and some time longer to discover a way off the service road that didn't take me past the army of law enforcement types that had gathered at the entrance to the quarry. Apparently none of them had heard the shots from the top of the bluff.

Afterward, I drove more or less southwest, not caring one helluva a lot where I ended up. I needed time to think, time to decompress. The days were beginning to run together, and I was afraid there were things I was starting to lose.

Eventually I ended up at a small bar in Glencoe and wondered if this was the joint that Ivy Flynn had called me from a lifetime ago. It was a pleasant enough place, and the pretty blonde bartender knew how to flirt without making a guy think there was something to it. I had two beers and a sandwich before driving back to Hilltop.

I changed out of my dirty clothes, showered, dressed again, and stretched out on the bed, my fingers locked behind my head. The sun was just a sliver on the horizon, and the motel room was engulfed in gray, yet I kept the lights off. There was nothing I wanted to see.

Tomorrow, I told myself. *Tomorrow I'll call Harry and he'll tell me I can go home, and it'll all be over.* Fuck Frank. Let Ishmael have him. What did I care? When he went down for messing with Granata, he'd go down for Mr. Mosley, too. It wasn't the justice I had been looking for, but now it was justice enough.

I closed my eyes.

The room was nearly pitch-black when I opened them again. The only light came from the parking lot and crept through a crack between my window drapes.

I had been awakened by Steve Sykora's voice calling for Pen, wondering aloud where she could be. I hadn't heard a sound coming from the receiver in my desk drawer since I entered the room and had forgotten it was there.

"Lucky. Where are you?" There was a wail in Sykora's voice that was almost childlike. I guessed things hadn't gone well for him during his meeting with the AIC, and the thought of it made me smile.

"Glad I could help," I told the empty room.

I closed my eyes again but didn't sleep. Instead, I continued to listen and smile as Sykora banged around his trailer. Yet after a few minutes I found myself pressing the tiny button that illuminated the face of my watch. Like Sykora, I was becoming concerned.

Where is Pen?

I must have asked that question a dozen times. Finally the phone rang. It rang only once before Sykora answered it.

"Yes?"

"I have her," Frank's voice said.

"What?"

"I have her."

"What do you mean?"

"I snatched your wife, what the fuck do you think I mean?"

Sykora didn't reply. I imagined him staring at the phone, his mouth open but words not coming out.

"You hear me?"

"Yes," said Sykora.

"I have your wife."

"What do you want?" Sykora was calm. A lot calmer than I was.

"You were always a guy to get right to the point. I like that."

"What do you want?"

"What do you think I want? I want money."

"How much?"

"Fifty large."

"Where do you think that's going to come from?"

Frank thought the question was funny. "From the FBI," he said, and laughed some more.

Sykora said, "The FBI has placed me on administrative leave without pay. I'm being investigated for what happened at the quarry this morning and for harboring a fugitive. Guess who the fugitive is, Frank?"

"Well, shit."

"What happened to the cigarettes, Frank?"

"Fuck if I know. Ask McKenzie."

"McKenzie?"

"Fucker was there, watchin'. Look, that don't matter. McKenzie don't matter. I kept my end of the deal. Now you're gonna keep yours or you ain't never gonna see your wife again. Got it?"

"You hurt my wife, Frank, you touch her, I'll kill you."

"Fuck. You don't think I heard shit like that before—

threats? Forgetaboutit. I'm still here, Fed. I'll always be here. So fuck that shit, okay? You can't go to the FBI? Is that what you're sayin'?"

"That's what I'm—"

"Fuck it, then. What we're gonna do is Plan B. Your wife says you have eleven-four in a money market account. I'll do you a favor. I'll only take ten thousand. It won't get me back to the Big Apple in style, but it'll get me back."

"Into Granata's waiting arms."

"You let me fucking worry about Little Al, wouldja? Just get the money."

"Banks aren't open, Frank."

"Banks open at 8:00 A.M. I'll call back at ten o'clock tomorrow and tell you where to deliver it. And don't fuck with me, Fed. You won't like what happens you fuck with me."

"I want to talk to my wife. I want to talk to her right now."

"Sorry, she can't come to the phone. She's all tied up." Frank thought that was funny, too.

"I don't talk to her, you don't get the money."

"You can talk to her tomorrow morning."

"I mean it, Frank. You hurt her—"

Frank hung up the phone.

Sykora screamed as if in great pain. I heard a crash. And then another. And then another. "Pen, Pen," he wailed, followed by a moan that spoke of all the sorrow there was in the world.

I checked the load in both my guns and left the motel room.

* * *

Steve Sykora flung open the door of his mobile home after I knocked. My impression was that he was hoping I was someone else.

He was an inch or two shorter than I was—with light brown hair. His eyes were dark, and he was blinking at me like he wasn't sure I was really there.

"I'm McKenzie," I told him.

He lunged out of the doorway toward me, his fist leading the way.

I managed to get under the blow and attempted to counter with a ridge hand to his solar plexus, but he was already behind me. I tried to turn, only he caught me in a headlock. I grabbed a fistful of his hair and pulled back hard. At the same time I stomped his knee from behind. His leg folded, and I drove his knee to the ground. He kept rolling, taking me with him. Suddenly I was on my back and he was kneeling on my biceps. My wrist was pulled backward—he could have snapped it with a thought.

"I'm a friend of Pen's," I blurted. I didn't know what else to say. "I'm here to help Pen."

"What do you know about it?"

"I know Frank kidnapped her."

"How do you know?"

"I bugged your trailer."

"You did what?"

"A UHF transmitter on your telephone line."

Sykora added pressure to my wrist. I closed my eyes, steeling myself for the excruciating pain I knew would come—only he eased up at the breaking point.

"Talk fast."

All the lies I had told in the past week and a half flashed before my eyes. None of them had done me much good, so I decided to try a different strategy—the truth.

"You're a sonuvabitch," I told him. "Frank and his thugs killed my friend and raped another, and you let them get away with it. I hope you all burn in hell. But Pen doesn't deserve any of this. So I'm going to help you get her back. I only hope she leaves you when we do."

"Leave me for you?"

"She doesn't even know who I am. I only know who she is because I've been listening to her put up with your bullshit for the past week."

"You're the one who burned me with the bureau, aren't you?"

"You bet your ass I am."

Sykora chuckled, an odd thing to do, I thought. He released my wrist and abruptly stood up. As I rubbed first my wrist and then my arm, he wandered to the trailer. He tried to slam shut the door, but it bounced back open again.

"I'm supposed to trust you?" he asked.

I didn't say if he should or shouldn't.

"Penelope," he moaned. "I don't know what I'll do if . . ."

The unspoken thought hung between us.

"Yeah, now you care," I told him.

"What's that supposed to mean?"

"Have you ever listened to her?"

"Of course I listen."

"I mean really listened to her? Listened to what she had to say about people, about life? Have you listened to her laugh? Have you listened to her music?"

"Not for a long time." His voice sounded far away.

"You and I—we deserve what happens to us. God knows Frank does. But Pen . . . not Pen. She doesn't deserve this. None of it. She's an angel come to earth. And she needs our help. So what's it going to be?"

"An angel come to earth," Sykora repeated. I admit it sounded way over the top when he said it. "You love my wife."

"No, I don't. But I could be talked into it real easy."

I was surprised by the truth of my own words. But despite what Ruth Schramm had said, Pen wasn't Audrey Hepburn and I certainly wasn't Humphrey Bogart.

Sykora took hold of the door as if he wanted to slam it again.

"What's it going to be?" I repeated.

He left the door open.

"Do you know where Frank is?" he asked.

"We can find him."

"How?"

"There's only one person in Minnesota who would help him. Guy called Brucie. I'm betting Frank's with him."

"And if he's not?"

"You can always pay him the ten thousand and hope for the best."

Sykora closed his eyes.

A moment later, he opened them again and started talking. His voice was brisk and sure, his words clearly enunciated. Yet he paced like he needed to urinate and the restroom was a long way off. His forehead and upper lip glistened with sweat. He reminded me of a poor poker player pushing chips into a pot he couldn't afford to lose.

"I know this Brucie," he told me. "He's one of Frank's boys. But I know nothing else about him. I don't even know his whole name."

"Neither do I."

"Then how do you expect to find him?"

"Do you have a couple of flashlights?"

Sykora glanced toward his mobile home.

"Yes."

"Bring 'em."

I told Sykora we were driving back to the quarry in Elk River. He asked why, and I told him he'd see when we got there.

For most of the drive north Sykora stared out the passenger window of my rented Neon. He felt like talking—maybe it was nerves—and I let him.

"These wiseguys, you stay after them long enough they come to know your name. They start to think of you as an associate, a playmate, a friend—like guys on competing basketball teams who play each other often. They send you gifts on your birthday. Frank, he once sent me a food dehydrator for making beef jerky and dried fruit. Do you believe that?

"When his power play with Granata went south, he sought me out, tracked me down to Minnesota. He offered me a deal—no witness protection, this was supposed to be between just him and me. He said he would help me get Little Al Granata and then he would return to New York and impose his will on the Bonanno family and we could go back to the way it was, me chasing him, like it was a game, cops and robbers. I took the deal.

"My mistake, one of many, I tried to do it on my own. I didn't want to bring the bureau in until I was ready. I was afraid they would queer the arrangement I had with Frank. I was under strict orders to ignore organized crime and concentrate solely on terrorists, you know. But I had a plan . . ."

"I know your plan," I told him.

"Think so? Tell me."

"The cigarette bazaar this morning. All those immigrants and foreign-born citizens. You bust them all for selling illegal cigarettes, sort them out. Maybe there's a Somali or a Palestinian who's using the profits to help fund some group with ties to al-Qaeda, whatever. Then you connect the cigarettes to Granata and accuse him of being in cahoots with terrorists. To hell with due process, you use the Patriot Act and other terrorist legislation to swoop down on him, punch his ticket to Guantánamo Bay. No charges, no lawyers, no rights, who cares? He's a gangster. The others, they're foreigners. No one's going shed tears over them. And you—you're a hero. Saving the world for democracy. They might even make a TV movie out of it."

Sykora turned in his seat and looked at me as if I were suddenly interesting.

"Oh, you don't approve? Well, too bad. We're trying to make the United States safe. And that means safe from the Mafia as well as terrorist groups."

"Safe for whom? Mr. Mosley? Susan Tillman?"

I was glad that he didn't answer, that he turned his head and stared out the window some more. If Sykora had said something about collateral damage, about breaking eggs to make omelets or sacrificing a few to save the many, we probably never would have reached Elk River. At least not in one piece.

Sykora was on my right, sweeping the tall grass and shrubs with his flashlight. We had been at it for five minutes before he asked, "What am I looking for?"

"You'll know it when you see it."

"Give me a hint."

"It's bigger than a bread box."

We had driven to the top of the bluff following the same ancient road Frank had used earlier. I parked many yards back from where he had because of an irrational fear that I would accidentally drive the Neon over the edge of the quarry. I blamed it on the acrophobia.

It was slow going. Clouds hid the night sky, and the only illumination came from our flashlights and the headlamps of the Neon. After ten minutes of searching I found my binoculars. I hung them over my shoulder by the strap and pivoted to my right, trying to remember where I had moved after I dropped them that morning. Toward that tree, I told myself, and a little that way, and . . .

"Jesus Christ."

I trained my light on Sykora. He was standing still, his flashlight holding steady on an object in front of him. I moved to his side.

"This is what we were looking for?"

"Yeah," I said.

"Ahh, Jesus . . ."

Danny seemed smaller now, more like a child than a man, curled into a ball, his limbs locked by rigor. His pale skin reminded me of cold mashed potatoes—not an appetizing sight. The blood on his body had dried, and the blood that pooled beneath it had soaked into the ground and turned a muddy color. Its odor was faint and slightly sweet, like a bad perfume. I set the binoculars on the ground and reached into my pocket for a handkerchief. I unfolded it over my hand and used it to pull Danny's leather wallet from his pocket.

"Did you do this?" Sykora wanted to know.

I ignored him.

"Did you?"

"Jake Greene shot him," I said.

"Who's Jake Greene?"

"Some guy from South Dakota."

I opened Danny's wallet. His driver's license was easily readable in a clear plastic sheath.

"Frank said you were here this morning," Sykora told me.

It wasn't a question, so I didn't reply. Instead, I asked, "Do you have your cell phone?"

"Yeah." Sykora reached into his pocket.

I set my flashlight on the ground next to the binoculars and took Sykora's phone. I held it with one hand, punching the numbers on the keypad with my thumb by the light of Sykora's flash, while holding Danny's wallet with the other. When Bobby Dunston didn't answer by the fourth ring, I knew he wasn't going to. Still, I waited, and in the middle of the sixth ring I was rewarded by a voice that said, "St. Paul Police Department, Detective Shipman."

"Jeannie?"

"Yes."

"This is McKenzie."

"They haven't arrested you yet?"

I was looking at Sykora when I said, "No, they haven't arrested me yet." Sykora frowned. "Is Bobby around?"

"Checked out for the evening."

"Maybe you can help me."

"Help you what?"

"I need a favor."

"What do you have in mind?"

"Can you pull up a guy for me on C-JIS, named Fuches, F-U-C-H-E-S, first names Daniel James?"

"You know, McKenzie, the St. Paul Police Department frowns on accessing the state's Criminal Justice Information Systems computer for personal use."

"Help me out, Jean."

There was a long pause while Jeannie considered my request. She said, "You know what I like about you, McKenzie? You're a quid pro quo kinda guy."

"I am?"

"Someone does you a favor and you're always sure to return it."

"I don't suppose you're familiar with the maxim 'A good deed is its own reward?"

"I must've missed that one."

I gave it a few moments' thought, then said, "If I'm not mistaken, you're a Sheryl Crow fan."

"Yes, I am."

"I hear she's coming to the Xcel Center in St. Paul next month."

"She is. Concert's already sold out."

"I can get you tickets."

"You can?"

"Main floor center."

"How?"

"I know a guy."

"Of course you do. Two tickets?"

"Absolutely."

"And perhaps you'll join me?"

I hesitated. "Perhaps I will."

"Hang on. I need to switch to a different phone."

Jeannie put me on hold. Nearly two minutes passed in silence while I waited. I was thinking, it wouldn't kill me if I took out Bobby's "young, beautiful, smart-as-hell" partner, but Nina might. Best to not tell her. I wasn't sure exactly what our relationship was, but I was going back to my life, and lately she had been one of the better parts of it. Best to keep it from Bobby, too. A moment later, Jeannie was back on the line.

"Let's see—Daniel James Fuches. Bunch of DWIs, a few dis cons, questioned for two burglaries and one armed robbery but nothing came of it, charges filed on a first-degree sexual assault, then dropped when the victim refused to testify—what do you need? Anything specific?"

"I'm looking for any kind of reference to a guy named Bruce or Brucie."

"Bruce or Brucie . . . Bruce David Fuches, arrested and charged along with Daniel on the sexual assault."

"They're brothers?" Even as I said it, I didn't believe it. Danny and Brucie looked so unlike each other.

"Brothers, cousins, uncles, I don't know."

"Let's take a look at him."

Jeannie sighed like she had plans and I was keeping her from them. Thirty seconds later she said, "Looking, looking . . . Here we go. Bruce David Fuches. A couple of burglaries, both dismissed, armed robbery dismissed, first-degree sexual assault, same deal as Daniel . . . one, two . . . five A&B's, four dismissed, but finally with the fifth he took a six-month jolt, year probation. These guys, both of 'em, a couple of low-level habituals."

"Gangster wannabes."

"Huh?"

"Never mind. Do you have an address?"

"Same as Daniel's."

"Thank you, Jean."

"I'll be looking forward to the concert."

"Me, too."

I deactivated the cell phone and handed it back to Sykora.

He smiled.

I said, "Shut up."

The address was in Norwood Young America. It was only about five miles from where Mr. Mosley had lived, but I didn't know that part of the area, and it took me a while to find it. Sykora didn't mention Danny during the drive. I thought that was good of him.

Bruce Fuches lived in a small clapboard house with worn shingles and white paint peeling from the clapboard. Even in the dark I could tell that the yard needed work. Sykora and I walked up the front walk. His Glock was out and resting on his thigh. My gun was still parked between my belt and the small of my back, but my sports coat hung open. When we reached the door, Sykora slid to the side, out of sight. I knocked. A light went on and the door opened.

"Yeah," a woman said.

She swung her head, and long black hair swept from one shoulder to the other. She was wearing blue jeans and a white T-shirt cut off just above the navel. There wasn't much muscle tone under the shirt. I was guessing the beer can she held in her hand had something to do with it.

"I'm looking for Bruce Fuches," I said.

"I ain't him."

I looked her over from top to bottom and smiled what I hoped was a charming smile. "I can see that," I said.

She smiled back, then wobbled a bit as if it had taken great effort. She placed a hand on the door to steady herself.

"You're a lot cuter than most of his friends," she said.

"So are you," I said, although when you think about it, it wasn't much of a compliment.

"I'm Wanda," she said.

"Hi, Wanda." She didn't ask for my name and I didn't give it.

"What do you want with Brucie?"

"I have some business with him and Danny."

"The Bobbsey Twins," she said. "Gonna make it big any day now. Least what they say like *every* day now. Couple a' losers, you askin' me. Hey, you wanna come in?"

She turned in the door frame to let me pass. Sykora concealed his gun behind his back and stepped across the threshold. Wanda saw him for the first time.

"There's two of you," she said, then smiled a smile that shaded off into a leer. " 'At's okay. I can do two of you."

The living room was small. A table and two chairs were set in front of the window overlooking the street, and a battered sofa was shoved against the wall opposite them. All the furniture was arranged so that it had a clear view of a TV set on a metal stand with hard plastic wheels. The TV was on and tuned to a reality program in which dozens of beautiful women were chasing a homely man they thought was rich—if you call that reality.

"Is Bruce home?"

"Naw. Think if Brucie was home I'd be . . . Listen, Brucie, he and Danny ain't coming back. Least not tonight. We'd be all alone. So whaddaya think? A threesome?"

"I like the sound of that," I said, feeling suddenly like the pizza delivery guy in a bad porno flick.

"Wha' 'bout you?" she asked Sykora.

"Yum."

"Well, then . . ."

"Wouldn't Bruce be upset?" I asked.

"You don't look like you'd be 'fraid of Brucie."

Little did she know.

"Lookit, he don't mean nothing to me no more," she said. "This place." Wanda waved at the room with her beer can. "He said he was gonna take care of me, only it's been the other way 'round. My alimony checks and my tips that's payin' for all this. Him and that wimpy brother of his, they don't do nothin' 'cept say how they gonna be big in the Mafia. The Mafia! You gotta be kiddin'."

"I appreciate that, Wanda. But I really have to find Bruce."

"Why?"

"Business, like I said. With him and Danny and Frank."

"Fat Frank," she said. "There's a piece of work. Think I offer to Frank he'd turn me down? C'mon, you guys gonna fuck me or what?"

"I'm just saying right now might not be the best time."

Sykora moved enough to catch Wanda's eye.

"You said Bruce wouldn't be back tonight. Where is he?"

There was an edge to his voice that made Wanda take a step backward. She glanced down at his hand, and her eyes grew wide. He was tapping his thigh with the barrel of the Glock.

"He's, ahh . . . he's . . ."

"Wanda," I said. "Hey, Wanda."

She tore her gaze from the gun and met my eyes. I smiled, going for reassuring this time, hoping Sykora hadn't panicked her into silence.

"I'm thinking, we take care of our business with Bruce, maybe we could come back later."

Wanda said, "Him and Danny, they got this place on Whitefish Lake they inherited from an uncle or somethin'. Up near Mille Lacs."

Sykora said, "Where?"

Wanda gave him an address and directions. Sykora put his gun away and asked her to repeat it. She did, and he wrote it all down in a spiral notebook.

"You're cops," she said. Her smile returned. "Well, why didn't you say so?"

"When did you last see Bruce?" Sykora asked.

"Are you gonna arrest him? Him and Danny? Cuz that's cool far as I'm concerned. Kinda solve some problems for me, you know."

"When did you last see Bruce?" Sykora asked again.

" 'Round noon today. Frank called and off he went," she said. "He woulda went with Frank and Danny early this morning, only Brucie, he had to meet with his probation officer."

"Have you heard from him since?"

"No."

"Then how do you know Bruce is at the cabin?"

"He said he was goin' there. Him and Frank, they talked on the phone for like, I don't know, a half hour, and then Brucie, he looked like he was really pissed at someone, he said he was gonna stay the night at the cabin and to not wait up. Like I'm gonna wait up for him. So, you know, it's like I said before, we're all alone."

"Maybe we should call him, let him know we're coming," I said.

"They ain't got a phone," Wanda said, which is exactly

what I wanted to hear. "They make calls, they go to this place what's just down the road."

Sykora turned and headed back to the car.

"Thanks, Wanda," I said.

"Hey, you," she said. She took a step toward me and lowered her voice. "When you come back later, don't bring him."

We were back inside the Neon, working our way to the freeway.

Sykora said, "So are you going back?"

"No, I'm not."

He smirked as if he didn't believe me, and I had to resist the urge to pop him one.

We were on Highway 212 heading north to the Twin Cities when Sykora said, "I'm still trying to figure it out."

"What do you mean?"

"Why you're here."

"I told you. I'm here for Pen."

"No, I mean, from the very beginning. Most people would have let it go, what happened to your friends. Most people would have let the police handle it."

"Probably I would have, too. Except the fix was in."

Sykora hesitated for a moment, like he was selecting his words carefully. He said, "Sometimes you need to make choices. Sometimes you need to let one guy go in order to catch a worse guy."

"Is that how you rationalize it?"

"There are a lot of murderers walking around free."

"None that killed any of my friends."

"Your friends are special?"

"Every damn one."

His mouth worked as if there was something he wanted to tell me, but apparently he decided to leave it unsaid. Just as well. Time was getting away from us. It was past 9:30. Even without traffic, from the wrong side of the Twin Cities it would take us nearly three hours to get to Whitefish Lake.

I told Sykora, "Maybe now's a good time to start talking about what we're going to do."

"I guess that depends on what we find when we get to Brucie's cabin."

"Now that we know where they are, we should arrange for backup."

"Backup?"

"From a much maligned organization called the FBI."

"Not a chance."

"Why not? Kidnapping is a federal offense."

Sykora turned in his seat and looked at me. "No," he said. At that same instant we passed under a light. I caught only a glimpse of his eyes, but it told me everything I needed to know. Sykora was going to kill Frank, and he didn't want anyone or anything getting in the way. Including me.

This was my cue to tell him something about revenge. Maybe repeat what the Reverend Winfield had told me. But seriously, who was I to talk?

Mille Lacs was probably the most important lake in Minnesota if not the biggest. Near the center of the state, it had long been a focal point in discussions ranging from Native American treaty rights to sportsman's rights to conservation to property taxes to the best place to catch walleye. In the winter, it would take you over an hour to drive across its ice. In the summer, you can't see where the lake ends and the sky begins. At night, it looks like it's full of stars.

Whitefish Lake—not to be confused with Upper Whitefish Lake, or Lower Whitefish Lake, or Little Whitefish Lake, or the other five Whitefish lakes in Minnesota—was located on the west side of Mille Lacs, near Wigwam Bay, so close that at one time it had probably been part of the larger lake. Even now it was pretty good size, about seven hundred acres. A former chairman of the Joint Chiefs of Staff had a place there. But while I knew where the lake was—I pass it when I drive to my own place up north—I didn't know my way around it, and Wanda's directions proved less than precise. Eventually we began searching for someone who might give us a more accurate course to follow. Stopping for directions isn't something I normally do, but we were on the clock. It was already 12:30.

The lights were still blazing at Big Oak Resort & Cafe, so we stopped there. It turned out to be one of those ma-and-pa operations that made most of its money between Memorial Day and Labor Day renting cabins and boats, selling bait and tackle, and serving food and drinks from a weathered lodge that looked like it had been standing since the Great Sioux Uprising. But that was the outside. Inside was new wood—floors, walls, tables, bar—all covered with a thick shellac that reflected light, making the room as bright as an operating theater. On the wall was a large poster featuring the names and profiles of all the fish catchable in Whitefish Lake—walleye, northern pike, largemouth bass, rock bass, crappies, sunfish, bowfin, bullhead, perch, shiners, suckers. Next to it was a large map of the lake and surrounding area. Sykora made a beeline for it.

"Gentlemen, you're just in time for last call," a woman said from behind the pristine bar. If she wondered what two guys wearing sports jackets were doing in a fishing resort after midnight, she didn't let on.

"Couple of Leinies," I told her.

She was a slightly overweight woman of about thirty with large brown eyes and reddish-brown hair with bangs, wearing jeans and a Minnesota Vikings sweatshirt. Her smile was infectious, and she reminded me of the kids working the booths on the first day of the Minnesota State Fair, all excited and enthusiastic. I wondered how she'd feel at the end of the season.

I mentioned, as I maneuvered around tables to the stick, that we seemed to be her only customers.

"It's a late Monday evening in May," she told me. "Weekends have been terrific since the fishing opener, and business will get even better next weekend when they open the bass season. But we don't do much in the middle of the week until after the schools let out and people start taking vacations."

Made sense to me. I took a long pull of the beer.

"Ask her," Sykora called from the map.

"Ask what?" said the bartender.

"We're looking for the cabin of a couple of guys we know on Whitefish." I attempted to sound more casual about it than Sykora did. "Only the directions they gave us aren't the best. We're wondering if you can help us out."

"Sure. Who are you talking about?"

"Danny and Bruce Fuches."

"Oh, them." The smile flickered on her face like a lightbulb that wasn't sure if it was going to burn out.

"Have you seen them around?" I asked.

"They were in earlier, Bruce and some fat guy thinks he's clever, kept insulting my resort."

"What does he have against this place?" I asked. "This place is great."

The bartender's smile returned to full wattage.

"Not just here. Minnesota in general."

"Jerk," I said and drank more beer.

"He wanted to use the phone, then got all bent outta shape because he thought I was listening to his conversation. I mean, who cares?"

"Some people's children," I said.

Sykora stood next to the wall map. He looked amped as if he wanted to run across the room, leap over the bar, and shake the woman by her shoulders. Instead, he asked in a calm voice, "Do you know where we can find them?"

"Well, here," the bartender said. She rounded the bar and walked to where Sykora was standing. She stood in front of the map, biting her lower lip while she studied it, then raised a long, delicate finger and pointed at a red square.

"That's us," she said. "Here." She moved the finger about two inches to the left. "This is the Fuches's cabin, at the very end of Little Whitefish Lake Road. Used to belong to old man Sevier. Now, he was a sweetheart."

"How do we get there?" Sykora asked.

"All this between us and them, where Fuches is, all this is steep hills and rocks. So what you need to do, you need to swing way around here"—using her finger as a pointer, the bartender traced a convoluted series of roads—"to here and then drive across to here. This is Little Whitefish Lake Road, where the cabin is. But you want to be careful you don't take Whitefish Lake Road by mistake, because that'll take you to way the heck over here."

Sykora looked like he was already lost.

"What's this?" I traced a thin line that extended directly from the resort to a spot on Little Whitefish Lake Road just short of the Fuches's cabin.

"That's a footpath, a trail."

"Will the path take us to the Fuches's cabin?" I asked.

"Uh-huh. If you don't mind the walk. See, what a lot of people do, instead of driving out of their way to get here, to get to my place—I have a very nice dinner menu—what they'll do, they'll take this trail through the steep hills and rocks and some swamp, too. It's a nice walk. Couple times a year, we go over, cut down the growth, keep it nice."

"We can walk there from here?" Sykora said.

"Sure. It's about, I don't know, a little over a half mile. It's dark out, but just stay on the trail and you'll be all right."

"Mind if we leave our car in your lot?" I asked.

"No problem."

* * *

We walked single file down the narrow path. We had flashlights but didn't dare use them, instead relying on the modest amount of moonlight that managed to penetrate the overcast sky. It didn't show us much, but it was enough to keep us from straying off into the thick brush that hugged both sides of the trail.

"It's quiet," Sykora whispered. I waited for him to add, "Too quiet," but he didn't, and I started thinking, a guy born and raised in New York City, this must be traumatic for him, a world without noise or lights. There were no sirens, no traffic, no radios or TV, no people and the sounds they make, no dogs barking in the distance—even the crickets hadn't grown large enough yet to make a racket. And although it worked to our advantage, suddenly I was sorry the night sky was hidden by clouds. Otherwise Sykora would really have had something to see. As it was, the only light visible appeared just as we reached the mouth of the path. It was about 150 yards in front of us and shone through the windows of a small cabin.

I had brought my binoculars and used them now to give the cabin a hard look. It was old and it was small, no more than twenty feet by twenty feet with a wooden facade badly in need of paint and a tattered shingle roof. The cabin was built on cinder blocks on the side of a hill. The blocks in the back were stacked two high; in the front there were five. The front door and a single window faced Whitefish Lake, with the road cutting between the cabin and the shoreline. There was a wooden staircase without a railing leading to the front door, which was only wide enough for one person. Despite the chill in the air, the interior door was open; light streamed through the outer screen door. There was a second window in the side of the cabin facing us. I studied the windows and door carefully.

Sykora squatted next to me.

"What do you see?" he whispered.

"Nothing. Wait . . ."

A large man suddenly appeared in the second window. He rubbed his face vigorously, stretched, moved forward out of sight. I swung the binoculars to the front window. He appeared there, slowly moved to the front door, and leaned against it, looking out.

"Frank?" Sykora asked.

"Yes."

Sykora moved toward the light. I grabbed his arm and pulled him back.

"Where are you going?"

"Pen's in there."

"So are guys with guns. Give it a minute."

"What for?"

"I don't see Brucie."

Sykora shook my hand free, but I grabbed his arm again.

"Wait."

Sykora stared at the cabin for a moment, then edged slowly back next to me.

"I'll go through the front door. You cover me from the window."

"Don't be foolish," I told him. "Look at the cabin. Look at how it's elevated. Standing on the hill, I won't be able to see above the windowsill, much less give you cover. Plus, we don't know where your wife is yet—will she be in the line of fire? And we don't know where Brucie is."

"He's in the cabin. Where else would he be?"

"Watching the road? Waiting in the dark to shoot us?"

"Frank isn't smart enough for that."

"Who says?"

"Listen. Are you listening?" Sykora was speaking with the intensity of a computer salesman hawking the latest hardware. "Frank won't be expecting us. I know this guy. The most vulnerable mark is the one who's been to the circus before. He figures he has experience, he figures he's too smart to get clipped. That's Frank."

"Frank? Or us?"

"Are you afraid, McKenzie?"

"You bet your ass I am."

"I'm not."

"Then you're an idiot. With all my misgivings about the FBI, I never thought they hired idiots."

"Pen's in there," he said again.

"Probably. And for her sake, let's get this right. C'mon. We don't need to rush this. We can take our time. Watch and wait. See what moves."

"No."

"Yes. Patience, man. It's a virtue."

"Who told you that?"

"Mr. Mosley."

"Fine," Sykora said, but I knew he wasn't fine.

Frank moved away from the door and retraced his steps past the front window and the side window before disappearing again from view. I trained the binoculars on the outside of the cabin and spent long, silent minutes sweeping the yard, hoping to see a shadow move. None did. A tiny hole opened in the clouds, allowing the full moon to light up the yard like a flare. I saw no one. Then the hole closed, and once again the cabin was seized in darkness.

I whispered, "There's a stand of trees on the right. I'm going to move over there, see if I can get a better view of the cabin and the yard. Wait here."

"Do you have your gun?" Sykora asked. He was gripping his own Glock with both hands.

I slipped the Beretta out of my holster, showed it to him.

"Good," he said. "Cover me."

"Wait."

But Sykora was done with waiting. He was on his feet sprinting toward the entrance to the cabin. I muttered a few obscenities and followed him.

Sykora ran quickly and didn't halt until he hit the side of the cabin next to the door with his shoulder. I heard the thud twenty feet away. So did Frank. He popped to his feet. I had been right about the window—I could see only his head and the top of his shoulders. He was looking toward the door.

Sykora flung open the door and charged through it.

Frank's shoulders hunched upward and his head slid to the side as if he were sighting down a rifle.

My shriek was loud and guttural, a variation on the word "no."

Frank glanced my way just as I fired onetwothreefourfivesix rounds at him through the cabin wall. I saw his head spin, and then he dropped from sight.

I dashed to the front steps, up the steps, and through the door, my Beretta leading the way. The living room was cramped with ancient furniture, and fishing gear hung from nails hammered into the cheap wood paneling. Frank was lying on his side in the middle of it, clutching his belly with one hand and reaching for a sawed-off shotgun with the other. Sykora was kneeling on the floor in the far corner in front of Pen. He had set his Glock on a sofa and was hugging his wife. She was naked, her wrists and ankles bound to a wooden chair with duct tape.

Frank heaved himself forward a half inch and tried again for the sawed-off. I fell to my knees next to him, grabbed the barrel of the gun, and slid it across the floor to the screen door. It hit the door and wedged it open half a foot. I pivoted on my knees, the Beretta in front of me, searching for Brucie. He wasn't there.

Frank looked at me like he was trying to remember my name.

"Fuckin' McKenzie," he said.

In the corner Sykora pressed his forehead against Pen's and chanted her name. Her eyes were red. There was a slight bruise behind her left eye, and the skin around the tape was red and raw. The severe light from the poorly shaded lamp on the table next to her caught her face, and for a moment I could see what she would look like when she was much older—still beautiful, with the kind of aristocratic grace that you gain only from conquering extreme adversity.

Pen said, "I'm okay, I'm okay. He didn't hurt me—yet."

The "yet" hung in the air like a threat.

I pointed the Beretta at Frank's face.

Frank said, "I never touched her. Never laid a finger on her."

"Where are her clothes?" I asked.

"Hey, now. There's no harm in lookin', is there?" He grinned like he couldn't help himself.

I studied his face. There was an intelligence there, yet at the same time, he seemed a couple of steps removed from what you'd call normal.

I took up the slack on the trigger.

Frank's eyes were wide, as if he were suddenly afraid to close them. His expression was unidentifiable. He said, "Don't, now. Don't. Don't shoot me. You ain't got any reason to shoot me. Girl's okay. You can see. She's right there."

I glanced toward Pen. Sykora had freed one hand and was working on the other.

"Mr. Mosley," I said.

"You mean the nigger? That's what all this is about, ain't it, McKenzie? That's why you're fuckin' up my life. The nigger. Only I had nothin' to do with him. I keep sayin' so, but no one fuckin' believes me." I remembered that he had said that to Sykora over the phone when he *wasn't* arguing for his life. "The lawyer's wife? That wasn't me, either. That was—you can't get no fucking good help in Minnesota, I'm tellin' ya. I told 'em just muss her up. But the boys, it was Danny and Brucie gettin' outta hand."

Brucie.

Again I pivoted on my knees.

"Where is Bruce?"

"You can't shoot me," Frank said.

Sure I can, I thought but didn't say. First things first. I looked down at him.

"Where's Bruce?"

He shrugged as if he had never heard the name before.

"Don't make me ask again," I told him.

Frank smiled. Smiled the same way Danny had smiled at the motel in Chanhassen. One of those smart-ass grins you see when a loudmouth poker player fills a straight flush with the last draw. And I knew. Knew even before I felt the barrel of the sawed-off brush the back of my neck.

"McKenzie," Bruce said, making my name sound like an obscenity.

Sonuvabitch!

"Gotcha," said Frank.

In the corner, Sykora lunged for his Glock.

"Don't!" Frank shouted. He added, "Don't do anything stupid," in a lower voice when Sykora held himself up. "Don't want the little lady hurt now, do we, Fed?"

Sykora looked at the Glock, his wife, back at the Glock. He raised his hands. Pen dropped her one free hand over her lap.

I glared at Sykora. *This is your fault,* my mind screamed. *The first two times were my fault, but this one is yours. Dammit. You just couldn't wait, could you?*

Frank worked himself into a sitting position.

"Okay," he said.

He made a gimme motion with his hand. I handed

him the Beretta. He glanced at it, handed it off to Bruce. Bruce slipped the gun into his pocket.

"You," he said, looking at Sykora. "On your knees. Put the Glock on the floor. Slide it under the couch." Sykora did what he was told, then positioned himself so that he was kneeling directly between Pen and Brucie, shielding her naked body.

"You," Frank said to me. "You just stay there on your knees."

Frank pushed his great bulk up and off the floor with terrific effort. I suspected it would have been hard going even if he didn't have a hole in his side. He crossed the room and sat in an overstuffed chair. I turned on my knees to face him. Sykora and Pen were now on my right. They would have had to run over me to get to the door located on my left and slightly behind me. Only it didn't make much difference. Brucie moved to Frank's side. He now had a clear line of fire at all of us, and with the sawed-off, accuracy wasn't an issue. No one was going anywhere.

Frank picked at his wound.

"That hurts," he said.

The cabin wall and his multiple layers of fat had reduced the impact of the 9mm slug. Instead of killing him, it had merely given him a bellyache. I couldn't believe I had only hit him once out of six tries. I needed practice.

"I should have aimed higher," I told him.

Brucie said, "He thinks he's funny."

"I noticed that," said Frank.

"Let me kill him, Mr. Russo."

"In a minute."

Bruce changed his grip on the sawed-off. He pointed it at my head with one hand. The other hand he filled with the seven-inch stainless steel combat knife he had threatened me with before.

"I wanna cut 'im. Make 'im cry like a little girl for what he did to Danny."

"Yeah, yeah, yeah. In a minute," Frank insisted.

Brucie smiled.

I adjusted my position.

"Stop," he said. "Put your hands behind your back."

I did. Then I sank backward, sitting on my heels. Because of the angle, my body now blocked Brucie's view. He couldn't see my hands slowly working my pant leg up, reaching for the .25 Iver Johnson that was taped to my ankle.

Frank poked his wound some more. There was surprisingly little blood. What there was he licked off his fingers with his tongue.

"Whaddaya think, Penny? You want some?"

Pen gave him no sign of anything but her anger.

He winked at her.

"You know what? This is really going to work out nice. Much better than I thought. Right, Bruce?"

"Sure, Mr. Russo."

"Uh-huh." He pointed at Sykora. "I knew you'd be coming. A pretty wife like yours, you didn't think I knew you'd be coming? True, I didn't think you'd be bringing McKenzie. But c'mon. Who woulda thunk that?"

"Let Pen go," Sykora said.

"I will, I will," said Frank. "I said I would. How come

no one ever believes me when I tell them shit?" Frank pointed again at Sykora. "I don't suppose you brought my money with ya? No? I didn't think so. But that's okay. Doesn't matter. Nothin's changed. The deal's the same. Tomorrow you're gonna go get it for me. Just like I said before. Do that. Get the money, bring it back here, and you and the missus get away alive. Whaddaya say?"

"Just like that," Sykora said. "I give you the money and Pen and I walk away?"

"Sure. Why not? I don't hold a grudge."

"What about McKenzie?"

"Fuck do you care as long as you get what you want?"

Everyone was looking at me now.

Frank grinned.

Pen said, "Jake?"

"Jake?" said Frank. "He tell you his name was Jake?"

"Yes," said Pen.

"Then he's a liar. Cuz he ain't Jake. This here is McKenzie. McKenzie who shot me. McKenzie who's been causing me nothin' but trouble since I got to this lousy neck of the woods. Me, who ain't never done nothin' to him. Nothin' at all. If I had, I'd say so."

"Let me cut 'im," Bruce said.

"Why not?" said Frank.

My father was a hunter. He tried to instill in me a hunter's patience. It was a life lesson, he said, learning not to rush, learning how to wait for your shot. It was a lesson I had learned well. But it was now or never. I threw a look at Sykora. A second's diversion. It was all I asked.

Bruce stepped forward. He raised his combat knife high in the air, prepared to slash down on me.

"Brucie," Sykora shouted and dove under the sofa for the Glock.

Bruce glanced at Sykora, calculated how long it would take for Sykora to fish the gun out, quickly turned to face me.

I rolled onto my shoulder and grabbed the butt of the .25.

If he had fired the shotgun at that moment, I would have been killed. Instead, he brought the knife down in a long arc, slicing nothing but air. Brucie didn't seem to mind that he missed. He was smiling the same damn smile he gave me in the parking lot of the motel in Chanhassen.

I yanked the gun free. Brought it up.

A half dozen shots—they sounded like howitzers in the small room. Only they weren't my shots, I never fired.

A half dozen bullets slammed into Brucie, stitching him from his hip all the way to his head. Blood and bone and brain sprayed Frank and the back wall. Bruce fell against Frank's chair as if someone had shoved him there, spun off, hit the wall behind the chair, and sunk to the floor.

Frank screamed and wiped at the blood and bone and brain.

Pen turned her head away, her hand clamped over her mouth.

I was lying on my side on the floor. Sykora was on his stomach. We both angled our heads toward the door.

Nick Horvath stood there with an Israeli-made 9 mm Uzi submachine gun in his hands.

He said, "I don't want any trouble with you two. Drop your guns, slide them away."

From the look of the magazine, I figured Horvath had about thirty-four shots left. I set the Iver Johnson on the floor and slid it across to him. A moment later, Sykora followed suit with his Glock.

Horvath smiled. He nodded at Pen and said, "How you doin', sweetie?"

"I've been better," said Pen evenly. The pain in her eyes hadn't reached her voice yet.

Horvath glared at Frank. "Did fat boy here hurt you?"

"A little bit. Not a lot."

"I'm terribly sorry about all this."

"It's not your fault."

"In a way it is. I could've stopped Frank in New York, but he slipped away from me."

"Butterfingers."

Horvath smiled at Pen like he was proud of her. Truth be told, so was I. She was handling herself extremely well. A brave front.

Sykora asked Pen, "Do you know this man?"

Pen said, "He's our neighbor. Nick Horvath."

The one who couldn't hit the broad side of a Ford truck with a baseball bat, I remembered.

"Ishmael," I said.

"I've been called worse."

"I understand now," I told Horvath. "The so-called kidnapping attempt outside Pen's trailer. You arranged that to gain Pen's trust."

"Yeah. Looks like it worked out better for you, though, huh?"

"You're the one who bugged her trailer."

"Yes."

"And you're the one who warned Granata that the FBI was going to hit his cigarettes."

"Uh-huh."

"I thought it was the gay guys down the road."

"I heard they broke up," Horvath said.

"Tell me something. If you knew the FBI had the quarry staked out, why send a truck at all? Even an empty one?"

Sykora answered the question for him.

"Granata wanted to send a message. He didn't want us to think the shipment was jacked or diverted. He wanted us to know that he knew that we knew all about it."

"It was a chance to say, nyah, nyah, nyah, nyah, nyah," Horvath said, and I flashed on what Sykora had told me earlier—*it was a game, cops and robbers.*

"You'll never get away with it," Sykora said.

"Oh, shut up. Never get away . . . You know what?" Nick pointed the Uzi at Sykora. "I'm not talking to you. In fact, I'm not talking to either of you. Puttin' Pen in danger. What a couple of schmucks."

"You followed us," I told him. "You heard our plans on the bug in the trailer and you followed us."

"Yes, I did. Shut up, McKenzie."

Horvath pointed the Uzi at Frank.

"Get up, fat boy."

Frank looked to be in shock, his face and clothes splattered with pieces of Brucie.

"C'mon, Russo. You want to die in fuckin' Minnesota?"

Frank slowly struggled to his feet and shuffled toward Horvath like an old man.

"Maybe we can work something out," he said.

"You keep thinkin' that, Frank," Horvath told him.

Nick spun the fat man around, then pushed him toward the door. Before Frank stepped through it, Horvath yanked his arm, halting him. He turned back toward us.

"Enough is enough, huh, guys," he said. "Enough bullshit over this fat fuck." He settled the muzzle of the Uzi on me. "When Little Al takes care of Frank, he'll take care of 'im for your people, too. And you." Nick swung the Uzi on Sykora. "You're just gonna have to find another way to become a fuckin' hero. Personally, I suggest you try doin' your job."

Horvath sighed like he was suddenly tired.

"I want fifteen minutes. Fifteen-minute head start. That's it. Whaddaya say?"

"Yes," said Pen. Her calm voice filled the room as completely as soft sunlight. "A fifteen-minute head start. I promise."

"Thank you, sweetie."

"Thank you, Nick."

"You take care."

"And you."

Horvath nodded. He pointed the gun at Sykora. "She's way too good for you. You don't deserve her."

He swung the Uzi on me.

"Neither do you."

Or you, I almost said but didn't.

A moment later, he was gone. I listened as Frank huffed and puffed into the darkness. When I couldn't hear him anymore, I came off my knees. I found my Beretta in Brucie's pocket and the Iver Johnson against the wall. I looked toward the door.

Pen said, "I promised him fifteen minutes."

So she did.

I moved through the cabin, trying as best I could to avoid Brucie's corpse, and found a bedroom. I pulled a blanket off the bed and went back into the living room. Sykora was removing the last of the duct tape from Pen's wrists and ankles.

"I'll make this up to you," he said. "I'll take care of this."

I remember saying pretty much the same thing to Sweet Swinging Billy Tillman. What a load of b.s.

I draped the blanket around Pen's naked shoulders.

"Thank you," Pen said.

"Give me your cell phone," I told Sykora.

He handed it to me.

"Fifteen minutes," Pen repeated.

Her eyes were red with tears that hadn't fallen, yet her voice still seemed unaffected, and I wondered if somehow she would manage to get a song out of all this.

I sat and waited.

Pen said, "Your real name is McKenzie?"

"Yes."

"Not Jake?"

"No."

"I liked Jake," she said.

You didn't know him the way I did, I thought.

A moment later, Pen rested her fingers on my wrist and I received the same unexpected jolt of electricity that I felt at the pool in Hilltop.

She said, "I forgive you, McKenzie."

I didn't realize how much I needed forgiveness until she gave it to me.

"Thank you," I told her.

Fifteen minutes later, I punched 911 into the keypad of Sykora's cell.

"Operator, give me the FBI."

At last, Pen began to weep, her husband's arms wrapped tightly around her.

Chapter Twelve

Give him credit, Sykora didn't try to explain or defend himself. He confessed to everything he had done and why he had done it. He even put in a good word for me. Lord knows I needed it. The fact that Pen sat next to him wrapped in the ratty old blanket seemed to make a difference to the hardened federal agents who filled the tiny cabin.

Still, neither the AIC of the Minneapolis field office nor a Justice Department attorney he had dragged to Whitefish Lake was pleased with me. The attorney spent a good deal of time pacing in front of my chair, listing all the federal and state crimes he could charge me with. I interrupted him after about a half dozen and reminded him of the recordings I had made of Sykora's phone conversations. That only made him angrier.

Finally he said, "I'm letting you go, McKenzie, but not because of the lousy tapes."

"Why, then?"

"Because if I charged you then we'd all be sonsuvbitches."

After I was released I returned to the Hilltop Motel and cleared out Jake Greene's clothes and surveillance equipment. I paid all of his bills with cash, including the rental on his car, and destroyed his credit cards, driver's license, and other ID. With any luck, he'd never know how badly I used him.

I retrieved my Jeep Cherokee from an impound lot—for about 5 percent of its original sticker price—and drove along Mississippi River Boulevard in St. Paul. I stopped under the railroad bridge near the Shriners Hospital. There was a catwalk under the bridge. I climbed out on it as far as my acrophobia would allow and dumped the gun I had used to kill Danny. I watched it splash and disappear under the water. Then I dumped all the copies of the tapes I had made of Sykora's and Frank's conversations. I would have liked to keep a copy of the song Pen had written, but the deal I had made with Harry took precedence.

Afterward I drove home. But I stayed there only long enough to shower, shave, dress, and arm myself with the 9 mm Beretta I kept in my basement safe before driving off in my Jeep.

There was still Mr. Mosley's killer to deal with.

The lawn around Mr. Mosley's house was freshly cut, and the hedges had been trimmed. I wondered if some parishioners from King of Kings had come over and tidied up the place. I parked my SUV and approached the front door.

I knocked. There was no answer. I held the latch down and pushed against the door. It swung open.

"Mr. Hernandez?"

I walked inside. The house was neater than I had ever seen it, neater even than when Agatha was keeping it. Someone had given the place a serious spring cleaning.

"Mr. Hernandez?" I called again.

No reply.

I stood at the base of the staircase and shouted upstairs.

"Lorenzo?"

Still nothing.

The kitchen was just as orderly as the rest of the house. Dishes washed and put away. Table and counter wiped. The floor where Mr. Mosley fell scrubbed clean of blood. Everything was in its place, including the ancient coffee percolator.

I went through the back door, the screen bouncing against the frame behind me. There was no one in the yard. I walked past the hives, ignoring—for the first time—the hundreds of bees that swarmed around me. I made my way to the bee barn where Mr. Mosley had kept the centrifuge that he used to extract honey from its comb, the pasteurizing machine that heats the raw honey to 155 degrees to kill bacteria, and his bottling operation. The huge door was open. Hernandez was inside. He was humming to himself as he polished the extractor's massive 16-gauge stainless steel drum. It was bright enough to bounce my reflection back at me.

I glanced around the barn. Like Mr. Mosley's house,

it was immaculate. Even the cinder-block walls and concrete floor looked as if they had been scrubbed.

"You've been working hard," I said.

My voice startled Hernandez. He dropped his rag and took two steps backward. He smiled slightly when he recognized me.

"McKenzie," he said.

I nodded at him and repeated, "You've been working hard."

Hernandez glanced around him. Pride shone in his face.

"I want to keep it nice," he said. "For Mr. Mosley."

"Sure."

Hernandez came toward me, his hand outstretched. I shook it. It was like shaking a frozen pork chop. Yet, while his hand was cold, his face suddenly seemed flushed. Beads of perspiration appeared on his forehead and upper lip.

"Good to see ju," he said, his accent sounding thicker than usual.

"Good to be seen."

Hernandez brought forth his handkerchief, unfolded it, blew his nose one nostril at a time, refolded the handkerchief, and returned it to his pocket.

"Wha' can I do for ju?" he asked.

"Let's talk."

"Talk? Okay." He pronounced the word "ho-kay."

He retrieved his rag from the spotless floor and moved to the counter Mr. Mosley had built against the wall of the barn. There were many tools neatly arranged on the countertop and hanging from nails in the wall—

frames, frame lifters and scrapers, bee brushes, uncapping trays and knives, tap strainers, smoker bellows, hive straps, and gloves. Several drawers had been built into the counter. Hernandez set down the rag and reached for one, hesitated, and left it unopened.

"Ju want coffee?" he asked.

"I could do with a cup."

"In the kitchen. I be wit' ju in a moment."

I left the bee barn and made my way back to the house. Once inside, I slipped the Beretta out from under my jacket and activated it. I sat at the kitchen table, balancing the nine on my lap. My hands were both flat on the table when Hernandez entered the room. He was carrying a small white and blue towel. The towel was stained and dirty, but it was neatly folded. Hernandez set the towel carefully on the counter next to the sink.

"Mr. Mosley always liked coffee black," Hernandez said. "Ju like it black, too?"

"Yes."

Hernandez opened a cabinet and pulled out two mugs. While his back was turned I adjusted the gun in my lap.

Hernandez poured coffee into the mugs. "Did ju find Mr. Mosley's killer?" he asked.

"Yes."

"Wha' 'appen to 'im?"

"I haven't decided yet."

Hernandez slid the mug across the table. I made sure he saw me reach for it with both hands.

"Wha' ju mean?" he asked.

"You know what I mean."

"I don't."

"Don't you?"

He shook his head.

"I had a suspect. I believe he's innocent, now—innocent of Mr. Mosley's murder, anyway."

"How ju know?"

"This guy—if he had done it, he would have said so. He's that kind of guy. Anyway, after he was eliminated, it was fairly easy to determine who the real killer was."

I leaned back in the chair, letting my right hand fall casually to my lap while slowly turning the mug in circles with my left.

Hernandez moved closer to the towel.

"Three things a cop looks for when a crime is committed—motive, opportunity, and means. You revealed the motive when you spoke at Mr. Mosley's memorial, when you said that working for Mr. Mosley helped you escape the poverty of Guatemala, that it allowed you to remain in the United States. But he was threatening to take your job away, wasn't he? Did you think if you lost your job you would be deported?"

I watched his brown eyes. I thought he would deny everything, proclaim his innocence, but for some reason he didn't bother.

"Opportunity—that came when you met with Mr. Mosley to discuss your employment situation. There were two mugs on the counter when Mr. Mosley was killed. He was pouring coffee for someone he knew. Someone he trusted enough to turn his back on."

"Ju can't prove anything," Hernandez said. But there was no force to his words.

"That brings us to means." I gestured at the towel with my chin. "I'm betting there's a .22 tucked inside that towel."

Hernandez looked at the towel, then back at me.

"Ju can't prove anything," he repeated, just talking now.

"The .22 proves it."

" 'Ere's no .22."

"Then you have nothing to worry about."

He looked at the towel again, inched toward it. The Beretta was in my hand. I settled it on his chest, aiming through the kitchen table. I had killed a man for a crime he didn't commit. But Danny had committed other crimes. He had raped Susan Tillman, the wife of my friend. He had tried to kill me. I had no regrets. Only I wanted no more of it, so I begged him, "Please . . ."

His hand hovered in midair.

"Don't do it, Lorenzo. Please, don't."

He stopped.

"Give yourself up."

He looked at me for a moment and dropped his hand to his side. He walked over to the back door. I thought he might try to make a run for it, but he just stood there staring at the hives.

Without turning he said, "Ju no cop. Ju can't arrest me. Ju 'ave no authority."

"I know."

"I don't 'ave to say nothin' to ju."

I took a sip of the coffee. It wasn't bad. Not as good as Mr. Mosley's, but better than mine.

I said, "Doesn't it hurt, Lorenzo? Keeping it all inside?"

He lowered his head and sighed. Something went out of him then.

"I loved 'im. Mr. Mosley."

"Why did you kill him?"

"I didn' mean to." Hernandez turned away from the door and walked back into the kitchen, settling near the towel. He had moved slowly, yet I tightened my grip on the Beretta just the same. "Somet'ing 'appen to me. Inside of me. I try to get rid of it, but it don' go 'way. I thought, Mr. Mosley, 'e make it go 'way. But 'e don't."

"You were afraid."

"I cannot go back to Guatemala."

"So you killed him."

"Sí."

I don't know exactly what I felt for Hernandez at that moment, but I didn't hate him. There was no hate left in me, no rage. I had used it all up on Danny and Brucie and Frank. I felt my grip on the Beretta relax.

"Why don't you lock up, Lorenzo."

"Wha' for?"

"I want you to come with me."

"Where?"

"I want you to go to Chaska with me and talk to a cop named Dyke."

"Ju wan' me to confess?"

"Yes."

"No."

"You'll feel better."

"No."

"You said you loved Mr. Mosley, you said you didn't mean to kill him . . ."

He moved closer to the towel.

"We'll tell them that. They'll believe you."

He looked at me. His expression was childlike. "Wha' will 'appen to me?"

"You'll be all right."

"I cannot go to prison."

"It's better than the alternative."

He studied me hard. He saw that my hand was under the table. He had to know that it wasn't empty.

"Please," I said again. "Come with me. We'll talk to the county attorney. I'll help you get the best deal possible. It'll be so much better."

"Better?"

"Better than reaching for the .22."

He didn't believe me.

The assistant county attorney for Carver County sat next to me at Mr. Mosley's kitchen table. He had run out of questions to ask and had packed up his tape recorder and notebook. Lieutenant Dyke was leaning against the kitchen counter, his arms folded across his chest. The three of us were watching the wagon boys zip Hernandez into a black vinyl body bag. Dyke sighed deeply and sidled up next to the table. He rubbed the tips of his fingers over the four ugly holes I had drilled through the wood with the nine.

"Well," he said.

"Yeah," I told him.

He worked a pinkie into one of the bullet holes.

"He never had a chance, did he?"

"No," I agreed. "But I gave him a choice."

"Looks like he chose poorly."

Just So You Know

Reverend Winfield spoke over the grave of Lorenzo Hernandez although no one else had come to hear him. He told me that even a killer deserved a decent burial. He said when the time came he'd be happy to preside at my funeral, too. I wasn't quite sure how to take the remark, and let it go.

Sykora resigned from the FBI and returned to New York with Pen. But he went out a hero, hailed for killing a suspected terrorist—that would be Brucie—who had targeted him and his wife after his heroic efforts helped shut down a cigarette-smuggling operation that was using profits to finance Islamic organizations with links to al-Qaeda. As evidence, the FBI singled out three Twin Cities convenience store owners—one Pakistani and two Saudis—who were prosecuted for donating money to a Moslem charity that the Justice Department claimed was funneling cash to the PLO.

Frank Russo's moldering body was discovered in the locked trunk of an abandoned automobile with Minnesota plates. The car was found in Hunts Point in New York, only a few blocks from where Russo had been born. It was labeled a "gangland hit," and despite the description of Nick Horvath that Sykora and I had supplied, and the physical evidence obtained from his trailer, no arrests were made.

Roseanne Esjay's story was never printed in the *Times*, or anywhere else for that matter. She didn't explain what had happened, and I didn't ask.

The Seeking Information Alert issued on me was obviated, and the AIC of the Minneapolis field office made it clear that for the good of the bureau my name was never again to be uttered in the hallowed halls of the FBI—at least that's what Harry told me. I had invited him and his wife for dinner, seating them next to Chopper, who seemed to delight his wife but made Harry nervous. He kept checking to see if his wallet was missing.

Nina, Margot, Bobby, and Shelby also came to dinner. Shelby returned my shoe box. I was happy to get it back.

Nina forgave me for not staying in touch. I always knew she would.

Shelby also forgave me, but not until after dessert. She told me when we were alone in the kitchen that the next time I pulled a stunt like this she'd kick my sorry butt up and down and around Merriam Park. She wasn't kidding.

Finally, after all the dust settled, I called Sweet Swinging Billy Tillman and told him that the men who had attacked his wife were dead.

"Did you kill them?" he asked.

I told him I was responsible.

He paused for a moment, said, "Thank you," and hung up. There was no enthusiasm in his voice. I have no idea what the news meant to him, or if it meant anything. I called several more times over the next few months, tried to visit, but the conversations were always abrupt and I was told to stay away.

I never saw or spoke with Penelope Glass again. But whenever I hear a song I like, I now check the liner notes to see who wrote it.